The
Love Curse

Heart struck

The
Love Curse
Book 2

Heart struck

Rebecca Sky

HODDER CHILDREN'S BOOKS

First published in Great Britain in 2019 by Hodder and Stoughton

1 3 5 7 9 10 8 6 4 2

A CIP catalogue record for this book
is available from the British Library.

ISBN 978 1 444 94007 7

Typeset in ITC Berkeley Oldstyle by Hewer Text UK Ltd, Edinburgh
Printed and bound in Great Britain by Clays Ltd, Elcograf S.p.A.

The paper and board used in this book
are made from wood from responsible sources.

Hodder Children's Books
An imprint of
Hachette Children's Group
Part of Hodder and Stoughton
Carmelite House
50 Victoria Embankment
London EC4Y 0DZ

An Hachette UK Company
www.hachette.co.uk

www.hachettechildrens.co.uk

To my   lil bro,
thank you   for pushing
me to follow my heart. And
to all those reading this, I
<-------------- hope ------------<<
you find what
sparks your
dreams
too
!

Anacreon, Fragment 358
*Golden-haired Eros once again
hurls his crimson ball at me:
he calls me to come out and play . . .*

One

The first thing I notice is the smell – warm and metallic, salty like tears. There's only one thing it could be. Blood.

The surface where I lie presses hard into my back; my bones and joints ache like I haven't moved in days. I don't know where I am, what's happening.

I fight my body's need for sleep and open my eyes. A harsh light floods my vision. I blink, raising my hands for a shield only to be yanked back by restraints. It's a struggle to lift my head and to move my mouth, panic forcing dry lips into a cry for help. Only a raspy 'Hello?' escapes – it sounds like I'm getting over a cough.

No one answers me.

My skin prickles with cold and a low electric buzz hums overhead. Soon my eyes adjust, settling on a glowing web contraption hooked to the ceiling, illuminated by the lamp above. I squint to focus and realize the webbing is dozens of clear plastic tubes filled with pastel-blue opalescent fluid. I follow them down until they continue past my line of sight. It's impossible to know where they go but the hollow ache in my arms

1

makes me worry they hook into me. 'What the—' I hurry to sit up, only to find my neck is strapped in too.

'H-hello?' I choke out, managing to twist my head far enough to see a small section of a sterile room with walls and ceiling the colour of a fog-filled sky, and the top of the machine with more tubes rising up. It becomes impossible to breathe.

I struggle against my bindings, thrashing and twisting and ignoring the pain like my life depends on it. The last thing I remember is the graveyard, my fake funeral, watching my family and friends saying their goodbyes . . . watching the Hedoness power leave them. Then something happened. Not just to me, to Eros and Ben too. The blue and yellow dart comes to mind. My back aches like a bruise where it hit me. I try to calm myself enough to listen for clues of where I am but my heart beats too heavy in my ears.

'Help!' I call, this time louder, rattling the wrist bindings. 'Ben? Eros?' Still no answer.

Beads of sweat form on my brow. Not being able to wipe them away heightens the sensation, like an angry river pouring over me. The buzz of lights, the fake sunny yellow glow, the unnerving slurp of the machine, the bleached-blue fluid glistening in the tubes; everything amplifies until it's all-consuming. I search past the conduits dripping the gods-know-what into me to the far corner of the room where yellow mould blooms over the walls in long gangling streaks, like the water damage in the attic of my family's New York townhouse. A lump swells in my throat. My family. I'm strapped to a machine with no idea where I am, while my family . . . I can't bear to think about what might've happened to them.

I try again with my bindings, fighting to get my hands free. My skin becomes raw from all the tugging. I picture Ben's red swollen wrists from the time I locked him to the boat rails with the furry handcuffs. I'll have to apologise next time I see him. *If there is a next time.*

A gentle thud jolts Ben from my mind. The door to my room slides open and a cool, smoke-tinged breeze pushes in. The air around me shifts to ice. I twist my neck against the collar, trying to see, and let out a hesitant 'Hello?'

'You're awake!' a strange voice says in an echoed muffle like he's speaking into a tin can. He takes slapping, uneven steps, whistling a familiar tune as he nears.

I crane my neck and make out the top of his head, bright purple hair twisted into a tight bun, bobbing with his movements. He stops beside the bed with his back to me, wearing all black, his long coat less like a trench coat and more like one you'd wear in a lab. He turns and leans over, studying me like I'm not here. I frown back at his gaunt skin and beady eyes rimmed with dark circles. It looks like he hasn't slept in days. I'm surprised by how young he is – maybe a year or two older than me.

'Who are you? What do you want with me?' I ask.

He stops whistling and loops around the gurney, not looking up from his clipboard. 'How do you feel?' he says with the same enthusiasm as an automated computer voice.

'What's going on?' I shake my bindings. 'What do you want?' My neck presses painfully into the strap as I strain to see him, catching the tail end of his eye roll.

He sighs. 'Heda will be here soon. She will answer any questions.'

'Heda?'

Cold fingers wrap around my wrist and I flinch away. Touching me should cause him pain. Then I remember my Hedoness power is gone. Ben's kiss saw to that.

My stomach fills with butterflies as a strange, unfamiliar part of me wishes for my power back. Then I could manifest it on command, use it to turn this boy and make him do whatever I say. With my Hedoness power I could easily get out of this situation, find Ben. I close my eyes, searching my body for any sign of the electric spark that once was. Instead something else, something dark and lonely, seeps into every part of me.

I choke back the urge to cry and fixate on his pale bony fingers that wrap around my wrist, tips pressing firm into my pulse, uncomfortably near my raw skin. 'Do you know where Ben and Eros are?' I ask.

His beady eyes narrow into slits. 'You ask a lot of questions.' He releases my hand and scribbles something on his clipboard.

4

'I need to know they're OK.' I go to sit and am yanked backward by the neck strap. 'Please,' I cough out, 'just nod if they're OK.'

He stares at me for a long minute, still as a statue, those bulging eyes the only thing that moves. Fear and loneliness threaten to swallow me whole. Finally, he nods, so quick I almost miss it, then scoots away from the table and goes to the machine.

I breathe my first full breath. They're OK. Wherever they are, whatever is happening to them, at least they're OK.

Something tugs on my arm, sending a bite of pain through me. 'Ouch!'

The boy's returned to the bed, his hands busy looping the tubes, each new coil stinging more than the last. He ignores my hiss of pain and starts whistling again. This time I recognise the tune as the classic *Take Me Out To The Ball Game*. Which seems an unnaturally cheery song for his task.

'Stop, OK?' I say. 'That hurts.' I stretch as best I can to see what he's doing but my bindings are too tight.

The purple-haired guy sighs. 'If you'll hold still, please, I'm unhooking you from the intravenous.'

I do as he says, fighting the urge to struggle every time another tube gets plucked from my body. 'How many of those are in me?'

'Four.'

'Four?'

'Overkill, sure,' he says. There's a twisted lightness to his words that only heightens the mechanical cadence. 'We really only need one. But I like the number four. Four is a home run.'

I fight the urge to roll my eyes at the terrible baseball pun.

He flicks a switch and the sucking sound stops. Only the scratching of his feet, the buzzing overhead light and our mismatched breaths fill the emptiness as the last of the iridescent liquid travels up the tubes. Despite how beautiful it shimmers in the light, until I know what the heck they're pumping into me I'll only feel fear.

'What is that? The liquid?'

'Heda will be here soon. She'll answer any questions.'

'You keep saying that. Who's Heda?'

He stops his work and looks over. 'Hedone.'

A shiver runs through me. 'Hedone? As in Eros's daughter? The first Hedoness?'

'The same,' he says, adjusting the tubing coil over his shoulder before turning and limping towards the door.

'Wait.'

His irregular footsteps slide to a stop.

'Can you at least undo my neck strap?'

His steps continue away.

'Please,' I say, hating the desperation that fills my words. 'I can hardly breathe.' The last time I felt this way I was crammed into the back seat of the old pizza delivery car watching my ma be taken by the police. It's not a feeling I want to relive.

He grumbles something then returns. His spindly fingers struggle to unhook my collar. Thankfully he continues, muttering under breath until the last hook is undone and the leather straps hang loose.

I reach to rub my neck but the restraints hold me down. I hiss through the sting of leather in open wounds. 'I don't suppose you'd unhook a hand too?'

He glares and steps away, his left leg dragging behind as he walks.

As soon as the door closes, I sit up, waiting for the dizziness to subside before repositioning myself on the metal bed, trying to get enough leverage to kick my wrist binding loose. I guide my leg behind my arm with my chin but pull a muscle in the process. It leaves me twisted and in more pain, with little leverage on the strap. Unhooking my foot is a struggle, but as I do, I realize my left hand is tied a little looser than the other. I use the slack, attempting to pinch the strap-end and slide down the gurney for leverage. It's a struggle to move the brace enough to reach it with my teeth.

Bending forward further strains my body; the leather becomes slick against open wounds. I'm inches away. I bend again, faster, doing crunch-type movements. On my second try I manage to snag a corner in my teeth. My momentum yanks me back. The strap slips out, and my spine slams into the table. I lie there a moment regaining my breath, giving my wrist a short break and stretching my neck before trying again.

I pull the bindings as high as they can go and push every last ounce of energy into my crunch. I shoot forward, grab the strap again, biting so hard my jaw aches. But I refuse to let go until I get a good enough grip to start threading the strap through the hook with two fingers. It begins to loosen. I wiggle my hand and it slips free.

My bruised and raw wrists leak the same iridescent fluid that was in the tubes. *No time to panic.* I have to find Ben and Eros and get out of here.

Wherever here is.

I unhook my other hand and swing my legs over the gurney. I'm in some sort of blue tracksuit. The only thing of mine I recognise are my Converse sneakers. But there's no time to worry about that now so I hop down, teetering for a moment, not sure if my aching legs can hold my weight, but they do, and I tiptoe over to the door and crack it open. I wince with every hinge squeak and peer out. It's an adjoining room, dull and empty except for a scattering of equipment that doesn't look like it's meant for this space, and there's a machine and metal bed like the ones in my room. In the centre, the purple-haired boy blocks most of my view of someone dangling from a chain attached to the ceiling by a giant metal hook. The person's toes barely brush the ground and dozens of tubes stick out of them.

The purple-haired boy shifts to grab something, giving me a better view. My heart sinks.

'Eros,' I gasp, instantly covering my mouth, afraid of being heard.

The boy doesn't turn. Instead he brushes Eros's curls, then dabs his lips with a wet cloth. He bends down to clean Eros's feet, giving me a clear line of sight. The liquid in the tubes makes Eros's skin glow a sickly blue, his facial hair is scraggly, his broken body now waif-like. If I didn't know he was a god, I would have never guessed. I'm filled with a sudden urge to bring him home for dinner and offer him a hot shower and clean clothes. I can almost hear Ma's voice. 'Another stray?' she'd say, half annoyed that I brought a stranger home but half proud that I'm doing the right thing.

The guy asks Eros a question and Eros struggles to reply, opening his mouth then closing it before resorting to a nod. His eyes catch mine over the purple bun and they fill with a warning. The boy's back stiffens. He turns, following Eros's gaze. There's nowhere for me to go, so I shut the door and rush to the bed, fumbling to secure one of my hands and slip my other back in the strap.

The door creaks and purple-hair guy pops his head in. He frowns, then comes over and tugs on the strap I didn't get to close. It flops open.

His dark eyes search my face for answers. 'Heda doesn't want any problems,' he says, tightening the strap. The leather digs in painfully. He pulls again, trying to connect to a tighter notch, and I panic, jerking my arm in his grip. His hand slips before he can secure it. This is my chance. I take it, and sit up.

Our foreheads collide with a smack. The boy grips his head and stumbles back. I ignore my throbbing skull and tug desperately on my hand but, even though he didn't finish latching it, the strap doesn't budge. I crunch forward, trying again to grab it in my teeth. The boy struggles to get back on his feet, his left leg twisting at an unnatural angle.

'What do we have here?' someone says from the door, their voice cutting and cold but somehow musical.

I turn to see an elderly woman wearing a blue silk robe, with long salt and pepper stained blonde hair that hangs loose over her shoulders. There's something about her that's so familiar. As she strolls towards me, her hair and robe float like they're caught in a windstorm, and I can't decide if I should be more afraid of her or the two masked guards, one in grey and one in red commando gear, who flank her, gripping electronic, sword-like weapons. My heart races and I tuck my knees in tight, wishing my hands were free so I could defend myself.

'Heda,' the purple-haired boy says, scrambling to his feet and pulling his leg back into place.

A shiver goes through me. *Heda?* How can this be Hedone, Eros's daughter, the woman we basically worshipped at St Valentine's? I've seen so many portraits of her but none that reflects the old woman in front of me. The closer she gets there's no denying she resembles Eros – the shape of her face and eyes and how she holds herself. But she doesn't look like his daughter, she looks more like his grandmother. It doesn't make any sense.

The purple-haired boy bows low, fighting back his leg's urge to shake, and steps aside, giving her clear access to me. Heda nods to the guards and they move forward. From this angle I can see the one in red is a woman and around the same size as me, just a little taller. My best chance at escape is to try and overpower her. I have a few seconds before they make it here and I'm not going down without a fight. Staying means I may never find out what happened to Ben and Eros. I do another crunch, catching the strap and biting down.

Heda laughs. 'My, aren't you a bendy thing.'

I pull so hard my teeth shake. The red guard is at my side in seconds, her gloved hands pushing my face back. I swing wildly but the other guard pins my arm. Soon the wrist and neck straps are secure, so tight that when I swallow my throat scrapes against the leather edge. 'Please,' I say, 'why are you doing this?' I glance past the guards to Heda, half sitting on a metal stool, her weight firmly on her feet like she might spring up and charge at any moment. Despite her age, I have no doubt she could. There's something about the way she watches, something feral. It makes every part of me rise to alarm.

Heda nods again. The red guard grabs a spool of fresh tubes and hooks them one by one from the machine to my arms. Her touch is rougher and more rushed than the boy with purple hair. Each new tube is a needle shoving into my already bruised skin, a cry I have to fight back. When she finishes, she stands behind Heda.

The boy with purple hair speaks up. 'She hasn't eaten yet, her strength is—'

'She'll be fine,' Heda says. 'I want a full batch.'

'Please,' I croak, 'before you do this, at least tell me Ben is OK—'

'Ben?'

I don't get the chance to ask about Eros or my family.

Heda rises from the stool. She takes long sweeping strides towards me, her back rigid like my nani's when her arthritis is kicking in. If Heda is in pain, her face shows no signs of it. She stops beside the table and turns to the guard in grey. 'Well done,' she tells him. 'Now, say goodbye to Rachel.'

I expect the man to return to his place beside the red guard. Instead, his gloved hands rise and unhook the chinstrap of his helmet. He pulls it off. Dark hair falls around his face, framing hollow eyes. And when his stare locks on me it's like being trapped inside a frozen breath. Everything goes out of focus. My heart seizes in my chest. My stomach sinks.

The guard in the helmet. The one who helped connect me to this creepy machine.

It's Ben.

Two

I grit my teeth and stare. 'What did you do to him?'

Heda smirks. 'What did we do?' She nods for Ben to explain.

'Rach,' Ben says. I'm surprised when his voice has its familiar cadence. 'They didn't do anything to me,' he finishes.

'No.' I turn my head, fighting the tight collar. I can't believe that.

'Rachel, look at me.'

I refuse, focusing my effort on not crying.

He sighs. 'Let me explain.'

This can't be Ben. He would never do anything to hurt me. 'Nothing you could say could make this right.'

'Tell her,' Heda says, walking around the metal bed so I have nowhere to look but at her. I close my eyes but Ben's face is there too. At least in my mind there's nothing hollow about his gaze; it is smart and thoughtful and ever watchful.

'Rach.' He speaks softly and puts his hand on my arm. I nudge it away. 'You don't understand,' he says.

'You're right, I don't.' I twist too hard, tearing the delicate skin of my throat on the rough leather strap. I clench my teeth through the pain and glare up at him. Warm blood trickles down my collarbone. This can't be the same boy who promised to remember me in death and spend eternity together in Elysium. I study his face, every familiar piece of it. But when my gaze returns to his eyes it's like I'm looking at a stranger. The watchfulness that was always there, a comfort through some of the hardest times of my life, is gone. The once strong and confident boy is a shadow, worse than when the Hedoness power took his will, making him a puppet eager to obey Marissa's every command. I know his face and every expression as if they were my own. Right now, as confusing as it is, they're telling me this isn't something forced. Whatever it is that's changed him was his choice.

How long has it been since that life-altering kiss we shared? What has he got into?

'Why?' I say, forcing my voice to be steady. 'Why are you doing this?'

His hand returns to my arm and this time I let him keep it there, burning into me, a reminder of all the times I yearned for his touch. Now that he can touch me, it only confuses me more.

He leans closer. Brushes a curl from my face, his unsteady fingers lingering in the hair behind my ear. 'I'm sorry, Rach, you know I'd never want to hurt you.' He lowers his voice. 'This is the only way.' *The only way for what?*

A sadness registers in his eyes, then a determination like he's trying to tell me something he can't, and it gives me hope that somewhere, deep inside, he's there.

I know I shouldn't ask about us. There was fear in the way he just touched me, like I'm some broken teacup with the pieces placed back together but not yet glued. It wasn't that he was afraid of breaking me, more that he was afraid he couldn't keep me whole. Whatever the reason he's acting as Heda's guard, I have to trust him. Even if I did ask about us, he wouldn't be able to tell me the truth, not here, not with them watching.

I glance back to Heda and her guards and the boy with purple hair and suddenly I need to ask, even if it's just to hear the words leave my mouth, to claim something of my own. 'Remember what you said at the graveyard, before we were taken?'

He keeps silent, his blue eyes fixed to the tubes going into my arm. Heda scoffs at my question. I hate her now even more than I did learning about her at St Valentine's.

Ben lets out a long breath, the kind he does before he answers a question he's been thinking hard about. I pull my gaze back to him to find his mouth closed and his eyes asking what it is I really want to know.

So I ask it. 'Do you still mean it?' I say, but what I don't say, and what I know he knows I'm asking is, *Do you still love me?*

His eyes flick wearily to Heda and his fingers fidget with one of the tubes. 'There will always be a part of me that does, it's just—'

'Just what?'

He flinches at the sharpness of my words. I know he can't speak openly here, but I'm frustrated and need to know why he's pretending to serve Heda. He of all people hates immortals and offspring of immortals; he'd never willingly help one. What changed while I was unconscious?

Ben lifts his chin. 'Since we can't be together any more, I—'

'Can't be together?' The question rushes off my lips in a panicked flood. His eyes tell me this is no lie. He truly believes what he's saying.

'I'm bored with this,' Heda interrupts, her words laced with warning. 'Back to work.'

Ben nods and flicks a switch on the machine, and the next thing I know the tubes are refilling with the luminous substance.

My eyes follow him everywhere but he keeps his gaze down, so I turn my glare on Heda. If she's going to do this to me, whatever *this* is, I won't give her the pleasure of seeing me squirm. When our eyes meet, I lift my chin. 'Will you at least tell me what that liquid is?'

'That's diluted ichor,' Heda says, her eyes locked on the tubes, her voice distant.

'Ichor?' The word is so familiar. I know I should know what it is.

'The blood of the immortal,' she says like I'm ignorant for not knowing.

A shiver runs through me. The last thing I want is blood of the gods in my body. I hated being a Hedoness, hated that the arrow in my blood turned my touch into something that forced people to love me. I hated everything that power made me. Now they're experimenting with me and putting immortal blood in. I just got rid of the Hedoness ability. I don't want another.

My heart races and I fight back the shakiness of my voice. 'Why are you putting ichor in me?'

Heda chuckles, a low, gravelly sound. 'Putting it in you?'

Something about her response makes my stomach flip.

She pats my hand. 'Seems my father didn't mention.' Her fingers shake against mine, like she's cold, or waiting for something.

Father?

'Eros?' I say, flicking my gaze to his door. 'What didn't he tell me?'

She starts back to her stool, nearly tripping in the process, and the red guard rushes forward, wrapping a protective arm around her. Heda leans into the guard, barely able to hold herself up. It's such a strange shift from the strong, fear-inducing woman who first entered this room. I strain to see her but the strap only digs further into my neck. I give up, dropping my head back down.

'Perhaps you should look more closely at the tubes,' Heda says, her voice shaky as she takes her seat on the stool, struggling to catch her breath.

It hurts to turn my head but I do, and focus on one of the lines entering my body. Tiny air bubbles travel in the shiny liquid. Then I see it, the bubbles, they're travelling away from me and to the machine.

The liquid isn't going in me – it's coming out.

'How . . .'

Heda laughs, coughing from shortness of breath, before managing to say, 'You know that vial of ambrosia he gave you?'

My mind goes to the first time meeting Eros, in the field of statues, and that shiny red vial he placed in my hand, watching it blend into my red leather glove. I can almost taste the sickly-sweet flavour, like a phantom memory fixed to my tongue. The day I drank it, in the midst of the angry mob outside the police station, was the very day Ben promised to never forget me.

'Yes,' I choke out.

'Ra-chel.' My name comes soft to my ears, a faint whisper, the voice so familiar. It's not until Heda, the purple-haired boy and her guards turn to the door that I realize it's Eros who spoke.

Heda glares at the boy with purple hair then turns to the guard in red. 'Go and shut him up.'

The boy holds open the door, standing between the two rooms as the female guard pushes past him with electronic sword in hand. There's a thump and Eros grunts in pain. I watch Ben, and even from this strained angle I'm certain I see him flinch.

'And he's out!' The purple-haired boy animates his words, smiling like it's funny to him, and I don't know if he's enthralled by his lame baseball joke or the fact that Eros was hurt.

'Fathers, am I right?' Heda shakes her head in annoyance and the boy smiles. She motions to me. 'Can she handle another full round?'

'She hasn't eaten,' the purple-haired boy says again, head cocked, gaze squinting as he assesses the request. 'It's a little early, but her blood pressure has been good.'

I watch Ben as they discuss my fate. His eyes are everywhere but on me.

'The ambrosia?' I repeat, needing to understand what's going on.

Ben's eyes flicker between anger and hurt, and it's a mirror of what I saw when he told me about his family's car accident – that he was left all alone, for ever an orphan.

'Right, yes,' Heda says. 'It's making you immortal.'

Three

When they leave, the room feels even colder and my heart aches worse than my body. That look in Ben's eyes is branded on my mind. He hates immortals – and I'm becoming one.

But the way he looked at me and touched my face – he can't be working for Heda. It's something more. It has to be something more.

They keep the door between mine and Eros's room open, and Eros's wheezy breaths mix with the sucking of the machine and the buzz of the overhead light to fill the silence. I glance up at the tubes; beautiful rainbow blue swirls of liquid. It's hard to believe it's coming from me. Ichor. *My blood.* Light blue, not red. What does this mean?

Warm liquid trickles down my neck. I push against the neck strap, wincing as the band wedges further into the raw flesh, and manage to look down at my hand. The strap that Ben fastened so tight isn't properly latched closed any more – my breath catches in my throat – this is the sign I was hoping for. He did this on purpose to let me know he's on my side but working as an insider, just like he did with the police back in NY when he left them clues to find. I'm not about to let it go to waste.

I wiggle my fingers until the strap flops open and my hand is free. Then I hurry to unhook the rest of me before pulling the tubes from my body. I wince through the pain, pressing my lips to keep from crying out and drawing unwanted attention. I wipe the liquid from my neck – pastel blue, shiny blood. I ignore the panic it stirs in me, wipe it on my shirt and rush through the door to Eros.

He's so weak his head flops and I have to hold it up. I hope he'll say something, tell me he's all right. All he manages is a slight nod to the wall where the chains that hold him from the ceiling are secured. I gently lower his head before hurrying over and pulling them from the hook. They slide through the loop and Eros collapses to the floor, the chains falling over him in a racket. I ignore the draw to escape coming from the main door and hurry back to make sure he's OK, pulling the pile of metal off and rolling him into a more comfortable position before removing the IVs from his arms. His blood is a bluer shade than mine, a deep royal colour, and the reflections from the halogen light send small rainbow fractures about the floor like some strange strobe. It's what I imagine they'd have at a school dance. We never had dances at St Valentine's.

'The . . . door,' he forces out.

I lower his head from my lap and go to the large double door opposite the interconnecting one. It's painted the same blue as my tracksuit. I drag the chains and loop them through the handles to hold them shut. It's not a permanent fix if Heda and her guards return, but at least this will buy us some time to recuperate and figure out a way to help Ben get us out of here.

When the last chain is secured, I return to Eros, kneeling beside him. 'So, your daughter,' I begin, pulling his head back into my lap. He arches his back so very little of him touches me as I brush sticky blond curls off his forehead and out from under the matt-black metal collar around his neck. 'She's . . . not what I expected.'

Not that anyone would expect a wild elderly woman to be the daughter of a young god. Though I suppose Eros isn't actually young, just looks that way.

He half laughs, wincing in pain as he does. It's then I notice the skin around the collar is enraged and blistering. 'What is this?' I say, reaching for the black band.

He pulls back. 'Don't!'

His breathing is heavy and he chokes as he struggles out of my arms and props himself on the leg of the metal table. 'Anti . . . magic . . . speech . . . inhibitor.'

'Why don't they want you to talk?' I ask, then remember that replying will cause him pain. 'Don't answer.'

He wraps his hand in his sweat-stained purple shirt and tries to pull the collar from his throat. 'Don't . . .

want . . . tell . . . you . . . truth.' His shirt starts to smoke and he hisses before dropping his hand. There's a freshly burned hole in the purple cloth.

'They don't want you to tell me the truth?' I repeat. He nods, tilting his head back and taking long deep breaths.

I have so many questions but I can't justify causing him pain to ask. Even if he nods his skin presses more into the collar. We need to get it off him. I must focus on the most important thing. My heart tells me to ask about Ben but I settle on, 'So how do we get out of here?'

Eros nods to the chained door and shrugs.

'I don't imagine that takes us outside of this place? Whatever this place is.'

His head drops, and I know that's a no. My attention is drawn to the sloppy pile of tubing I pulled from him and the deep blue translucent puddle forming on the polished cement floor.

'How is Heda older than you?'

'Aging . . . demigod, not full immortal,' he manages.

I cringe when he says 'immortal' like it's the dirtiest of all bad words. 'Why did you do that? Why did you trick me into taking something that made me immortal?' I blurt.

His head snaps up, his bright blue eyes full of an apology. He pats my hand, stopping to catch his breath. 'Only . . . way . . . save . . .'

'The only way to save me?' I finish for him, pulling my hand away. He knows how I felt about the Hedoness power. I was pretty clear about wanting to be a normal girl and not wanting any powers. 'So you save me by making me the very thing I hate. Kinda twisted.'

He nods. 'I know,' he whispers. 'Sorry.'

I want to say his sorry doesn't change the facts.

Eros watches me and I'm reminded that he can read my thoughts. I don't really care right now. All I care about is getting out of here.

'Any idea how we can get rid of that collar?' I ask, absently rubbing the raw skin on my wrists.

He shrugs, his eyes lock on my wound. 'How?'

'How did I free myself?'

He nods.

'I'm not sure. I think Ben helped me.'

'No,' he says, loud and sharp and hissing through the pain. 'Ben not help.'

He knows something, and by the look on his face it's something I'm afraid to know. But he's wrong if he thinks Ben's with Heda.

'Forget . . .' Eros struggles, pulling me from my thoughts. 'Forget Ben.'

I stand and pace. I can't really trust Eros. He made me immortal without even telling me. For all I know he has some twisted motive to turn me against Ben. I'm not going to turn on Ben, I'm going to find a way to help him get us out.

24

First, I have to figure out what's going on, where we are.

In the next room, the machine beside the bed they tied me to starts flashing red. I go to it and pry open the compartment to find a big plastic gallon container half full of ichor. It's strange to think that that was once in me. That I no longer bleed red.

I return to Eros. 'Why is your blood so much bluer than mine? Is it because you're fully immortal?'

'Yes,' he says, gritting his teeth. 'And it would be . . . darker . . . more potent . . . royal . . . without this collar.'

Voices carry from the other side of the chained double door. My first instinct is to re-strap myself to the bed, but Eros isn't chained to the ceiling and I don't have time to do both.

The door rattles. I rush over to the metal stool and hold it like a cricket bat, taking slow steps back to Eros. He tries to stand but needs the table for support.

'Rachel?' says a familiar voice from the other side.

The last time we spoke was on the phone and she'd just smashed into a police road barricade with my cousin Kyle. I don't know whether to laugh or cry.

'Marissa?'

'Are you OK?' she says. 'What's blocking the door?'

'Where are we? What's going on, Riss?'

There's a long pause. 'We're in one of the Committee's facilities,' she finally says.

'Which facility?' I ask. The main ones I know of are in London and Greece.

'Open the door and I'll tell you all about it.'

I give Eros a look, wondering if I should open it. He shakes his head no and any hope of help slips away. 'Why am I not surprised that you're working with Heda and her goons?' It takes energy to keep my voice from shaking.

'Goons?' She sighs the same way she did back at St Valentine's before she'd give me one of her 'embrace the gift' speeches. 'I'm sure this is all confusing,' she continues, 'but you need to know that Heda isn't here to hurt you.'

'So, draining my blood was for fun?'

Marissa clears her throat. 'She's just trying to help. Please let me in.'

I look back at Eros and he shakes his head again. But I can't help my curiosity. Maybe Marissa is my key to finding out what's going on.

I go to the door and loosen the chains enough to open it a crack. Cold smoky air rushes in.

'No . . . stop . . .' Eros chokes.

I ignore him and peek out. Marissa wears a grey guard uniform without the helmet. Her trousers are cuffed to show off her navy heels, her sleeves are rolled and she uses a ribbon as a belt. Even her attempt to spruce up these clothes falls short – she looks like a weird combination of guard and Banana Republic sales clerk. She holds a tray with a bottle of water, an apple and a wax-paper-wrapped sandwich. 'You hungry?' she asks.

I haven't had time to think about hunger but now that she mentions it: 'I could eat,' I say.

'Open the door and I'll bring it in.'

'Just pass it through,' I tell her.

'I owe you an apology,' she begins, instead of handing me the food. 'For the Kyle stuff—'

'I hope you aren't referring to turning my gay cousin and making him love you as *stuff*.' My chest tightens as anger surges through me for him once more.

'I'd love to apologise face-to-face,' she says. As if to prove her friendship, Marissa shoves the tray close enough that I can reach the sandwich. I drop the stool, pull it through the gap and greedily unwrap it to find something that looks like Ma's homemade samosas but with a flakier crust. I rip it in half and hand one piece to Eros before taking a big bite of the other. I eye her curiously. 'It's good,' I say. 'Thanks.'

'Spanakopita. I thought you'd like it.'

The food feels rough against my dry throat. What I'd give for a big mug of Ma's masala chai right now. The bottle on her tray is so tempting I debate opening the door. Behind me, Eros chokes on his mouthful.

I nod to the bottle. 'Pass the water.'

'Let me in and you can have it. I need to make sure you're OK.'

'Why? So you or one of Heda's goons can re-strap me to the machine? Look at my neck, Rissa. Look at my arms.' I hold out an arm showing her the faded bruises and tilt my head, exposing my neck.

She sucks in a breath. 'I'm sorry, Rach. Heda told them not to harm you.'

Eros chokes out a laugh at this.

Marissa frowns at the sound, then shoves the door as far as she can to see him. 'You've unhooked Eros?' Her eyes fill with worry.

I push the doors, knocking her back. 'Why are they doing this to us?' I persist.

'Rachel, please.' Marissa's face softens into a false smile. 'Let me in and I can explain everything. It's not what you think.'

She thinks I'm dumb enough to fall for another of her lies. 'I'm over people telling me that.' I tighten the chains before heading to Eros and taking a seat on the metal bed – ignoring the ichor-stained strapping and the sweat outline where a body once lay. 'At least tell me how long I've been in here.'

'In there?' she says, choosing her words carefully. 'A couple of days.'

'And before here?'

'I don't know, Rachel. They've finally let me come to

check on you. Is this really how you want to spend our time together? We have so much to catch up on.'

'Yeah,' I say, 'like how you got away from the police.'

She doesn't reply so I press further. 'You were arrested, Riss. And now you're here working for Heda?'

'Actually –' Marissa peers through the crack – 'it wasn't a police barricade. Not exactly. I mean, it was, but it was under the Committee's control.'

'What?' I gasp, turning to Eros to see if he knew this. He doesn't make eye contact.

I flashback to sitting in the uncomfortable altar chair in Mother Superior's office as she lectures me on the importance of the Committee. '*Over the years, the Committee learned that it was easier to control the gods with the help of Hedonesses. Now that the gods no longer interfere in our world, the Committee's efforts have turned to world politics, trying to spread peace by placing Hedonesses in influential and strategic positions.*' Is this what she meant, when she said their 'efforts have turned'?

I glare through the crack at Marissa. 'So the Committee that's supposed to be appointed by the gods to govern Hedonesses and keep the world at peace works for Heda now?'

Marissa fidgets with her hair. 'Heda has supporters everywhere . . .'

She keeps talking but my mind wanders to my family,

my ma and the distrust she had for the Committee. I try to hold back my worry for them.

'Great, what else don't I know?' I ask. 'Where's my family?'

She flinches. 'If you open the door, I'll tell you everything. I promise, Rachel, I won't let anything bad happen to you.'

'Anything worse, you mean?'

Her face drops. 'Heda never wanted to take ichor from you against your will but our time was running out. She didn't have a choice.'

I'm about to reply when what sounds like an army's worth of heavy boot-steps approaches. Eros's eyes widen.

Marissa gasps, steps back from the door and bows. 'Let me in, now,' she whispers firm, head remaining down. And I know I should listen to her. In all my years of knowing Marissa, I've never seen her humble herself like she's doing now. It's almost like she's scared, and if Mother Superior's angry lectures back at St Valentine's or being arrested and held in a police cell didn't scare her, whatever's coming must be bad.

'Open it,' she repeats, 'before they force their way in and it's too late.'

Four

I drop the last of my spanakopita, pick up the stool and stand at the door, peering out at the approaching guards. The majority seem to be women, which isn't at all surprising considering only women can be Hedonesses.

I spot Heda, being helped along by Ben and the guy with purple hair. She leans her whole weight on them as she wobbles forward. It's like she's aged ten years since I last saw her.

'Why are you in the hall? Who's tending to them?' she asks Marissa. Her words are wild and desperate. It's then she notices me watching through the door and she pushes away from Ben, attempting to stand on her own, teetering and unfocused. Heda stops to regain her breath and my eyes find Ben's. He gives me a half-smile.

For a heartbeat it's like all the questions between Ben and me disappear and it's just the two of us, an arm's-length away. It takes everything in me not to rip the chains from the door and throw my arms around him. Then his gaze flicks down and his smile slips away. I'm almost certain he's looking at my hands clutching the stool, at the scarred flesh from the tight straps. He steps closer to Heda and grabs her arm with a new resolve. It's a stab in the back seeing him help her. But my heart believes he's trying to do right by me, he's playing a part to keep me safe. He left my wrist unhooked after all. That couldn't have been an accident. It has to mean something.

I try to catch his eye and my attention is drawn behind him to a face – framed in a familiar halo of corkscrew curls – looking down at a small black box with gold markings in her grasp.

'Paisley?' I call, afraid I'm wrong and it isn't my friend, and even more afraid I'm right and that Heda has her too. Ben's head snaps up but I focus on the girl as her eyes scan the line of guards to see who called her. It is Paisley, there's no doubt. I bang the door with the stool. 'Paisley, over here!'

'Rach, stop,' Ben warns.

Paisley's eyes find mine and she smiles, then Heda turns and says something I can't make out and the smile slips from her face. Paisley nods, glancing back to offer a quick anxious look before falling into place in line behind Heda and the gathering cluster of grey guards, her grip even tighter on the box.

Heda steps closer, peering past me, her gaze coming to focus for the first time on Eros. 'Open the door, Father,' she says.

Eros pushes on to his feet, rocking in place as his legs get used to his weight. When he starts walking, it's in slow, wavering steps.

He can't seriously be listening to her. He stops beside me.

'What are you doing?' I ask.

He reaches for the door.

'Don't even think of opening it.'

His fingers wrap around the chains.

'If they hook you up again don't blame me,' I say, walking back to Eros's bed and taking a seat on the edge, stool still gripped in my hands like the four metal legs can keep back Heda's army, *or stop me from running to Ben*.

When Eros gets to the door he stares through the crack at his daughter. His shaky hands come to rest on the knot of chains. 'I love you. I will always love you. But you're . . . a . . . disappointment,' he says. It's the firmest his voice has been but his stiff posture gives away that he's in pain.

'That disappointment is mutual.' Heda lifts her chin.

Eros doesn't unhook the chains like I expected. Instead he closes the door and pulls them tight, wrapping the excess around his arm.

Someone bangs on the other side.

'Open it,' Heda orders. 'Take it off the hinges if you need to.'

I stand alert at this. Last time she came in here, she had Ben and the red guard re-hook me to the machine. My strength isn't back yet; the small amount of food wasn't enough and all I have to protect myself is this metal stool. I make my way to the other side of the bed and eventually Eros drops the chains and follows. We stand shoulder to shoulder, stool raised, as they slam into the door. The chains rattle, the gap gets wider, one of the guards slips in through the crack. Eros attempts to step in front of me but I nudge him back, raising the stool like I'm not afraid to use it to whack the guard away.

But I am afraid.

I'm afraid they will tie me to the bed.

That they will insert the IVs and drain my blood, and they won't make the same mistake as last time – my straps will be double-checked.

Ben and the purple-haired boy follow the guard through the gap. The stool shakes in my grasp but I feel safer now that he's coming closer. The boy with purple hair stops just inside the door and unchains the handles, letting the rest of them in. They pass him and Ben and fill the small space between us.

I try to catch Ben's eyes, see what's happening, get some reassurance, but the guards are too many. Eros pushes me behind him as he backs up, pulling the bed with us like the small metal platform is enough to keep them away. I secure my grip on the stool, feeling not unlike a lion tamer guiding my beasts. And the guards are beasts. They hold weapons: long glowing rods that crackle with electricity.

I can imagine what being touched with one of them feels like. I don't need a demonstration to know I don't want it.

Marissa helps Heda to the front, closer to the bed barricade. Heda points to the adjoining room where they first held me, then motions the boy with purple hair to go before turning back. 'Drop the stool and let's have a civil conversation,' she says.

'Drop the lightsabres,' I say.

Ben steps forward. 'Rachel, please.'

Heda raises her hand and the guards stop moving. Still Ben continues his approach, stopping beside Heda, who's using Marissa for balance, her attention focused on the guy with purple hair unhooking the tub of blood from my machine.

'It's not a full batch,' he calls over.

'No time to wait.' Heda adjusts her grip on Marissa, using her like a crutch as she teeters over to the purple-haired guy. 'The stool,' she demands, snapping her fingers.

A guard's arm snakes out, grabbing the stool at lightning speed. I'm so unprepared it slips effortlessly from my fingers. She rushes it over to Heda who sits upon it and holds out her arm.

The boy struggles to secure the ichor under one arm as he returns. He takes a crooked step, pulling his black lab coat tight to his body. 'You really should use your father's blood. You need the vitality, not—'

'You know what I need,' she says. Marissa rolls up the blue silk sleeve and he gives in, hooking a fresh tube to an IV port that's already in Heda's arm. He attaches the other side of the tubing to a nozzle on the tub, opens the valve and soon my blood flows up the tube and into Heda. Eros steps closer, the warmth of his body the only thing comforting me in this bizarre moment.

After most of the tub empties into her, her eyes roll back and she stops shaking. She stands on her own – some colour returns to her cheeks and the fire returns to her eyes. 'Better, for now,' she says, taking the container of ichor from him and inspecting its dregs. 'But I'll need some of my father's soon.'

The boy shuffles forward, purple hair shining in the overhead light. 'You should absorb the arrow first, see how it sits with you.'

The arrow?

Heda lets out an annoyed sigh. 'Fine. Process what we have from my father's batch. We can't waste a drop.'

He nods, reaches for the tub of my ichor, but she holds it close and points to Eros's machine. He shuffles over and opens the compartment, working to remove the tub of Eros's blood.

When Heda looks back at me, she seems younger somehow, like she just got a facial or something. I have the sudden urge to hide under the table.

Eros holds me like he's in my mind, understanding my terror, and normally I'd be mad about that, but right now his grip is the only thing keeping me from caving in to that fear.

Five

Heda stands up with ease and extends her arm for Marissa to unroll the sleeve, her eyes locking on Paisley and then the box in her grasp. It freaks me out that this sudden change in her has something to do with my blood.

I need to know why. 'You're stronger . . . my blood? How?'

'Not yours. Eros's ichor makes me stronger, yours quenches my thirst.' She grins, watching me as she grabs a knife from Ben's waistband and stabs a nearby guard in the side. It happens so fast I'm not sure if it's real or if I imagined it. But then the guard clutches her side, a crimson pool blooming over her grey uniform, and falls to her knees.

I take a step back against the wall. Eros grabs my hand protectively. I pull away, half because I'm mad at him for my being here, and half because I don't want to look weak in front of Heda and Marissa.

Marissa reaches for the tub containing the dregs of my blood and Heda pulls it closer. But then she glances at the boy carrying Eros's jug and motions Marissa over to that. Heda's grey gaze stays locked on me, burning into my skin. Her voice fills my mind. *Two, maybe three litres,* it says, like she's assessing how much she can bleed without killing me. It's so clear and real that I wonder if maybe she said it out loud and it wasn't my imagination, but I didn't see her mouth move.

I glance at Eros, wondering if he heard it too, but he's watching Marissa give a swig of his blood to the injured guard. Lustrous blue. The royal liquid pours into the woman's mouth. Her hands loosen from her stomach to clutch the container, her lips seal around the spout and she chugs like her life depends on it.

It's grotesque. But I can't take my eyes away.

She drinks until she's drained the container then sticks her finger in as far as it will go, swiping at the residue and licking it off.

'Is there any more?' she asks.

Heda laughs. 'You've had enough.'

'It was only a two-inch stabbing,' says the boy with purple hair. 'A half cup would do the trick.'

'The trick?' I blurt.

They turn to me.

'Show her,' Heda says.

The guard stands and pulls up her crimson-soaked shirt to reveal a flat, injury-free stomach. There is no sign of a knife wound or bleeding. My knees weaken and I grip the cold metal gurney for support, feeling its chill rise up my arms and filling my entire body.

The blood. It healed her.

'How . . .?' I glance at Paisley, hovering in the entrance to the room, holding the little black and gold box like her life depends on it. I wouldn't be surprised if it did – Heda keeps looking at it every few seconds. Whatever is in that box, however the guard was cured, it's making fear creep up my spine and settle in.

'The benefits of being an immortal,' Heda says. 'You'll soon see ichor makes you stronger.'

Soon. I shudder at the thought.

Heda smooths her blue robe and heads to the door. Marissa goes ahead, leaving the room before them; the rest wait for Heda to pass.

She takes her time, stopping beside Paisley, pushing the sleeves of her robe up and running her hands over the black and gold box. The way Paisley shifts uncomfortably confirms that whatever is in it is dangerous. My mind flickers with an image of me leaping over the bed, knocking the guards aside and grabbing the box – instead I merely cower behind Eros.

Heda smiles, like she knows just how afraid I am, then tilts my ichor tub to her lips and drinks the last dregs before handing the empty container to the boy with purple hair. 'Get them out from there, string them up with chains and refill their tubs.'

'Both of them?' he asks, glancing at me.

'Both,' she says. 'It's time Rachel learns how serious I am.'

My heart races. All I have is the bed and Eros, and he can barely stand on his own, let alone help me fight them off.

Ben doesn't make eye contact but he subtly positions himself between me and the encroaching guards, his hand resting on his weapons belt.

Over the shouted orders, the uneven footsteps and the heavy breaths of everyone in the small room, floats a whisper . . . '*The box*'.

I swear it's Paisley who says it. I search the crowd for her and find her behind Heda, shaking like a deer caught in headlights, but brave enough to hold the black and gold box out towards me.

The guards are closing in. They've pushed past Ben, who stands unsure, his weight shifting from one foot to another, looking like he's going to charge to my rescue at any moment. But I know if he does help me it will only put us both in jeopardy.

On his next scan of the room, I catch his gaze and motion for him to stay back. There are only two ways out of this: I can either let myself get caught and chained to the ceiling then hope that Ben will come up with a way to save me, or I can fight.

The path to Paisley and whatever is in that box is narrowing. I don't have time to hesitate. It's now or never. Eros gives me a light nudge forward as if he knows my dilemma, and I take it as my sign to go. I

41

jump on to the metal bed and spring towards the gap in the guards.

I land, steady on my feet, like this is something I've done countless times, my instincts taking over and surprising not only the guards but me too. I grab the stool and swing it wildly, taking down three before the others even know what's happening. Most of them go to the door, thinking I'm trying to make a break for it, and that leaves Paisley unattended.

I close the distance to her. Heda's frantic orders keep changing and the guards don't know which to obey, so she growls and lunges at me herself. I use the stool to hold her back and take the box from Paisley with my other hand.

Heda's fist comes flying at us. 'You let her have it!'

I dodge her swing and sprint for the bed, box firmly in grasp. The guards are back on their feet, charging me from behind. Heda shoves Paisley, then grabs her by her hair. 'You'll pay for this!'

My heart fills with guilt. I can't believe I didn't wait for Paisley. 'Leave her alone,' I shout, as I slide behind the metal bed and lift the box lid. As I do, a hush falls over the group; it's like they even forget to breathe. If it weren't for the feeling of Eros's chest rising and falling against my arm, I'd think I was back in Little Tokyo with all the statues.

Inside the box there's something wrapped in red

velvet. I pick it up, feeling a heat and vibration through the cloth – like dozens of little needles against my hand. I use my sleeve as added protection from the sting and push the cloth back to reveal a twisted black arrow armlet.

My textbook from St Valentine's comes to mind. *Eros's Arrows: Infatuation and Indifference.* Infatuation, Eros's gold arrow. Indifference, his black. This can't be the long-lost Arrow of Indifference?

I can't seem to get away from Eros's arrows.

I pull the velvet further back, turning it to get a better look. One of the black metal tail feathers wiggles loose. It falls off, landing on the ground near my foot. I step on it, hoping no one saw, and wave the armlet for distraction.

'Don't touch it!' Heda shrieks.

'Or what?' I say, bare hand hovering over it to spite her.

'Don't,' Eros chokes. His throat catches my eyes and I can't help noticing how the arrow armlet and his collar are both the same dull black colour. He told me his collar is a magic inhibitor and I immediately wonder if the arrow armlet is the same. The truth is I don't want to touch it. It's already burning me through my sleeve, and by the look of Eros's neck I can see what it does to raw flesh.

Before I can figure out what to do, the guards at the door part. Everyone turns to see the red guard waltz in.

She heads straight for Heda, pulls the knife from her waistband and holds it to Paisley's throat.

I swallow the lump of fear in mine, only to feel it bob up and down in my stomach instead.

Heda dusts her hands and steps towards me. 'If the armlet is not in the box and handed to me by the count of three, Paisley dies.' The red guard shoves her knife deeper against Paisley's throat until a single crimson drop streaks down her neck.

'Stop!' I shout.

Heda holds up her hand and the red guard eases off.

I lift my chin. 'I'll give it to you, but I want out of here; Paisley and Eros too.' I glance at Ben to see that familiar frayed-edge look of abandonment flash in his eyes. He has to know I'll come back for him. But asking Heda for his freedom now will only put him in danger.

'You're wasting my time.' Heda rolls her eyes and drops her hand, and the red guard's blade pushes back into Paisley's neck.

'Wait!' I cry, not able to stand the tears pooling in my friend's eyes.

'What for?' Heda says, bored.

'I need to know my friends and family are safe. If you can ensure that, I'll willingly give you more of my blood – I won't fight it.'

'And you'll give me the armlet?' she asks, eyebrow raised.

'Yes, take it.' I toss it to her, listening to it clank across the ground and feeling instant relief as it leaves my hands. Paisley's eyes widen and I realize how foolish she must think I am for giving it over before Heda agreed to my terms. But she doesn't know about the piece burning through the sole of my shoe.

Heda glares at Paisley. 'Hand it to me,' she says. The red guard shoves Paisley to her knees. Sucking back tears, Paisley crawls for the armlet. The necklace Marissa once lost, the spaceship with fangs, dangles around Paisley's neck once more. She must have had it replaced. It reminds me of school and how much simpler things were then.

Paisley picks up the arrow in her bare hands. I flinch, expecting her to cry out in pain, but she doesn't. It's like it's just any chunk of metal to Paisley.

Heda wraps her robe around her hand like a boxer preparing for a fight and extends it to Paisley, who places the black arrow in Heda's palm. I want to run to Paisley and protect her from them but I'm afraid it will only start another battle.

Heda holds the arrow like a child holds a butterfly – carefully, but with fear it will float away – and she comes over to the bed, folding it in the velvet and setting it in the box. I grit my teeth, hoping she doesn't notice the smell of burning shoe that's starting to fill the space. When she closes the lid and turns back to the red guard,

I let out a breath of relief and bend down, pretending to tie my Converses, while really pinching the piece of black arrow in my sweatshirt sleeve.

I use the bedframe to block their view, but Paisley is still kneeling on the ground at my eye level and she watches everything I do. When Heda turns her back, Paisley smiles at me, then screams.

'What's wrong with her? Stop that racket at once!' Heda says.

The red guard grabs Paisley's arm and pulls her up. Paisley continues to wail dramatically, giving me a much-needed distraction. I quickly roll the fragment into my jogging bottoms' thick elastic cuff, before securing it between my sock and shoe for safety. I hope to the gods it doesn't burn through to my leg. As soon as I'm done, Paisley stops and whimpers softly.

Heda hands the box to her red guard and gives Paisley a onceover, eyes landing on the crimson stain across her neck. 'Get that looked at,' she says.

Paisley grips her throat and nods.

Heda smiles, crooked and content, then turns to me. 'Come,' she says, waving me forward.

I don't move.

She lets out a long breath. 'Do you not wish for me to honour our agreement and reunite you with your family?'

'What?' I take a stuttered step forward, butting into the bed, not sure if I can trust what I'm hearing. 'My family's here?' Last I saw them was at my fake funeral. 'Who? My ma, my dad? Kyle?'

No one answers. But the look in Ben's eyes is all the answer I need.

'Where are they?' I ask, worried that they'll take me to another room like this to find them hooked up to equally disturbing machines.

'Guest quarters are down the hall. I can take you, if you like,' says Heda, her posture once again strong.

I nod and take another cautious step to her, this time moving out from the protection of the bed. No guards rush me. Everyone stays by Heda, waiting.

'I'll follow you,' I say.

She smirks and nods, continuing on. Eros steps around the table after me. We take hesitant steps forward, side by side. When the pair of us are close to the door, Heda turns to the boy with purple hair. 'I need a replacement of the ichor we lost.'

He gestures to the guards. 'You heard her.' Five of them rush over. I brace myself for another fight. Then they grab Eros.

He struggles, and even though he's bigger than them they easily overpower him. The door is open, my family down the hall. I could leave now.

Eros cries out in pain.

My body reacts on instinct. I grab one of the guards and try to pull her off. Paisley's tear-filled eyes find mine in the struggle. The red guard holds the box in one hand and Paisley's arm in the other. I tug harder on the guard and get an elbow to the chest. I stumble back, sucking in large mouthfuls of air. I don't wait to regain my breath before diving back in and securing my handhold. Across the fray, Heda whispers something to Ben then turns and leaves. The red guard drags Paisley after her.

'Rachel,' Ben says, my name shaky on his lips, 'you can stay and fight Heda's guards or you can come and see your family.' His voice practically pleads with me to go.

My body aches to be here, defending Eros, but my heart is with my family. Our eyes meet through the chaos, Eros's so blue and full of sorrow. 'Go,' he forces out, wincing. He stops struggling, surrendering to the guards, letting them loop the chains round his arms and waist. The skin around his black collar is redder than before. I'm thankful he made the choice for me.

'I'll come back for you,' I say.

He nods as if to say he expects nothing less. Turning away is the hardest thing I've had to do yet.

Ben waits for me at the door. Every step I take away from Eros is heavy with guilt. The rattle of chains, his painful breaths, the guards' conversations – it fills me to the point of bursting. *'I'm sorry,'* I think.

And I swear I hear him say, *'I know.'*

Six

Ben closes the door, trapping us in the icy hallway. I hug my arms and walk beside him, keeping as much distance as I can. My mind and body are at constant odds; my body wanting the comfort of his touch, to absorb his familiar scent, feel his warmth, while my mind screams that he could reach out and grab my hand too, and he doesn't.

As if reading my confusion, he nods over his shoulder to another grey guard a few metres down the hall. I keep my eyes forward and walk stiffly so as not to move the piece of black arrow tucked up in my trouser cuff. Instead of saying all the things I want to say to Ben, I take in my surroundings and try to memorise my way back to Eros.

The hall is stark and white but stained with dirt. The cement floor's cracked, like at one point it was a working industrial facility. The faint scent of sulphuric smoke blasts out with cold air from large vents. It stinks but it covers any burning smell coming from the black shard. We walk under a hanging sign in a language that's familiar but I can't quite pinpoint. The English translation is hand-painted beneath it, *Shipping and Receiving Bay*, and an arrow points in the direction we're going. We pass many blue doors, and I count them all. Ben slows his steps, turning to me every once in a while like he's got something to say, but I keep my eyes forward. I can't risk giving into my need for comfort, and if I look at him I know I will.

Still, the need to break our silence overpowers me, and I think maybe I can get some information out of him before the other guard catches on. I glance back to see her a good way behind, then ask in a low voice, 'What's the story with the black armlet?'

He shakes his head and motions over his shoulder at the guard.

'She can't hear, just tell me.'

Nothing, no response.

I sigh. 'I'll find out on my own.'

Ben's whole body goes rigid, and in a blink he's holding my shoulders and pressing me into the wall, his body inches from mine. My chest rises and falls with heavy breaths, warmth fills all of me. This is the closest we've been since our graveyard kiss.

My eyes land on his lips and trace up his face. 'I miss you,' I whisper.

His gaze is cold, but it flicks to my mouth and lingers there a little too long. That and his uneven breaths give away that he's struggling with our closeness too.

'I know you have a piece of the arrow,' he says, low, a warning. 'I saw it fall.'

Of course Ben saw. He sees everything.

'It's dangerous,' he continues. 'Don't touch it and don't let Heda know you have it. Do you understand?'

I open my mouth and am about to reply when heavy footsteps rush up behind us.

'Everything all right there?' the guard asks, electric rod charged and in hand.

I don't want Ben to get in trouble or lose Heda's trust. The fact that she has a guard trailing him makes me think she doesn't have very much trust in him to start with. So I do the only thing I can think of.

'This jerk won't leave me alone.' I shove Ben. 'I told him I changed my mind; I'm not giving any more blood. It's cruel of Heda to take it.'

Ben's eyes widen, registering what I'm doing. 'Actually,' he says, pushing off me and standing alert, looking so much like a soldier that I almost don't recognise him, 'taking blood isn't cruel when that blood has the power to heal sickness and help people. What's cruel is preventing that help.'

He's so serious about his answer that it makes me question if he really thinks Heda is doing the right thing.

'Is that what she's doing, helping people?' The need to press him further fills me to bursting. 'Her method of taking it sure feels cruel.' I hold out my bruised arm,

51

only to see all the bruises faded and the skin around my wrists nearly healed. 'W-what about that thing around Eros's neck?' I add quickly. 'It's literally burning his skin.'

The guard looks at Ben like I'm dense. 'If he cooperates he gets a salve that makes that burn go away,' she says.

I roll my eyes. 'How kind.'

'Yeah,' Ben says. 'It is kind. Heda doesn't owe him anything.'

I push off the wall, fists clenched. I don't care how good an actor he is, enough is enough.

The guard steps forward, rod raised at me. 'Should we take her back to Heda?' she asks.

Ben runs his hand through his hair, leaving a stray strand hanging over his eyes. 'Nah,' he says, flashing the girl one of his charming grins. She can't help smiling back. 'I have it under control,' he continues, turning back to me. 'And we better stick to the arrangement made. Isn't that right?' he asks, lowering his voice. 'You still want to see your family?'

I nod and swallow the lump creeping up my throat. Ben's too good at playing this part.

The guard stays with us, flashing Ben little looks, as we continue down the hall. We stop before the next set of doors, larger than any we've passed so far, and worn down with years' worth of rust. I counted ten doors from the ichor room, an easy number to remember.

52

There's a sign above the handle, with painted words in English: *Containment Room*.

Something about that makes me shudder.

Ben pushes the intercom button on the panel next to the doors.

'Scan your key card,' comes a static voice.

'Don't have one,' Ben says into the speaker.

'Name and clearance?'

'Benjamin Blake, clearance 278HUM-18.'

A small panel in the large door clicks open.

He pushes the button again. 'Bring out container 112.'

'Roger that.'

Ben turns to me. 'Listen, Rach—'

'My family's in there?' I ask, confused about the sign on the door and Ben's request for a container.

'Yes, but—'

I push past him, ignoring the scream of the tall steel door's hinges, and find myself on a large cement balcony overlooking a warehouse with endless rows of shipping containers stacked floor-to-ceiling. There's a small wooden paddle boat propped up on the railing with life preservers hanging off it and words written on the side in the same language as the signs. The stale scent of sea salt and corroded metal fills the air.

But I don't see anyone.

Panic fills me. 'Where's my family?'

Ben pulls a tablet off the inside wall and turns on the screen. He flips through until he finds what he's looking for, then holds it out to show me – live footage of individuals in small boxy cells. They have a bed, a light and a curtained-off area in the corner which I assume is the bathroom. At first I'm not sure why he's showing me that, then I glance back out at the sea of metal.

'They're all . . .' I point to the containers. My heart feels like it's being squeezed.

'Yes.' He nods.

Endless rows of shipping containers – filled with people.

My lungs become so starved for oxygen that no matter how many breaths I take I don't seem to get enough. 'My fam—' I can't even finish the question.

When he comes to the stream of someone I know, he holds it up for me to see. At first, through my tear-clouded eyes, I don't recognise the person on screen, but then I'm certain it's Paisley's ma. He swipes the screen to show me Mother Superior and some of the other sisters from St Valentine's. I want him to stop swiping but he doesn't.

Not until he comes to my dad.

He holds it out for me to see. Dad lies on a mattress on the floor, tracing his finger along the wall. My heart races with a mix of sadness and anticipation. I cannot wait to meet this man. My real dad, the one I've been

54

denied my whole life. Another male form enters. The intruder turns and faces the camera, using the reflective surface to fix his hair.

'Kyle,' I gasp. 'They have him too?'

'They have everyone,' Ben says. His words have no remorse, but his eyes look like they could cry at any moment.

'Turn back to my dad,' I say.

And he does.

Dad looks nothing like the frail pushover of a man I used to know. Even now, while a captive of the Committee, he looks more angry than scared.

I'm angry too. 'Why are they being held?'

Ben looks like he wants to tell me everything but the guard tailing him makes it impossible. Instead he points over my shoulder and I turn to see a large, claw-like crane lift one of the weather-worn containers. It swings it our way and lowers it on to the large empty space before us on the balcony. The number 112 is painted in yellow beside a small window. Something moves behind the glass, then the inside light flicks on, illuminating a familiar form.

Seven

Our eyes lock and I run to Ma's cage.

'Rachel!' Ma places her hand on the glass pane, eyes full of tears.

I put my hand over hers and cry too. 'Hey, Ma.'

Her long hair, normally pulled into a bun, hangs loose, and they've made her wear a blue tracksuit like mine. The gold and black beaded necklace I've never seen her without is gone. It's so strange seeing her like this, so unlike herself, so helpless.

Her lips tremble, still they spread into a large smile. 'When they told me you were alive, I didn't believe it, but I had to take the chance.'

I pull back, shocked at her words. 'You came here because of me?' I wave to the container. 'This is my fault?'

'Please. You know I would go to the Underworld and back for you.'

'Be careful what you wish for,' Ben says quietly from behind.

I ignore him and focus on Ma. 'They have Dad and Kyle?'

'They're all right,' she says, patting the window as if it were my hand. 'I see them daily when we're brought to the meal room.'

'Is Nani here too?'

Ma shakes her head. 'I haven't seen her.'

The smell of burning cloth begins to overpower the salty and sulphur smell of the container warehouse room. I look down at my trousers to see a trail of smoke rising up. The arrow can't stay as it is, I'll be burned soon. The guard next to Ben won't take her eyes off me, so bending down and pulling it out isn't an option. Instead I use my other leg to pretend to scratch my foot and attempt to get the shard out. Ma frowns at me.

'Rachel? Are you OK?'

'Yes, I—' The chunk flicks out and skitters just out of reach. The guard didn't seem to notice, but Ben crinkles his brow inquisitively.

Everything in me screams to hide the shard, that it might be my only leverage against Heda, but to be safe I'd better ignore it right now. Instead I step closer and lower my voice so the guard next to Ben won't hear. 'Ma, what's going on here?'

She glances at the camera mounted on the ceiling of her container and leans into the glass, covering her mouth from its view. 'Hedone's taken over the Committee. She's drugged or coerced everyone to come here. It was madness. For weeks the Quiver chat rooms were filled with stories of a blue and yellow helicopter showing up and Hedonesses and their families going missing. You can't trust anyone.'

'That,' comes Heda's grainy voice from behind us, 'is a most important lesson.'

Ma's eyes widen, and I whip round to see Heda with her gaggle of grey guards along with the boy with purple hair. Bringing up the rear is the red guard, leading Paisley by the tip of her electric sword. Heda's carrying the black and gold box herself this time, which makes me worried about why they've brought Paisley.

'Good to see you've been reunited,' Heda begins, 'but now that we've said our hellos, let's get down to business.'

Ma slaps the glass. 'You leave my daughter alone.'

'Is that any way to show your thanks? It's because of me that you got released from jail, after all.'

'She doesn't look very released from jail,' I say, shuffling towards the arrow shard that fell out of my trouser leg and hoping no one notices.

'Touché,' says Heda. 'Let's just say Priya owes me.' She is no longer the frail woman who needed a hit of my blood to stand on her own and that freaks me out.

'I owe you nothing!' Ma says.

There's something more than captive and captor between them; the way Heda said my ma's name tells me that much. I've also never seen my ma lose her cool like that.

'Why are you holding them?' I ask again, pulling Heda from her staring match with Ma.

'My darling, they're collateral.'

'Why?' I practically spit. 'What do you want with us?'

'You already know what I want.'

'Ichor,' I whisper, looking to Ma as I say it.

Ma's face drops. 'Is it true then? What they're saying about you? Did Eros—' She cuts herself off. The look on my face must be all the answer she needs. 'Oh, love,' she says. Ma has witnessed my hatred of the Hedoness ways, my rejection of the power of the arrow. Now, I'm immortal and, as my blood has proven, that comes with a whole other beastly power. Ma puts both hands on the glass. She doesn't need to say anything for me to know what she's thinking; the worry in her eyes speaks enough.

I turn back to Heda, angry about my family being once again behind bars. I'm just not sure what she needs from me. If it's ichor, Eros's is much stronger. 'What do you want from us?' I gesture to the sea of containers filled with Hedonesses, using the movement to bring me the rest of the distance to the arrow shard and shielding it with my foot.

Heda grins. Her fingers caress the box lid, running along the seams and gold markings like they're following a sacred path. She slowly opens the lid, not bothering to cover her hands as she pulls out the matt-black arrow bangle. The metal absorbs what little light hits it and the room seems to darken. She doesn't scream in pain as she slips it over her bare skin but her face twists in discomfort. It hurts her to touch it. She takes deep pulsing breaths but she doesn't let it stop her. Heda guides her hand through until the bangle is in place, carefully, reminding me of when I was a child and tried on the jewellery Ma told me not to touch. The tip of the arrow points out over her middle finger and she holds it up, turning it in the light. The guards nearest her step back.

She glides forward, arrow hand raised like a sword. 'Even after everything you've taken from me, this –' she spins the armlet – 'will ensure I get what I want.'

I haven't taken anything from her, unless she's meaning when Ben and I ended the Hedoness power.

Heda smiles at my confusion and scans the room, keeping the arrow hand raised. 'Le-Li, come here, will you?'

The boy with purple hair hurries over. His eyes lock on the arrow and he whispers, 'You shouldn't keep that on too long.'

'Don't tell me what to do,' she says, her eyes hardening with each word. She turns to me and forces a smile. 'You've met Le-Li, my special boy.'

'Unfortunately,' I say, hugging my arms and feeling every needle bruise that was once there.

She ignores me and adjusts the arrow encircling her wrist. 'His mother is a world-renowned biologist, but because his father is a god the Committee tried to hunt him down and kill him. Luckily, I intervened. We couldn't waste such a valuable asset.'

I glance at Le-Li, trying to see the divinity in him. He lowers his head and smiles like someone who's been posing for a picture for too long, his mouth cemented in some strange forced grin.

'In fact, his father is my favourite god,' Heda continues. 'The only one that can pluck ether out of stars and forge it into weapons.' She turns to Le-Li. 'Isn't that right?'

Le-Li nods.

'Show her,' she says, putting her armlet-free hand on his shoulder. He flinches and lifts his shirt and trouser leg to reveal an unusual hodgepodge of metal contraptions. I'm almost certain there's a tape deck where his heart should be and his leg is made up of two steel baseball bats. I understand now why he limps. 'Meet the son of Hephaestus, the god of the forge, known for his half-human, half-machine automatons.'

'Automatons?' I say, not quite believing I'm seeing a boy who is half metal parts.

Heda smiles. 'Remarkable, isn't he?'

Le-Li takes her words as a cue and pushes the button on his tape-deck heart. What sounds like a sports game broadcasts into the room. Not any sports – baseball.

'Turn that off,' she says. He does, then lowers his shirt. 'Le-Li is the last living automaton. Which is a shame, they're handy little helpers. They do whatever they are instructed to do.'

Well, that explains a few things.

'Plus, his father taught him everything he knows about weaponry and anatomy. Heph is remarkable. He made Eros's arrows, you know.' She continues talking, but I can't take my eyes off Le-Li – half boy, half robot thingy.

Heda waves, drawing my attention back to her. '. . . Zeus's bolt, any god who's anything has one of Heph's weapons.' She pauses, her eyes going to the black arrow with reverence. 'I suppose you could say he made this, too, with the help of Le-Li, who turned it into an armlet.'

Le-Li smiles, proud of his work.

'My little automaton's skills in weaponry and biology are remarkable. He used his father's forge to recreate a more containable source of Zeus's bolt.' She waves to the red guard, who pulls out her weapon, turning it on so it flashes an electric blue. 'And don't even get me started on what he can do with DNA. With Le-Li's help, I will do the impossible. I will take the stardust out of you.'

'What?' I lift my chin.

'Do you want to know what I'll do with it?'

I don't reply and she sweeps an arm to Ma's shipping container as if to prove her point. 'I'll use it to make weapons.'

My mind swirls with thoughts as I try to figure out why I'm on this side of the containers and not with everyone else. Heda needs ichor to keep her immortal, but she has Eros for that. There must be something in my blood that's different, something she craves more than immortality, something to make her weapons.

Suddenly Le-Li's strange comment to Heda after she drank my blood replays in my mind. *'You should absorb the arrow first, see how it sits with you.'*

The arrow. My legs shake, threatening to collapse me to the ground.

It can't be that. Ben and I ended the Hedoness power, we broke Eros's curse – the power of the arrow is out of our blood. But what is it then? I want to cry, I want to scream. If somehow it is still in me and Heda thinks she can take it out of my blood, then it could mean she wants to put it back in everyone. How would that even be possible? My whole body vibrates with anger. It worsens when I remember the glazed look on Heda while my blood went into her.

'Find someone else to fill your fix!' I snap back. 'I'd rather die than help you.'

'Good, that makes my job easier.' Heda raises her finger and the red guard shoves Paisley into the arms of another and springs forward. I manage to kick the shard of arrow towards Ma's container before her gloves encircle my arm. Ma's hands are outstretched behind the glass.

'Let me go,' I say, elbowing the girl. Her grip on me tightens. Suddenly I'm back in New York, the jail, Officer

Ammon's hands digging into my arm. I'm not going through this again.

'I'm afraid we can't do that,' Heda says. 'But give us your cooperation and you won't get hurt.'

I shove the guard but she holds her footing. Two guards in grey approach from behind her, electric rods raised. One of them tries to grab me and I twist, knocking the rod out of their hand, but not fast enough to avoid contact.

I'm jolted back.

The pain fills me with the same familiar sting as the Hedoness power. It's tearing me apart from the inside out, molecule by molecule. I cry, double over, clutching my hand, trying to catch my breath. The red guard jabs me in the side with her weapon. The two guards in grey do the same. Jab after jab, my insides fall apart. White lights shoot behind my eyes. I focus on the pain, willing it to exit my skin, *begging it to*.

This time, when the guards grab me, the cry becomes deafening. Defeat washes through me – this is my life now.

Then I see them. The guards. On the ground, clutching their stomachs and screaming. It wasn't me who cried out. Somehow, something has happened to the guards.

'Get her now!' Heda says, waving her arrowed hand in a wild arc.

I push up to see a new surge of Heda's guards. I'm surrounded. Their weapons raise, confining me to an electric cage. Someone jabs me in the back. I collapse forward into another rod. Bolt after bolt fills me as they ram their weapons into my body.

I jerk uncontrollably. In the distance I hear Ma cry my name and Paisley beg Heda to let me go. I'm afraid this pain will never end.

'Stop!' Ben shouts.

They listen to him and pull back. I drop to my knees, choking in mouthfuls of air.

'Stop?' asks Heda, unimpressed.

'There's a more effective way to get what you want from her,' he says.

'And what's that?' Heda asks, amused.

'Your collateral.' Ben pulls out the tablet and pushes a button. 'Bring out container 300.'

'An interesting choice,' says Heda.

Six glowing rods circle my throat as I catch my breath and watch the crane pick up another container. I'm afraid to know who's in this one.

Heda grips the box with one hand and the red guard with the other. I didn't even notice the guard get up off the floor. The colour seems to drain from every part of Heda, even her hair is quickly turning white. I can only assume that wearing the black arrow takes her strength somehow.

The crane lowers the container, setting it adjacent to my ma's.

'No!' Ma cries.

That's when I see who's in it. The one person who will be most upset with what I've done – the person who most wanted me to embrace being Hedoness.

'Nani.' I gasp.

She stands in her window, confused by the scene outside. 'Rachel? What is the meaning of this?'

Before I can reply, Ben leans close. 'Now will you cooperate?' he says, his eyes almost pleading.

Though I believe with every fibre of my being that he's putting on an act, I can't help the anger rising up in me. He of all people should know the pain of losing family. Offering them as an alternative is not OK, even if it is his only way to protect me. 'You wouldn't dare!' I bolt for him but stop when I come too close to one of the rods.

A slow clap comes from behind. 'Looks like I won't be needing this.' Heda slips off her arrow and opens the box that is now being held by the red guard. She places the armlet in the box with the tenderness of a mother laying a baby to sleep, then turns back to us.

'It seems I have underestimated you, Benjamin Blake.'

Eight

The guards back up as I struggle to stand in the small space they've given me. Paisley wiggles away from the one holding her and rushes over. She pushes through the weapons to my side; her arms slip around me for support.

Heda glares at the guard who let Paisley go and rests her hand on the box lid as if threatening to reopen it. 'What is your answer, Rachel? Will you cooperate, or will your family pay the price?' This was her plan all along. She only allowed me to see my family to know what's at stake if I don't help her.

I take deep breaths and struggle to lift my head. Ma and Nani's worry-filled faces press to the glass, eyes swollen from tears. They're all I have now. 'My family,' I struggle to say. 'Let them go.'

'Rachel, no!' Ma yells.

'No debating,' Heda says, and I know by her tone that she means it.

'All of them together and safe, then. If you can promise me that, I'll do it. I'll cooperate.'

Heda shakes her head. 'You don't seem to know what *no* means.'

I bite the inside of my cheek and take a deep breath. 'You need me and if you want me those are my terms.'

'Is that all?' asks Heda, sarcasm dripping from her words.

I glance out to the sea of containers. 'No one gets hurt. None of them.'

'I think you overestimate your power. You do see the armed guards surrounding you, don't you?'

Paisley's grip on me tightens.

'No,' I say, lifting my chin. 'You're underestimating me.'

Heda's back stiffens. It's obvious she doesn't like to be challenged in front of her guards. 'And how's that?' she hisses.

Heda wants what's in my blood, but there's something else she holds dear. Something else I have.

The black arrow.

I still don't fully understand what it does. Heda says it will get her whatever she wants, and it hurts some people to touch it but others, like Paisley, can touch it no problem. I look to Ben, hearing his warning reply in my mind, '*Don't tell Heda.*' But I have no other choice; she's threatening my family. I lift my chin and try to stand strong though Paisley is basically the only thing keeping me upright. 'I have a piece of your armlet.'

'What!' Heda whips open the box. When her eyes land on the missing chunk of feather, an infuriated growl escapes her throat. 'Search her!' she says.

The guards surge forward.

'They won't find it,' I blurt. 'It's not on me.'

Ben flashes me a worried look.

Heda takes a shuddering step closer. 'You are fit for another ichor donation, aren't you?' She lowers her voice. 'Your family is depending on it.'

'Does this mean we have a deal? My family will be safe, all the Hedonesses will be safe?'

'As long as you cooperate with me, they will be safe.'

I know she won't let them go. She made that clear when she set her red guard on me. But I can at least protect my family until I come up with a better plan, or Ben finds a way to get us out. Hopefully that happens before Le-Li manages to take whatever it is Heda needs from my blood. I glance at Le-Li then at Ben – playing the perfect role as her guard – the boy who once professed his love for me. 'Yes,' I say. 'I'm ready.' Ben doesn't even blink.

'Good.' She turns to Le-Li. 'Take her to back to the ichor room and check on my father while you're there. And Ben –' she looks at me – 'have the rest of her family brought here. This is as good a place as any for them to be together.'

Ben speaks the order into the tablet and the crane instantly unlocks from Nani's container and twists to grab another.

'Go now,' Heda orders.

Le-Li waves us forward and I cross my arms.

'Let me see them first.'

Heda sighs. 'The time for making deals is over. I am a woman of my word, and I trust you will be the same.'

I can tell I've run her patience to its very end. The last thing I need is to start another fight. I don't trust Heda not to hurt my family just to get back at me. So I nod and take a step towards Le-Li, my legs collapsing in the process. Paisley jumps forward and catches me before I fall. I lean into her, my body still weak from the electric beating it just received.

'Help her to the room, Paisley.' It isn't Heda who says it. It's Ben. Though there's no sign of concern in his eyes I take it as a kindness.

The red guard starts after Paisley but Heda stops her. 'I need you here with me to search for the missing piece.' She pats her black box then nods to Ben. 'You go, and make sure they give Le-Li no trouble.'

I stop in place, worried what the shard search means for my family.

Paisley nudges me forward. 'There's nothing you can do but pray she doesn't find it,' she says.

Paisley and I hobble into the hall as the crane sets another container down. I turn to see who it is but Le-Li closes the doors behind Ben. I glare at him and adjust my arm around Paisley before continuing towards the ichor room.

The hallway is colder than I remember. I walk close to Paisley for warmth, counting each of the ten doors we pass to distract my mind from wandering back to my family. I'll have to trust that Heda kept her word and that the cranes were going to retrieve Kyle and my dad.

We stop before the ichor room and I pull away from Paisley to stand on my own. I'm feeling stronger now, somehow. Le-Li unlocks the door and Ben holds it open for us. When I see Eros, once again chained, the urge to turn and run fills me. At least this time they've given him the stool to sit on. Still, he looks exhausted and struggles to lift his head. He glances up through limp curls, his pain-faded blue eyes offering a half-smile.

Paisley's hand rests gently on my back. It brings me more comfort than she knows. I feel less alone with her here. Sure, Ben's here too, but he's not actually with me, not like Paisley is. It's nice having her near. I would've been a prisoner of the Committee long before now if it wasn't for all those Quiver conversations with Paisley where she fed me with the information to avoid capture and tried to help me get my ma back. At least I know there's someone I can trust.

'No trouble, remember?' Le-Li says, putting one hand on my shoulder and motioning me towards the bed in the adjoining room.

The need to fight still pulses in my veins, my heart beats faster than normal. I yank away from Le-Li and march over to the table next to Eros, plop myself down, roll up the sleeve of the tacky blue sweatsuit and hold out my arm.

'Where do you want the IV?' I ask.

Ben leans in the doorway, watching everything I do with a newfound curiosity, like he's not sure if I'm really giving in or what.

Le-Li drags over the machine from my old room. He puts only one tube in me this time. He flicks a button on it and the mechanical gurgle fills the room. His movements look rigid and I wonder if they were always that way and I'm just noticing it more now that I know what he is. I have so many questions for him. For starters, I'm not entirely sure what an automaton is. Was he born half metal or made that way?

He shuffles back to Eros and I lie down, watching the blue bubbles, wondering how my family is now, hoping they're all together, even if in their shipping container prisons.

Paisley leans on the edge of the bed and tucks a tight ringlet behind her ear, only to have another spring out. I miss the little flowers she'd pick from St Valentine's garden and stick among her curls. 'Hey,' she says, giving me a half-smile.

'Hi,' I reply.

'So.' Her eyes go serious for a quick second. 'What was up with the guards?' she says in a whisper. 'One second they were attacking you and the next they dropped to the floor.'

'I have no clue.' A shiver goes through me as I think back to the jolts of electricity that rammed into my body.

'It was weird.' She flicks the tube going into my arm. 'Sucks this is all happening.'

'Yeah, I'm not a fan.' I glance at Ben. His eyes are on us, lips twitching like he wants to say something, but he doesn't.

She frowns, looking like she's trying to find something to raise my spirits. 'That was pretty awesome what we did earlier with the arrow armlet,' she says, her eyes fixated on the spot where Heda forced her to the floor to grab it. 'We make a good team.'

'We do,' I say. 'If we could've picked friends in school, I bet we'd have been best friends.'

She smiles up at me. 'We can pick them now. And you know what, we're more than friends or a good team, we're partners in crime.'

'Oh, are we?'

'I cause the distractions, you screw Heda over. Win-win.'

I laugh.

'So what are you going to do with it?' she asks.

My eyes return to the door, remembering Ben's warning about the arrow. 'Not touch it, that's for sure.'

Paisley lets out an airy laugh as she watches Le-Li swap out a full tub of Eros's blood for an empty one.

I prop myself up on my elbows, lean towards her and lower my voice. 'Why does Heda need so much of our blood?'

She looks between the boys and me with hesitation.

'Is it all for her health?' I continue. 'To keep her young or whatever?'

'It's a little more than that,' she says.

'Paisley,' Le-Li calls, his voice low in warning. 'I need you, now!'

Paisley offers a shrug before hopping down and heading to Le-Li. I pick at a loose thread on my blue top and think about the odd exchange. When she comes back a few minutes later she's carrying two small glass vials and a syringe.

'I hate it, but I'm supposed to give you these and I'd better obey,' she says, setting the vials on the bed beside me. She sticks the needle into one of them and drains the liquid into the syringe, squirts out the excess air, then turns back to me. She's comfortable with the syringe, like she's done this many times.

'I'm diabetic,' she says, catching the curiosity in my eyes. 'I self-administer a lot of shots. Well, I used to, before they started testing—'

'Paisley!' Le-Li shouts from across the room.

Testing?

She glances to him then back to me. 'This will feel cold going in.'

'What is that?' I ask.

'Vitamins and something to help you sleep.'

'We can skip the sleeping meds. I've done enough of that lately.' I don't even want to think about what they do to me while I sleep. Someone changed me into this blue tracksuit, after all.

'They're mixed together.' Her eyes fill with a sorry she doesn't speak.

'I told them I would comply. They don't need to put me to sleep and I don't need vitamins.'

'Yes you do,' says Le-Li.

'I feel fine,' I say.

Le-Li's full attention is on us now. 'You were in a fight and there was adrenaline flooding your blood. That is nasty stuff to work around. It'll skew all my experiments – total strike-out.'

'Experiments?' I repeat.

'Blood is easier to work with if taken while you're asleep,' he continues. 'There are fewer stress hormones. And you haven't eaten or had proper rest. The vitamins will help with that.'

He nods to Paisley, and before I can ask what *work* he's doing with my blood, she pushes the needle and empties the clear substance into my port.

It does feel cold going in. It shivers to my soul.

She refills the syringe. As the last of the liquid flows into my body it's like a heavy weight is placed on me. I try to sit up and can't. All I'm able to do is twist my head. My eyes find Ben's cold hard blue stare. I imagine it how it used to be, full of care and endless questions, and that helps calm me a little.

He steps away from the doorframe suddenly, standing alert, the look on his face sending me back into a panic. Then I see her – Heda and her entourage of guards whisking into the room, her blue robe filling with air like sails and giving the illusion she's floating.

Paisley quickly leans over and whispers, 'Pretend to be asleep.'

I furrow my brow in confusion.

'Now,' she adds, grabbing my hand then whirling round to face them.

I'm not sure what's happening, but I trust Paisley. The last thing I see as I close my eyes is Ben, leaning in to whisper something to Heda.

'Has she received the medication?' Heda asks.

'Yes,' says Paisley. Her grip on me stays firm.

'How long ago?'

'She's falling into REM as we speak.' Paisley gives my hand a quick squeeze as if to tell me to act more asleep. I take deeper, slower breaths, my chest rising and falling like waves, and soon the urge to sleep does fill me. I focus on Paisley's hand, trying to stay awake.

'Good,' says Heda. 'Le-Li, we couldn't find it and now I'm agitated. I'd like a little taste, can you arrange that?'

My heart races. I hope she means she couldn't find the piece of the black arrow I kicked towards my ma's container.

'I can,' he says. 'But—'

'But?' Her words cut through the room like a knife.

'Right away,' says Le-Li in a monotone.

His steps swish across the floor then the door to the machine opens and closes. 'Paisley, darling, are you ready for your next tests?' Heda swallows, smacks her lips, then grunts in approval.

Paisley's hand shakes in mine. 'Yes,' she says quietly.

'Very good. Le-Li will ready the operating theatre for you. Go to him.'

Another chill runs along my body. Whatever they're doing to Paisley can't be good.

'Yes,' says Paisley, her voice wavering.

'Now,' Heda says, annoyed.

Paisley gives me a light squeeze then lets go. The urge to jump from the bed and stop her fills me. But I honour her request and continue to fake being asleep, listening to her sad footsteps petering out towards the door followed by the shuffle of Le-Li's as he joins her.

Nine

My head spins. It's harder to fight the urge to slip into sleep.

'Leave us,' Heda commands.

There's a series of footfalls and the door clicks shut. A long silence follows, broken only by Eros's gurgled breaths. Then his chains rattle and he cries out in pain.

'Father,' Heda says in a sigh, 'will you tell me now?'

I bite the inside of my lip to keep awake, ignoring the metallic taste. Whatever they have to say to each other, I need to hear it.

'You . . . know . . . I . . . cannot.' The faint sizzle of burning skin drifts across the room and Eros hisses. It must be from his collar. But it isn't his neck that hurts him the most, sorrow hangs off every word. Whatever it is that pitted them against each other, daughter against father, must be breaking his heart.

I think of my own father. A man I've always wanted to know but couldn't because he was under the Hedoness power and didn't even notice I existed. Now that he wants to know me too, we're kept apart by others. It seems cruel and somehow ironic.

'All along,' Heda says from behind me, 'you had what I needed. I could have been returned to Mother but you gave it to that girl.' She practically spits the word *girl*. I know she's talking about me and the ambrosia. *The immortality.* And that leaves the question: why *did* he give it to me and not his daughter?

'Since . . . when do you . . . care about your mother?' Eros gasps in shallow breaths.

'You know nothing,' Heda snaps.

'I know . . . you broke . . . her heart.'

'I broke her heart? What am I supposed to do? I can't just go and be with her? Tell me, Father, please, because I'm all ears. Last I checked I'm not allowed in Olympus. None of the demigods are. What's left of us, anyway.' Heda's voice shakes. 'Hera created the Committee to hunt us down and kill us, and you did nothing to stop them.'

'I left your mother . . . love of my life . . . for you.' There's a waver in his voice, a sorrow, like his heart is breaking all over again. 'To end . . . Hedoness curse—'

'Curse? That *curse* was the only thing that kept me alive.'

'You care more . . . about power than family. I tried—'

'You tried? Is that a joke?' Heda's robe swishes against the floor as she paces. I bite down harder on my lip. More blood fills my mouth and trickles down my throat.

But I fight the pain. I need to stay awake. I need to hear this.

'You could have given me the ambrosia and made me a true immortal, and then I could have returned to Olympus and been with you and Mum,' says Heda.

Sorrow fills me, reminding me that I am becoming an immortal now and everything that means – watching my loved ones wither and die, being a slave to the powers in me once again. It's all too much to bear. A tear escapes over my cheek. I reach up to wipe it away and as I do so the bed rattles. I drop my arm, freezing in place.

Heda stops talking. There's a shuffle as she turns on the cement floor. 'Check on her,' she orders.

Someone rushes to me and grabs my wrist, testing my pulse, then puts an ear to my mouth. I know it's Ben before he speaks. The familiar way he smells – of paper and the ocean – it fills my head to bursting.

'She's still asleep,' he says. 'But it doesn't seem like deep sleep.'

I'm surprised he's here. I didn't hear him come back in. I thought it was only Eros, Heda and me.

'Give her another dose,' Heda commands.

Ben's hand stays on my arm, a forbidden touch, his thumb rubbing circles over my skin. It makes it even harder to concentrate on Heda and Eros.

'Your mother . . .' Eros continues, 'so . . . depressed

after you left . . . she threatened to throw herself out . . . out of Olympus.'

'Father,' Heda sighs. 'Mother's immortality is contingent on her being in Olympus – she can't leave, she'd die.'

Eros doesn't respond and after some time Heda starts tapping her foot, annoyed. 'So why would she give that up?' she asks, sounding bored by the whole conversation.

'Because of you . . . she couldn't bear life without her daughter.'

'And you, Father, could you also not bear life without me? Is that why you abandoned the love of your life in her depressed state?'

The cold sting fills my arms again and I realize Ben's putting more sleeping meds into me. I'm already struggling to stay awake; this is going to make it impossible.

'Sorry about this, Rach,' Ben leans down and whispers, his warm breath tickling my ear. 'If you want peace, prepare for war.'

I fight the urge to frown and ask him what he means, but then his footsteps carry away from me and Eros's voice fills my ears.

'I had to fix my mistake . . .' Eros grunts through the pain, 'end the Hedoness . . . Zeus made me a promise . . . if I could find someone to give his heart to a Hedoness . . . he'd end the curse and reunite our family—'

'Zeus. Ha! It's his fault this is all happening. He had affair after affair and spread his half-blood offspring everywhere.'

I wince at the disgust in her voice when she says *half blood*.

'Of course Hera would be ashamed of her husband's actions,' Heda continues. 'She's the one who started the Committee. She wanted her shame erased. And every other demigod monster with it!'

I fade in and out, only getting some of what they say. If I understand correctly, Zeus's wife ordered all the demigods out of Olympus then formed the Committee to hunt them down and kill them. But then Zeus made a deal with Eros that if he ended the Hedoness curse he'd be reunited with his family. Why did Zeus go back on that? One thing is clear – it's the first time I've recognised something of myself in Heda. We're both full of heartbreak and anger, we both feel betrayed by people we love. I think of Ben and my mind drifts through memories of him, folding them into the dark.

Eros's chains rattle, jolting me back from the edge of sleep. I try to open my eyes but it's as if they're glued shut. My arms too heavy to move. Eros takes a long, raspy breath.

'Don't worry, Father,' Heda continues. 'When I'm done here I'll show Olympus exactly how wrong they were about us demigods. We're not weak. We deserve immortality and not just whatever this prolonged aging is. We are stronger than they ever imagined.'

The pull of sleep weighs me down.

'This is your plan?' Eros coughs. 'You want to sneak into . . . Olympus. And what?'

Eros and Heda become distant voices on a radio.

'Sneak? No,' she says, her voice crackling in the static of my dreary mind. The darkness collapses in on me and I'm dragged down. As I finally surrender to it, the last thing I hear her say is, 'I will break down their door. And they will bow.'

Ten

When I wake, I open my eyes, disappointed to find I'm still in the ichor room. It's quiet, too quiet. I take my time sitting up, stretching, willing the dizziness to leave. My fingers grip the edge of the bed as I wait for the room to stop rocking. Eros lifts his head and offers a half-smile.

'Are we alone?' I ask.

He nods.

Ma's frequently recited words flutter through my mind, *'When you surrender to love, Eros will find you. Eros looks out for his own.'* If Ma saw him like this, she'd realize what a joke that is. I carefully step down, holding my tube so it doesn't yank the needle from my arm, and head for the door. It's locked.

I return to the gurney and we stay in silence, me on the metal bed, him on the stool. I flick the tube and stare at the ichor leaving me. I'm so confused about what it does, what Heda needs it for. If I'm right, she's going to find a way to get the Hedoness magic from my blood. But that begs the question, how is it still in me? I glance back to the spot Heda stabbed the guard then gave her Eros's blood to drink – to heal. Ben's words fill my mind, '*Taking blood isn't cruel when that blood has the power to heal sickness and help people.*'

'Does it really do that?' I blurt.

'What?' Eros chokes out, following my gaze to the ichor bubbling up the tube.

'Heal people,' I add.

'All immortal blood heals.' He watches me through his floppy blond curls. 'But you aren't . . . immortal yet.'

'What?' My heart races. It's hard to hope that what he's telling me is true.

'Not yet,' he says. 'But you're transitioning faster than expected.'

My eyes lock on the bright blue fluid feeding his machine and I can't help comparing it to the pastel blue of mine. 'Oh,' I say, first disappointed and then confused. I need to know if my theory is correct. 'Then why does Heda need my blood? Isn't yours stronger?'

'You took the ambrosia before you ended the curse.'

My stomach flips. 'What are you saying?'

'Ambrosia immortalises magic. Magic is the source of life. Even though you and Benjamin broke the curse, the Hedoness ability—'

'It's still in me?' I'm going to be sick. Then the image of all those containers filled with Hedonesses and Heda's words about taking the magic from my blood and

85

weaponising it fills my mind, and my stomach twists twice as hard. It's my worst nightmare. 'And she needs it, why?' I ask, hoping I'm wrong and she has no plans on restoring the curse.

'She was accustomed to its power. She craves it now that's it's gone.

That explains why she acts like an addict around my blood.

'But I don't feel it: no electricity, no power.' As I say the words there's a stirring. I push it aside as nerves.

Eros stares at the floor. 'When you're in transition, you only feel the abilities you want to feel.'

'That's it then, I'll be a Hedoness for ever.' Then I register what he's telling me. The room seems to close in and my chest tightens. 'Abilities? As in more than one?'

He doesn't look up. 'Every immortal is different. But we all have base abilities.'

I remember the time he seemed to come out of nowhere at the statues in Little Tokyo, and then again in the graveyard; how he appeared in the tree. 'Why don't you use your powers and leave then?'

Eros points to his neck. 'This collar, it's made from the arrow of indifference.'

'The black arrow,' I whisper and he nods. 'And that means you can't use your abilities?'

'Yes.'

'You're speaking better,' I say, realising his sentences have been unwavering and he hasn't winced in a while.

'It doesn't hurt as much. My skin must be scabbing. I'm sure it will burn through soon though.'

I glance down at my arm, the yellow and purple bruise around the IV port and the tube coming out. Maybe if they suck enough of this out of me I won't have to worry about fully transitioning and getting all those powers. I look back up. 'What are the base abilities?' I'm afraid to know the answer. I never wanted the Hedoness power and I don't want any others.

'There's eternal youth, obviously. Healing, teleportation, mind reading—'

'Mind reading?' All those times I thought I heard someone in my head – Eros, Heda . . . No, it can't be. This can't be happening.

'Love? Are you OK?'

I try to catch my breath but no matter how much I inhale it isn't enough.

'I realize this is a lot,' he says. 'You don't have to worry about the other abilities. The first is immortality, which you've already experienced.'

I cock my head in confusion.

'The surviving getting shot.'

'Right.' I did do that.

'The rest shouldn't manifest for months, maybe even years. It's not an overnight transition.'

'OK,' I say, wondering if I should tell him about the voices or leave it. It's probably nothing.

'Perhaps you won't even transition and they will all go away,' he adds, wiping his head on his arm to get the curls out of his eyes.

My heart quickens. 'What do you mean?'

'There's a way to undo immortality.' He lowers his voice and leans closer, balancing his weight into the chains. 'Heda would not want you to know this. It's probably why she's put me in this damn collar.'

Eros's voice rings in my ears, my mind looping the words 'undo immortality'. I grip the side of the bed as the room spins.

'H-how?' I force out, my body shaking.

'You don't look so good. Maybe you should lie down and get some rest. This has been quite the—'

'How?' I repeat, firmer, squeezing the metal edge like it's the only thing anchoring me to reality.

'There are two ways, but one is impossible and the other you won't like.'

'Tell me what's possible.'

He sighs. 'All right. Before you fully transition, you need—'

A light on my machine starts to flash red then an alarm goes off, high-pitched and jarring. It's hard to hear Eros.

'It's full,' he says. 'Your tub of ichor. They'll be coming for it.'

I fight the urge to cover my ears. 'What do I need to do?' I say desperately.

He hangs on to the chains and shakes his head. 'You won't like it.'

'Just tell me.' I'm tempted to march over there and wring his neck, collar or no collar.

'Don't say I didn't warn you.'

I throw up my hands. 'Eros!'

'You need to consume the life force of a mortal relative.'

He says it so offhandedly that, paired with the distraction of flashing lights and a wailing siren, I'm not sure I heard correctly. 'What does that even mean?'

'You can get away with drinking a cup or so of their blood if you haven't used any of your powers yet. Gross but no one really gets hurt.'

I think about all the voices I've heard and the incident with the guards. It might already be too late.

'And if I have used my powers?'

'Using them speeds the transitioning process. What could take months will happen in days. In that case you'd need to consume something stronger.'

'Like what?'

He rolls his eyes and shakes his head.

The door rattles as someone unlocks it.

'Hurry,' I beg.

The door swings open.

I hold Eros's stare, eyes pleading for an answer.

He taps his chest, the chains rattle alongside the alarm, the red light making them seem like they're coated in blood. 'Their heart,' he says in one final blow.

My arms buckle and I almost fall back on the bed. 'I'd have to eat their heart?'

My mind spins, my stomach clenches. I fight the worry that it's too late, that I've already used my powers, that someone would have to die to fix it. Instead I focus on the most important question. 'What relative? All of mine are part Hedoness, not immortal but not mortal either.' And as I say it, I know.

I gasp out, 'My dad.'

Eleven

Le-Li turns off the alarm and unhooks the machine. 'This couldn't come at a better time.' He grunts as he lifts the full tub of ichor on to something that looks like a tea cart. 'We're so close,' he says to himself.

'Close to what?' I ask, watching him kneel to connect an empty container.

He smiles, his beady eyes glistening. 'The answers.'

'Answers?' I ask. Perhaps this means they haven't found a way to take the Hedoness power out of my blood. A new wave of hope fills me, maybe it isn't in me after all.

He closes the compartment door and stands, tucking his hands in his lab coat pockets, his fingers rapping against his metal stomach. 'Did you know we had to use special needles in you?' He doesn't wait for my reply. 'A mixture of surgical steel and dust shavings from the arrow of indifference.'

I glance at Eros when Le-Li says this, then at the collar around his neck. Eros shrugs into his chains.

'It's so your body doesn't reject them,' he tells me. 'We had that problem at first. You being self-healing and all.'

But what he says has me thinking. Eros's collar inhibits magic, the needle shavings keep me from healing, Heda didn't want me touching the arrow armlet and she freaked out when she found out I had a shard of it. Could the little broken feather be my key to stopping my transition into immortality?

I shudder at the thought. Even now, knowing shavings of the black arrow are in me makes me sick. I want it out. I don't want either of the arrows in me ever again. 'Listen, I've complied. I've given you more blood. Can I go and see my family now?' My stomach rumbles and I realize the only thing I've eaten is the small chunk of spanakopita, and I have no idea how long ago that was. 'And some food, too?' I add.

'I think that can be arranged. I'll return with an answer.' Le-Li's purple bun bobs as he nods goodbye, whistling as he shuffles the cart into the hall.

The door clicks closed after him and I hop off the bed, being careful not to rip out my tube. As much as I want it out, I don't know when he'll be back. I coil the slack and make my way to Eros, brushing the sticky hair from his face. 'What can I do to help? Want me to lower the chains again?'

'Why bother?' he says. 'We won't be alone long.'

He doesn't even finish his sentence before the door's pulled open and Marissa pops her head in the room. 'I was just with Paisley. She asked me to come and check on you. How are you feeling?'

I've been so inwardly focused I completely forgot about Paisley. The worry I had when I last saw her comes rushing back. 'What are they doing to her? They said something about tests.'

Marissa slips inside, shutting the door behind her, and comes over to me. 'Tests?' she asks, picking her nails like she has no clue what I'm talking about. It's so obviously a lie, I have to fight the urge to roll my eyes.

'They're testing your friend with your blood,' Eros answers for her.

'What? Why?'

'Oh, *those* tests,' Marissa says as if it suddenly came to her. '*Tests* is a strange thing to call it, really. You know how ichor heals? They're using it to help Paisley.'

Paisley told me she didn't have to self-administer insulin shots any more. If my ichor helped heal her diabetes, then at least something good's come from this. But if that's all that was going on, why did Paisley seem uncomfortable about it? 'Why use my ichor, why not use Eros's?'

'We need to know how potent yours is getting,' she says, not mentioning anything about Heda wanting the Hedoness power from me.

'So this –' I wave to the tube of ichor exiting my body – 'it isn't just Heda wanting immortality? They really are using it to help people?' I need to know if I can trust them, if they'll tell me about Heda's plans to weaponise my blood. They weren't there when she told me that so they don't know I know.

Eros's head jerks up. His eyes lock on mine.

I cross my arms, careful not to catch the tube. 'Well, is it?'

He takes a slow breath and purses his lips, glancing warily at Marissa. 'Heda needs what's in you,' he says, choosing his words carefully.

Marissa glares. 'Rachel, you should return to the bed. I'm not sure walking around is beneficial to you or the machine. I'll get Le-Li. He needs to check that everything is working properly in here,' she says.

I ignore her order and take another step towards Eros. 'Wouldn't want to take anything away from the addict,' I say sarcastically.

Marissa whips back around. 'I wouldn't call her that.'

'I know it's not just immortality, or healing people, Marissa. I know she craves the Hedoness power in my blood.'

Marissa doesn't reply but Eros squeezes the chains tighter, like he's confirming my thoughts. 'If only that was all it was,' he says, his voice is full of cynicism. He exhales, slow and loud, then looks up. 'Love, your blood is the closest Heda can get to the Hedoness power,' he says. 'Because of my foolish mistake hiding the arrow of infatuation in her mother.' His voice softens at the mention of his wife, Psyche, Heda's ma, and his eyes drop to the floor. 'Heda was acclimatised to the arrow since her conception. When you and Ben reversed the curse, recalling the arrows magic, her withdrawal has been unbearable.'

It's the closest I'll get to the truth at this point and it makes my heart light to know I can trust Eros.

'I-I think I should get Heda,' Marissa says, her voice laced with panic. 'She can explain all this.'

Even after all the years of Marissa's lies, there's a need in me to give her one more chance to disclose the truth. 'What aren't you telling me?' I ask.

Eros looks from Marissa to me, his eyes shifting from hard to soft and maybe even a little sad.

She glances warily at Eros. 'Nothing, I've told you everything.'

It saddens me to know that no matter how much I prod, Marissa will never tell me. My eyes find the girl I once called my accountability partner and everything clicks together. All the rage I felt towards her comes rushing back. 'I should have known, Marissa. This is all so you can be a Hedoness again? That's why you're helping her!'

'Don't be stupid, Rach. That's not why.'

The room starts spinning. I remember Heda's words in the container room. 'Her weapons,' I repeat.

'Her army,' Eros says.

All those containers – all the Hedonesses – my ma, my nani.

'Heda might be able to make them Hedonesses again –' I'm practically yelling at Marissa – 'but they'll never serve her. Not now!'

'But they will.' Eros lowers his head. 'She has my bow and arrows. With them, she can make anyone do anything.'

A shiver runs through me. I stare down at the bruise on my arm, around the needle – the tiny sliver of one of those arrows.

'We have to stop her,' I say.

'Don't talk like that,' Marissa warns.

'You know what you need to do,' Eros says.

At first I'm not sure what he means, then he taps his heart and it all comes back. If I reverse my mortality, then she can't make Marissa or anyone a Hedoness again. I can also try the black arrow shard, but I don't know how to make it work or if the effects will be permanent. If those options don't work, there's only one thing I can do to stop this.

I can't wait around for whatever Ben's plan is. I have to escape before Le-Li takes the Hedoness power from my blood and makes an army of Hedonesses with it. I shudder at the thought of a legion of women with the ability to steal men's wills under Heda's control. The damage that would do would be catastrophic.

Twelve

I rip the needle from my arm, leaving the tube dangling from the ceiling and watching the ichor spill over my skin and on to the cement floor. Eros lifts his head, furrowing his brow in question. I push past a shocked Marissa and march for the machine. 'How do I turn this thing off?'

'Rach, don't.' Marissa rushes after me in a series of heel clicks. She tries to grab me but only gets an armful of sweatshirt.

'That's Le-Li's . . . department,' Eros finishes through gritted teeth, pain evident in his voice.

'Your neck?' I ask, trying to see him around Marissa who's positioned herself between me and the machine.

'I think the collar's wearing . . . through the scabs,' he answers.

Seeing him like this gives me more determination. I need out of here. We need out of here.

I follow the power cord from the machine to the wall.

'Rachel, stop!' Marissa commands. When I don't listen, she throws up her hands. 'Unplugging the machine will notify Heda.'

I nudge her back. 'You didn't care about Heda coming here five minutes ago when you threatened to go and get her.'

'I'm trying to help you.' She takes a calming breath and tugs on her ribbon belt, then glances at Eros. 'Be careful who you trust.'

'Right.' I wrap my hands around the cord. 'Because trusting you has been so good for me.'

'Rachel,' she sighs. 'Rachel, stop. I wouldn't do that.'

I stare at her. 'We have a long history, Riss. By now you should know that if there's something you wouldn't do, it's probably something I would.'

Eros chuckles and Marissa crosses her arms. 'I'm trying to have your back.'

'I've got my own back,' I say, tugging the cord from the wall. The words feel good coming out. For the longest time I've depended on someone else to be in charge: my ma, Ben, Eros, sometimes even Marissa.

The machine beeps then clicks off. I half expect the red light and alarm to sound but they don't. I bite the inside of my cheek to fight the smug smile I'm tempted to give Marissa and head over to Eros, pushing the chains and the hair away from his neck to get a better look. The skin under the collar is raw and oozing pus.

'Now to get this off you.'

'Don't!' Marissa says, jolting forward and grabbing my arm. She's more upset about this then my unplugging the cord. But of course she is. With his collar off, his powers are usable again. With his powers he could stop her, he could stop all of them.

I yank my arm free and reach to touch the collar. Eros pulls back. 'Don't,' he says. 'The arrow of indifference hurts worse than those rods they use.'

'This isn't right,' I groan. 'None of this is.'

Marissa rests her hand on my shoulder and it's so surprisingly gentle that I don't pull away. 'This is all messed up, I know. But you need to keep your word and give Heda your blood. There's so much more at stake now.'

I roll my eyes. 'You mean you want to be a Hedoness again.' I step aside and her hand slips away.

'No, I—' She stops herself and takes a seat on the side of the metal bed. 'You're right, I do. But that's not what I'm worried about.'

It's the most honest I've ever seen her. Her face, which is normally twisted into a protective mask, is now vulnerable somehow. I'm tempted to believe her.

'Then what? What are you worried about?'

'You, you weirdo.'

I frown. 'Forgive me if I have a hard time believing that.'

She lets out an airy laugh. 'I know I can be a little selfish sometimes, but—'

'Sometimes?' Eros says.

'A little?' I say, pressing my lips to keep from smiling and taking a seat beside her.

She smacks my arm playfully, and for a second I forget where we are and what we've been through, and it's almost like being with an old friend.

'I deserve that,' she says, smiling.

And I begin to return the smile but then I remember she's the reason I'm here. She kissed Ben, she turned Kyle. Her actions led the Committee right to my door. Whatever friendship we had has been betrayed so many times I don't think it can ever be repaired. Besides, we were never really friends, we were only ever accountability partners.

I clench my hands, take long slow breaths and slide down the bed, away from her. She picks up on my change in demeanour and glances at the puddle of ichor on the floor. 'Is there anything I can do to make things right?' she asks.

Eros catches my eye and I know he's trying to convey something but I'm too confused to figure it out. And before I get the chance to, his voice fills my head. '*Love, don't buy it.*'

'No!' I say, hopping off the bed and squeezing my head. 'No! Don't do that.'

'What's going on?' Eros asks, puzzled by my outburst. That fact that he doesn't know gives me hope that the voice was just my imagination.

'Rachel? What's happening?' Marissa is beside me, rubbing my back. 'Maybe you should sit down, you don't look so good.'

'I'm fine.' I pull away from her and pace the far side of the room.

'Rachel?' Marissa says.

'*Rachel?*' the voice in my head repeats.

'No, no, no!'

'Rach?' Paisley's musical voice calls from the door.

I stop, swing round, certain there's no one there and I'm imagining Paisley now too. But then Ben pushes her into the room in a wheelchair and the tension in my chest suddenly subsides.

'She shouldn't be here,' Marissa says.

But Ben ignores her and drives Paisley further in. He looks at the knot of dangling tubes, then at my arms, his eyes returning to mine with a frown.

'It fell out,' I lie.

'You OK?' Paisley cuts in.

'I should be asking you that,' I say, giving Ben a quick glance before crouching down to face her. 'What's wrong?'

Paisley fights to hold up her head – a fragile version of the girl I used to know. Her once beautiful umber skin is now a sick chalky shade and dark circles surround her eyes.

'I'm fine,' she says. Then she turns to Ben. 'Can I talk to her alone?'

Marissa gives us a closed-mouth smile, then heads to Ben and hooks elbows with him.

Ben shakes his head. 'I'm supposed to take Paisley back to—'

'Give them five minutes,' Marissa says, smiling at me and pulling him to the door.

She's trying to convince me that she really does have my best intentions at heart but she's going to have to do a lot more than this before I believe her. I watch them leave, noticing how good they look side by side. Marissa always wanted Ben. I can't fight her about that right now.

Paisley clears her throat and I peel my gaze from the door. Her friendly brown eyes fill with understanding. 'Let's sit,' she says, motioning to the bed. I stand and start towards it before realising she's struggling to push the wheels. I help her the rest of the way and take a seat on the cold metal edge.

My eyes flick to the door, wondering if Ben's waiting outside or if he's left.

'He meant a lot to you, didn't he?' she asks.

I can tell she cares more about this than her last question. 'Ben?'

She nods.

I glance at my feet, the Converse sneakers, the very ones I was wearing on the day I first met him. I never thought they would bring us here.

He means everything. But even though I trust Paisley and Eros I can't bring myself to say it out loud, not when anyone might be listening from behind the door. 'He used to,' I manage. *He used to mean everything.*

'Yeah, Marissa told me. She said you two were in love. That you're the ones who found a way around the Hedoness powers. I can't imagine what it's like to have a love like that and lose it.'

I shiver at how easily she says *lose it.*

She coughs and takes a moment to catch her breath before continuing. 'I swear you're living out *MVAL*.'

'*MVAL*?'

'*My Vampire Alien Life.*'

I chuckle. 'I should've guessed that.' I picture those perfect-looking people from her favourite TV show, going on extravagant dates and drinking human blood. My eyes lock on the tube hanging behind her. 'I don't think so.'

'No, seriously.' She follows my gaze over her shoulder to the ichor machine. 'Not just the drinking blood.' She stares down at her hands as she says it, but when her eyes find mine again the familiar spark of mischief is there. 'It's the otherworldliness, and this whole thing with you and Ben reminds me of the episode where Harry learns his soulmate Britt is betraying him and he tries to kill himself.'

My hands twist in the blue sweatshirt. I've never seen that episode but I can imagine how Harry feels. If the one person who is supposed to get you – all of you, the dark pieces and your best – doesn't want you any more, then who will? A lonely voice, buried deep within me, whispers that this is my truth: maybe Ben isn't pretending to work for Heda, maybe he really is. But Harry had one thing wrong. Death isn't the answer. At least not for me.

Paisley gasps, realising what she said. 'I didn't mean you should try to kill—'

'I know,' I say. I would have never expected Ben and me to end up like this.

'Well, do you?' she asks.

'Do I what?'

'Love him.'

Her question catches me by surprise, not because of what she asked but because even through everything my first instinct is to say yes. The memory of him holding me down while the red guard tightened my bindings until they cut into my flesh is there, but it isn't Ben in my mind. It's just one of Heda's goons. He's never harmed me before Heda, even when he thought I was one of Paisley's vampire aliens. I freeze, feeling the table's leather strap brush against my hand – a strap like the one he left unfastened. I run an absent finger over the freshly healed skin on my wrist, confused by it all.

'Yeah, I guess I do,' I say. 'Well, the Ben I fell for. This Ben –' I say, nodding to the door – 'I'm not so sure of.' I pause, thinking about what he whispered to me when administering the sleeping meds. 'He said the most random thing.'

Paisley looks up, a spark of curiosity in her big brown eyes. 'What?'

'He said, "If you want peace, prepare for war." What do you think it means?'

Paisley laughs. 'Of course he'd quote the *Punisher*.'

'The *Punisher*?' I remember our boat trip to NY, the comic he bought when he told me about his mother and how she taught him Spanish with *Punisher* comics. Was this his way of confirming he's on my side? My heart races at the thought.

Paisley sits forward. 'He has a stack of *Punisher* comics in his room. Carries one with him to most meals. That boy needs a hobby.'

I let out an airy laugh.

'Well,' Paisley says, 'do you think a part of him still loves you?'

I look at her, studying her face, the concern in her eyes, and I want to tell her my truth, all of it. Instead I say, 'Is it wrong that a part of me hopes he does?'

She doesn't answer, so I twist on the bed to be closer to her. 'Paisley?'

'I was remembering how the sisters at St Val's used to say, "Love is the most powerful magic."'

I'm confused how this conversation looped around to our high school.

She smiles up at me from the wheelchair. 'I always thought that was cool.' She pushes herself forward, her shaky arms struggling to hold her weight. 'Maybe there's something more to it.'

'Like what?'

'Like, I dunno, maybe your love can save Ben.'

I glance over at Eros. He hangs his head, giving us what little privacy he can. 'Maybe,' I mumble. But a part of me hopes she is right, that love is the most powerful magic and that my love, whatever twisted and confused mess it is, is enough to save us. I fight back the sudden urge to laugh, finding irony in that. After all the time of being a Hedoness, having a magic love and hating it, now I'm wishing that my love *was* magic.

Thirteen

The door pulls open and Marissa saunters in. My heart sinks. I didn't realize how much I needed this moment with Paisley. It's the most normal I've felt in a long time, and now it's over. Ben follows her, hesitating in the entrance for someone else. I expect to see Heda after all of Marissa's threats and am strangely relieved when Le-Li's piled-high purple hair comes around the corner. I jump off the bed, grab the tube and jump back up, hoping he doesn't look closely.

Luckily he's distracted by Eros and drags his metal tea cart over to the god. It's neatly stacked with empty ichor containers and rows of vials, the clear liquid sloshing with the wheel's jerky movements. I fixate on the tiny glass vials of sleeping meds, ready to pour me into the dark.

I can't let that happen. If they put me to sleep again, they'll hook me back up to the machine and continue draining my blood until they find a way to transfer the powers. I glance at the door and debate taking my chances with running. I'm fast, but I'm also weak from lack of food and blood loss. My gaze lands on the belt of weapons around Ben's waist. Would he help Le-Li stop me? Ben held me down and strapped me to the table once before.

'Back for more?' I ask Le-Li, hiding the ichor tube behind my back before he realizes I've unhooked myself. My heart races. I'm hoping to hear that he does need more blood – more blood means they don't have what they want yet. That there's still time.

'Yes,' he says, not looking up from Eros's machine and adding under his breath, 'So close, I'm so very close.'

'So you haven't done it yet?' I ask.

Le-Li's head cocks as he ponders the question.

Ben rushes forward, sidestepping the drying puddle of my ichor and grabbing Paisley's wheelchair handles. 'I need to return Paisley to her room,' he says. He obviously doesn't want Le-Li to tell me that he hasn't been successful in isolating and extracting the magic in my blood.

'*Or maybe,*' the voice says, '*it's that he's trying to keep Le-Li from realising you know what he's been up to.*'

I fight the urge to shout *No!* and squeeze my head until the voice leaves for ever, but I'm not even sure if I'm hearing it or it's my imagination. And the last thing I need is more attention drawn to me. For whatever reason, neither Marissa nor Ben have given away that I'm unhooked and my machine is off. I'm grateful for that, because I definitely won't find a way out if I'm forced back into the leather bindings, and I don't want to know what Heda would do to my family if I don't hold up my end of the bargain.

'Can we stay just a little longer?' Paisley asks.

I smile, knowing Paisley feels the same about our stolen time together. She is a true friend, and that feels much better than the forced friendships I've had in my life.

Ben stops Paisley's chair next to the supply cart, waiting for Le-Li to answer.

'There's no need to rush,' Le-Li says, slipping Eros's full container from the machine. 'I'll be here a while yet. Have to switch this over, then clean Eros's wounds.' He grunts as he stands, admiring the container of bright blue blood in his hands. 'This will give Heda a couple of years,' he says quietly to himself. He balances the container of ichor on the edge of the tea cart, waves Marissa over and hands it to her. She struggles to get a grip on it. 'Take it to Heda,' he orders.

She tries to give it back. 'I'm not your errand—'

Le-Li slaps the top of his thigh, filling the room with a resounding metallic smack. 'Now!' As soon as the command leaves his mouth, his shoulders curl in, like he's trying to make himself smaller or he's ashamed of the outburst, or both. 'I'm sorry.' He turns quickly, colliding into Eros and rattling the chains. 'Sorry,' he repeats. 'I have a lot going on and I don't want to disobey Heda. I need extra help, and—'

'OK, OK.' She huffs and takes a shaky step back, bumping into the cart.

Three vials fall over the edge and land in Paisley's lap. It's the chance I've been waiting for. Ben's busy holding the door for Marissa and Le-Li is focused on cleaning around Eros's collar. I try to catch Paisley's eye but she's busy carefully replacing the vials in their row on the cart.

I wave, freezing when Le-Li starts turning towards me. He stops halfway to adjust Eros's chains.

'Paisley,' I whisper, flapping my arms like a wild woman. She still doesn't notice. 'Psst.' I kick the side of the table. Only Ben glances over. I drop my gaze, staring at my feet, waiting for him to return his attention to Marissa. When I look back up, Paisley is watching me, her hand frozen mid-task, about to place the second vial on the cart.

I nod towards it, eyes wide and pleading.

She lifts the jar to its row and I shake my head *no*, waving her to bring it to me. After a few seconds her eyes widen in understanding and she slips it, and the other one, under the hem of her shirt. I make a gesture in the air like a needle going into my arm, then point to the cart. She frowns at first, but then she looks over her shoulder, before reaching into the supplies for a syringe.

Ben closes the door and Paisley panics, pulls her hand out, knocking vials in the process. The rattle makes Le-Li turn around, his hand going instinctually to the Taser hooked at his side.

'Take Eros's collar off!' I yell, forcing his attention on me. It's a risk he'll notice I'm unhooked but it's our only chance. 'Look what it's doing to him. Cleaning isn't helping.'

Le-Li shakes his head. 'There's nothing else I can do.'

'It's literally burning his skin,' I say, glancing quickly at Paisley, whose hand is in the cart going for the needle. My heart races. We might actually pull this off.

'What about that salve stuff,' I continue. 'Ben said there's something that could help him.'

Le-Li looks at Eros, true concern in his eyes. 'I will ask Heda—'

'She'll say . . . no.' Eros exhales loudly through the pain.

Le-Li twists the cloth, water dripping on the floor. He pulls the cart to his side and reaches back into the bucket. I look to Paisley in question. She gives me the thumbs up and relief pours through me.

Le-Li calls over his shoulder to Ben. 'I'm almost done. Take Paisley to finish her testing,' he says, dabbing Eros with the cloth. 'I'll be there shortly.'

Ben nods and starts pushing Paisley towards the door.

'Wait!' I say, gripping the bed's edge to keep from jumping down and giving myself away.

The boys look at me with confusion.

'I'd like to give Paisley a goodbye hug before she goes.'

'Fine,' says Le-Li. He motions Ben to push her over to me and adds, 'Be careful, you don't want to pull a tube.'

'I will,' I say, my heart racing. Then Le-Li kneels, bringing the cloth to Eros's feet in the same gentle manner as he did the last time I saw him do it. It still is a weird thing to witness, but right now I'm thankful for the distraction. I let out a breath of relief and slip off the bed, tiptoeing over. Ben rolls his eyes at the tube clutched in my hand but I ignore him and bend down, shielding Paisley's body with my shoulder.

'I got four syringes. Want me to fill them for you?' she whispers, tapping the bump on her stomach where the vials are.

'I'll take a couple filled,' I say under my breath, adding more loudly, 'I'm going to miss you so much. I hope we can see each other again soon.' I look up at Ben, then over at Le-Li. They don't seem to notice. But Eros has his eyes fixed on Paisley, and his lips twist to the side in a smile.

Her hands shake under her shirt but she manages to fill them quickly. Then she helps me transfer them from her shirt to up my sleeves, rolling the spare vial into my waistband.

'Thank you, BFF,' I say to her.

'See you soon, partner.' She smiles, mouthing, 'Be careful.'

'You too,' I say, worried about how weak she still is, how all the colour hasn't returned to her face. I give her a quick hug, a real one this time. 'Bye.'

I want to say more but Ben pulls the chair back. I hold up the empty ichor tube and mouth 'Thanks' to Ben. It means a lot that he hasn't turned me in.

I swear he gives me one of his crooked grins before pushing her into the hall. The door clicks closed and Le-Li stands. I need to return to the bed and keep up the pretence that I'm hooked to the machine. I take a quick step, eyes glued on Le-Li, and jump over the puddle of light-blue blood.

My waistband unrolls.

The contents fall to the floor – glass shattering on impact.

Fourteen

Le-Li drops his cloth and turns to the sound. Clutching a syringe in each hand, I pivot quickly on my heels, heading for him. If I don't inject these drugs into him before he sees me untethered, then there's no point trying. Because when he wakes up, he'll know what I did, and he'll make sure I'm caught and never left unattended again. Or worse, he'll make sure Paisley is punished for helping me. This is my only chance.

His hand reaches for the Taser at his side. My heart sinks. I'm not going to make it.

Still I charge, arms forward, needles out. Either way, I'm going to try to get out of here.

Le-Li's back is still to me, but he's inches from spotting me and I'm still a few feet away. His Taser is out of the belt and in his hand. He grips it uncomfortably, like it's something he hasn't held before.

There's a low rattle, like broken wind chimes, and Le-Li falls forward, face down, with a *humph*.

Eros is standing, though shaky, chains balled in his fists. 'You're welcome,' he says.

I take the opening, hurrying to close the gap, holding Le-Li down with my knee. As he struggles against me, a sharp section of his patchwork back drags across my shin. I jab both needles into his neck – the first fleshy part I can find. He cries out in pain but I manage to keep him secure while I wait for him to fall asleep. I know what it feels like, and even though he's part metal, with double the dose I hope he'll fall fast.

When Le-Li stops struggling, I drop the empty needles and slump to the floor beside him, fighting back the urge to cry as I clutch my now raw shin. I hate that I've hurt someone, even someone who works for Heda. It doesn't feel right.

'Love, you don't have time to mope,' Eros says. 'Now hurry.'

'Want me to unplug your machine?' I ask.

'No,' he says. 'I want her to have my blood. She needs it.'

That raises a whole new set of questions. But he's right, I don't have time to stick around here. Le-Li won't be asleep for long and this is a chance I can't pass up.

'I'll come back for you.' I get up and head for the door.

'Go,' he says.

Before I leave, I unhook his chains, listening as they fall through the loop on the ceiling. Eros exhales hard. I grab Le-Li's Taser and a handful of vials, quickly filling a few more syringes. The sweatsuit doesn't have pockets so I store them in my bra.

'Eros, if you hear me knocking can you get to the door to open it?'

'I'm not sure,' he says. 'But to be safe, jab something –' he pauses to catch his breath – 'in the locking mechanism so it doesn't shut.'

'Good idea,' I say, looking around for what to use and settling on one of the syringes. I grab another off the cart then prop the door enough to jam the needle in the latch and break it off. I test it, opening and closing the door, until it doesn't click shut.

I pop my head out, glancing both ways. The hall's empty so I step out, letting the door shut quietly behind me. I half expect alarms to sound. When they don't, I turn back and test the handle to see if my jerry-rig of the locking mechanism worked – it opens. No need to find a key card or key. I shut it again and start down the hall.

It's quiet. Too quiet. Cold, smoky air blasts through the large vent in the wall across from me. I hook the Taser's handle under my waistband then tuck my hands in my sleeves, hugging myself. If my experience with the meds is any indication, I have about half an hour before Le-Li wakes up, maybe more with the double dose. I need to find my family and get out of this place.

A high-pitched beeping makes me freeze. The noise stops as suddenly as it starts. I let out a breath of relief and continue, taking quick light steps so my Converse sneakers don't squeak on the cement floor. My heart races so hard I'm certain someone will hear and come running. Every few metres there's another vent blasting cold air. I hug myself tighter, wishing I had a blanket to wrap around me. I put my ear to the next door I come upon, wondering what's behind it. If it's a way out. I hear nothing.

The beeping returns and this time I realize it's coming from down the hall. I keep going, trying a nearby door. It's locked.

I backtrack to the door closest to me, the one I just passed. It's a risk as I'm heading in the direction of the beeping sound. Also locked. I rub my arms and keep walking.

If I've kept the right count, I've travelled six doors away from the ichor room. I let out a strangled breath when voices carry up the hall. Three, maybe more of Heda's guards approach.

From the other direction, the beeping noise.

I'm surrounded.

I have no choice but to return to Eros. This whole plan was a failure.

The guards' voices grow louder, as does the beeping coming up from behind me. My hand goes to the Taser. I'll fight my way through if I need to.

I'm a few metres away from the ichor room when I see them. There's too many for me to take on.

They don't notice me yet, but if I run the distance and pull open the door they will.

The vent wheezes another icy blast. I hug myself tight, the Taser pinned under my arm, hesitating about what to do. Then it hits me.

The vent.

I rush over and pull at the cover, relieved when the corners pop out on my first try. I yank it far enough to slip under, tucking my legs in tight and twisting to pull it closed behind me. It's cramped in here, the Taser presses uncomfortably into my hip and this close to the air, I'm freezing. I have to focus to calm my breathing and keep my teeth from clacking as I cling to the grate. I pray to the gods the guards didn't notice me getting in here.

Every warm breath that leaves my lips evaporates into an icy cloud. My fingers are going numb and I'm afraid my grip will slip, the grate will fall and my hiding place will be discovered. Each time my skin brushes the cold metal it stings like frostbite but there's no way to adjust my position. I watch over my arm, through the slats, as the beeping noise grows louder. Soon a four-wheeler towing a flatbed cart comes into view.

The guards approach from the other side and the driver stops right in front of my vent to talk to them; the beeping dies with the engine.

'How's it going?' one of the guards asks.

'Same old, same old,' the driver says. 'Bident made another mess. I'm taking it to be incinerated.'

'Oh yeah?' another replies.

The driver points to his cargo. 'Stabbed the girl right through the stomach. Guess they thought the ichor treatments would do the trick. Surprise, surprise, she didn't heal.'

I follow his finger to the black body bag plopped sloppily on the flatbed and gasp.

One of the guards cocks an ear towards me. I freeze, not even daring to breathe and hoping the rattle of air conditioning was enough to cover any sound. After a long second he turns back to the group. They keep talking but I tune them out, too numb and cold to listen. Did I do this? Was it my ichor that got that person killed?

Eros's suggestion that I drink my father's blood to reverse my immortality never sounded better. What's a little blood when it could stop whatever this is? A shiver runs through me. A little blood. That's assuming I haven't used too many powers and the blood is no longer enough.

'We have to keep up hope,' I hear another female guard say. 'We're getting close.'

'Yes,' they agree.

It seems like forever before the guards and driver part ways. As the flatbed pulls away I notice a tuft of hair sticking out of the black bag. Something about it is strangely familiar. Then, when the cart hits an uneven patch of floor, the bag flaps open and I see her face. A scream bubbles up my throat. I drop the vent grate. It slides to the ground with a metal screech that echoes in this small space. Right now, I don't care about the sound, or the possibility of getting caught, or the cold that envelops my body to the soul. All I care about is the girl in the body bag, with the familiar hair, and the stomach sliced open to test my healing blood.

But my blood didn't heal. It got Paisley killed.

Fifteen

I've never felt a pain like this. I'd take a hundred beatings with the electric rods, a thousand even. This is years of longing, of endless guilt, swirling and diving and pecking at my soul. Paisley's dead. She's dead. I don't think I will ever feel OK again.

I should crawl deeper into the vent so the guards can't grab me and pull me out. But my arms and legs are frozen, knotted together, and even if they weren't, I'm too numb to move.

Their conversation drifts in waves.

'. . . What was that?' a guard asks.

'One of the damn grates fell off again. I'll radio a janitor to come fix it.'

'This place is falling apart.'

'It was falling apart before Heda got here.'

'I heard it was condemned . . .'

They could be standing at the mouth to the vent, watching me, waiting for me to come out so they can strap me back to my machine. I wouldn't know, and I couldn't see even if I wanted to. My eyes are blurred over

121

with tears; there's only black when I open them. It's like vultures pecked them from my skull. The only eyes filling my mind are Paisley's warm brown ones. The memory of them only lasts a second. I struggle to keep it there, at the front of my mind, fighting against my subconscious need to replay what really happened to her – her body, shaky in a wheelchair, having my blood forced into it – her body, rammed through with a sword, red blood, the colour blood should be, splattering in an arc – her body, wrapped in black plastic, her smiling eyes now hard marble stones. The only sane thought I have left plays in a loop. 'Whoever it is they call *Bident*, I will make that monster pay.'

Sixteen

It's avenging Paisley that gives me the strength to pull myself together. I wipe my eyes and glance into the hall. It's empty, no guards. Somehow, they've missed me. I force my arms to move, my legs to bend, and I slide out, collapsing on to the concrete floor. I slip the vials of sleeping meds and the syringes out of my bra and stuff them into the vent for future use. Everything aches, from my soul to my bones. In my daze I put the grate back over the vent and somehow I end up outside the ichor room, one hand on the door handle, the other on the Taser.

I push the door open, stopping to pop the bent needle out of the latch and weave it through the bottom of my shirt. As I drift over to the bed, I sidestep Le-Li on the floor. Eros points. 'The Taser.'

I toss it to Le-Li, hitting him on the leg.

My eyes don't rest on anything. They float around the room, mapping out all the places Paisley once was – by the cart, next to the bed, in and out of the door – she's everywhere. I plug the machine back in. It screeches to action, the dry suction sound filling the room like a baby trying to get milk from an empty bottle. I grab the tube and the IV connector I'd ripped out earlier, and I crawl on to the metal bed. I shove the port roughly into my arm, light blue blood pooling. The pain is sharp, my body tells me that by twitching, but my mind's too dull to feel it. I close my eyes and am trapped inside my mind, and the only thing that meets me there is the corpse of my friend.

'What's wrong?' Eros asks. His gaze widens when I turn to him and he sees my face. I'm thankful that he doesn't press for an answer. I don't think my mouth is ready to speak the words. Eros nods to Le-Li, stirring on the ground, letting me know he's waking up. I hook the tube into the sloppily inserted port, feeling the sting of cold as it begins to draw my blood, and I lie back on the bed, watching sickly blue ichor rise up and fill it.

Le-Li wakes, realizes he's on the floor and rushes to push himself up. He stumbles, still groggy from the drugs, grabbing the cart for support as he sets his leg back in place then rubs his neck. I close my eyes and pretend to sleep. I know what's coming. Questions. I don't have the energy for questions.

'You slipped on that patch of ichor and hit your head,' Eros lies for me.

'I did? I remember—' Le-Li pauses. 'The chains?' he says in an unsure whisper. 'I need to go.'

The door opens and Le-Li's footsteps echo away. Before the door clicks shut, another set cautiously approaches.

'Ben,' Eros says, less as a greeting and more to tell me who it is. But I don't need him to tell me, I know the way Ben walks and breathes and the gentle touch of his hand on my arm, shaking me. I ignore the urge to grab him and let him hold me, to nuzzle into his shoulder and cry, absorbing his familiar scent and the rhythm of his heartbeat, and I rip my arm away.

The absence of his touch on my skin is colder than any frostbite.

'Rach?' He shakes me, his voice gentle. 'I know you're awake,' he says. 'I've seen you sleep enough times to know the difference.'

I keep my eyes closed out of stubbornness and because I don't want him to see the sadness in them. Because he will, he's Ben, and even if we are in this weird situation, that doesn't change the fact that he can read me like one of his comic books.

There's a tug on my arms as he unhooks me from the machine. His warm breath is inches from my face. His presence is everywhere. My entire body fills with the need for him. I know I could just tilt my head and our lips would connect. Their magnetic pull is only a whisper away.

'What are you doing?' Eros asks.

Ben doesn't reply. He brushes a curl from my forehead and wraps an arm under my knees and my shoulders and he lifts me off the bed. I cry out, not from pain, but from the heartbreak of being safe in Ben's arms when Paisley is anything but safe. My body's limp, too picked-over by the loneliness to question him, so I let him carry me to the door.

'Where are you going?' Eros asks again.

Ben turns back to say, 'Something terrible has happened. I'm taking her to her family. She needs them now.'

Seventeen

He carries me down the cold hallway, each step driving the loss deeper into me. I keep my eyes closed, not wanting to see where we're going. I know it's the same direction that the flatbed and the body bag went. There's a faint beeping sound still ringing in my ears.

So much is gone. All the things I never properly appreciated when I had them – Paisley's chattiness most of all, especially the way her eyes glisten when she talks, *talked*, about her favourite shows and our many late-night Quiver chats. Mostly I'll miss that for the first time in my life I found someone who was kind to me and expected nothing in return. I'm overwhelmed with the urge to find this Bident person and ask them why they did it. Why they killed her.

Ben slows his pace. We must be close because Marissa rushes over. I can tell it's her by the clicking heels and familiar scent of her rosemary and mint shampoo. It's odd that she got the brand she uses delivered here, wherever here is – and I'm ashamed of myself for thinking about something as trivial as shampoo right now.

'Rach?' Marissa puts her hand on my cheek, wiping at a fresh tear trail.

The last thing I want is a fake friend pretending she cares. I squeeze my eyes tighter, turning my face into Ben's chest. *Regretting that choice instantly.* Now that I'm closer to him, touching him, as I wished so often I could, it's confusing and only further breaks the broken pieces of my heart.

A soft sob escapes my lips. Paisley, Marissa, Ben, being trapped in Heda's facility, it's all too much.

'You told her already?' Marissa says.

Ben adjusts my weight in his arms, pulling me closer. 'No, she was like this when I found her.'

Marissa's cold hand brushes my neck as she strokes my hair. 'Poor thing, the blood extractions must be taking their toll.'

At the mention of blood, the image of Paisley in a body bag shoves back into my mind.

I focus instead on Marissa's confusing behaviour; her words sound genuine, but she's never seemed to care how things impacted me before. Not unless it benefited her to do so. My guess is she's trying to get Ben's attention once again.

'Can you open the door?' Ben asks, breathing with exertion. 'I don't have a key card.'.

'Oh, did you misplace it?'

'Never got one.' He adjusts me again, my head resting

higher up on his chest, under his chin. 'The door,' he repeats. 'She's heavier than she looks.'

'I can stand.' I wriggle out of Ben's arms. But grief has drained me and my steps are weak and flimsy.

'I didn't mean—' Ben stops mid-sentence when I stumble.

Marissa catches my arm.

I pull away. 'I got it,' I say, leaning into the rusted blue door, watching the paint flake under my touch.

'OK.' Marissa slings a duffle bag over one shoulder and backs up, arms raised, key card in hand, and waves it in front of the scanner. The doors click open. She takes a step, reaching for the handle, pauses and turns back to the intercom. 'Can you bring out container . . .' She looks at Ben. 'What's Paisley's mom's container? I'll have it brought up.'

I grit my teeth and ball my fists. Now, more than ever, I want to be far away from Marissa. How can she talk so offhandedly about Paisley? Right in front of me.

'Why would I know?' Ben says, glancing warily my way.

Marissa's asking about Paisley's ma doesn't reveal anything that the body bag hasn't already, but I don't tell him that.

'What are the orders?' the intercom voice asks.

Marissa frowns at Ben. 'You knew the numbers of Rachel's family. I thought you'd know others—'

'I don't, I only . . .' His face hardens and his posture goes stiff. 'I was keeping an eye on them –' he clears his throat – 'for Rachel.' His words don't match his body language and it's too much for my brain to process right now.

'The orders?' the intercom repeats.

Marissa brings her mouth back to the speaker. 'Bring out Mrs T-Turn, Turning, Turnel?' She stops.

'Turner,' I say, and as I do, grief punches me in the gut.

I'm going to have to face Paisley's ma. What do I tell her? It's because of my blood that Paisley's dead.

Ben offers me a hand, winces and stops. 'Ouch.' He picks a bent needle out of his shirt. It must have unhooked from mine on the way over. 'Strange,' he says, watching me inquisitively.

'Please, just let me in.' My arms are too rubbery to lift, let alone open these large doors. I want to go to my family. I need to see them, be held by them, cry into their arms. They're all I have left.

'Do you want a hand?' Marissa asks.

'No, I'm fine.' I sense Ben's gaze on me and I glance over, quickly returning my eyes to my sneakers, not wanting to be caught up in the emotions that come when he looks at me that way. Instead I count the blue paint peelings from the door that have settled on my scuffed white toes.

Nothing lasts for ever.

Marissa leads us into the container room, dropping her bag beside the door. I follow her into the once-empty balcony that now has five weatherworn shipping containers in the shape of a giant question mark. Four of them are neatly placed, making the semi-circle, in the centre is the wooden paddle boat propped up with life jackets so it doesn't tip. The fifth container juts out at an angle from the end. Five. I count them: Ma, Nani, Dad, Kyle; the fifth one must be Mrs Turner's.

I take a shaky step forward, wanting to run the distance to my family. Ben follows close behind me. I sense his hand, hovering inches from my back like he's expecting me to fall.

Eighteen

The closer I get to my family, the surer my steps are. Nani's container is nearest the entrance. It's the only one with a window facing my direction. The others can't see I'm coming. She stands in it, with a blanket wrapped around her shoulders like a pallu, watching me approach. Her black hair, with wisps of salt and pepper that frame her face, hangs perfectly straight over her shoulders, shining like she just rubbed oil through it. Her gaze flicks between Ben and me; her hands press against the glass as I get nearer.

'Rachel?' she calls, her entire face lighting up.

My eyes pool with tears and I hurry my pace. The last time I saw her was at my fake funeral and the last time I hugged her I was a child heading home from my visit in Gujarat. The urge to hug her again fills me to bursting. It's been hard having her overseas. The distance makes it easier to lose touch. The hours can slip into days, then weeks, and soon it's months before you connect again. But Nani never let that happen. She called every Sunday like clockwork. I regret all the times I went for an evening run to avoid those calls. Losing a friend makes you reprioritise a few things.

Nani leaves the window and rushes to the door. She throws it open and picks up the hem of her tracksuit bottoms, the same way Ma does before running in her sari. I'm about to dive in and wrap my arms around her, but she stops abruptly.

'Nani?' I frown, taking another step closer. 'You coming out?'

'I must stay here.'

'Why?'

'I . . . I . . . because I must.' Nani glances at her feet, toe to the line. She lifts one up and tries to move it forward. Then her foot shakes and she drops it.

'You must?'

'Where were you?' she demands, ignoring my question. 'You had us worried sick.'

I missed this. I miss her desire to know everything. 'I love you too, Nani,' I say.

Her usual stern face slips into a half-smile and she waves me to come over to her. 'Come, we have much to discuss.' She glances at Ben when she says this and her eyebrows raise. 'Like what my favourite offspring has got herself into.'

'I won't tell Ma you said that,' I say. I really want to see my ma and meet my real dad, the dad not under the Hedoness spell, but this stolen moment with Nani feels right. We didn't always see eye-to-eye but I understood that she had my best interests at heart, even if her idea of what was best differed drastically from mine. The biodata envelopes she mailed by the dozens or her quest to make me the most powerful Hedoness – she wanted the best for me; she genuinely thought I was the best. I could use some of Nani's belief in me now. And maybe Nani has an idea how we can get out of this place. She knows more about the Hedonesses and the gods than anyone I've ever met. I should have paid more attention to my lessons.

There's a long bell, like the ones between classes at St Valentine's, and Nani's head shoots up. 'Lunch,' she says, and steps out of the container, passing me like I'm not even here.

'Nani?' I turn to watch her and realize Ben's still there, right beside me. 'Where are you going?' I call after her.

She continues her march to the far wall, a single steel door. 'Lunch,' she shouts back.

Ma's next to pass me, then Dad and Kyle, even Paisley's ma. Kyle tosses a balled sock in the air and catches it as they follow Nani, leaving me in their wake and ignoring my calls like I'm some phantom they don't see.

'It's the anklets,' Ben whispers to me.

I turn to him, mouth moving to ask 'What?' but no words come out.

'Did you notice the gold band around their feet. They're made from the arrow of infatuation,' he explains.

The arrow of infatuation, the source of the Hedoness

power, the weapon that can make anyone do anything. The weapon that's still in me. But now that its magic isn't coming from Heda's blood, who's controlling it?

Eros's words flit through my mind: *'She has my bow and arrows. With them, she can make anyone do anything.'*

She has the bow and arrows.

And the 'anyones' she's controlling are my family.

Nineteen

I follow after my family. If their gold anklets are forcing them to do something stupid for Heda, I want to know what it is.

'Rach,' Ben calls.

'Don't try to stop me, Ben.'

'It's just, I need to tell you something.' He doesn't mention Paisley but I'm certain that's what he means.

'I know.' I keep my eyes ahead, watching the white door with red paint that reads *Emergency Exit* shut behind Mrs Turner. 'But right now I need to make sure my family is OK. Can you tell me after I do that?'

'Right, of course.' He rushes ahead and holds open the door, waving me into a stairwell.

'Thank you,' I say, confused at the kindness he's been showing me today. He's letting his guard act slip and the real Ben is showing through the cracks. Is it because my friend died and he feels guilty, or is there something more?

I follow the sound of my family's footsteps, taking the metal stairs down. Ben is never more than two steps behind.

'Where are they going?' I ask.

'There's a cafeteria on the bottom floor.'

'And they go when they hear the bell?'

'Yeah. It's kinda like they've been programmed to respond to a number of different sounds.' Ben lets out a loud sigh that makes me think he doesn't approve of what's going on. I'm tempted to stop and turn so I can see his face but for some reason I pick up speed instead. My weary body struggles.

'We won't lose them,' Ben says. 'I know where the cafeteria is.'

I nod and catch my breath, then continue at a normal pace. It strikes me that I'm unsure whether I'm running to catch up with my family or to get away from Ben. All my jumbled feelings for him have only intensified since Paisley's death. I'm positive this is just like the time he left his jacket in my house for Officer Ammon to find, that he's only pretending to serve Heda so he can look out for me. Deep in my soul there's a whisper confirming that's what it is.

We get to the bottom landing and there's only one door so I open it before Ben has the chance and come face-to-face with the wall of stacked shipping containers. From the balcony I never noticed the small metal ladders leading up to each container's door. I can't imagine my Nani having to climb down one of those and am thankful her container is on the balcony floor and not four storeys high like some of these. It didn't look this big from the balcony.

I spot my family ahead, merging into a queue of prisoners that forms between the wall and the stacks of containers, leading to the cafeteria. They all wear the tacky blue sweatsuits, hair hanging wild. I'm surprised to find that Dad and Kyle aren't the only males being held.

'They collected anyone who knows about the Hedonesses,' Ben explains.

'Anyone?' I repeat. Are Officer Ammon and my aunt Joyce in a container somewhere too?

He nods. 'Yeah, apparently she had every Hedoness under surveillance.'

Of course she did.

More and more of the prisoners merge into the queue.

'We should hurry or we'll lose them,' I say. When we get to the end of the line I rush past, looking for my family.

Someone shouts, 'To the back.' Suddenly the people in the queue hold out their arms, making a barricade of limbs. I get trapped between two strangers and the wall.

'Just trying to get to my family,' I say.

'To the back,' they repeat in sync.

I turn to find Ben, waiting in the queue, a few others lined up behind him.

'I didn't have time to warn you,' he says.

I glare at the woman holding her arm out. Then I remember that she's being controlled by the anklet and my face softens. I wonder who she is, what part of the world she comes from. I point to Ben and she lets me pass.

'Clear,' she yells with a thick German inflection. Instantly they drop their arms.

The accent makes me miss Heinz and Frieda and their quirky statue-filled home, and that treasured time Ben and I shared on the boat they sold us. Things sure are different now.

When I make it to Ben, he's fighting back a smile and I'm not sure if it irritates me further or calms me.

'Heda really likes order,' he tells me. 'She's obsessive about it.'

'I can see that.' I cross my arms and tap my foot, waiting in the stupidly long line. The containers on the bottom level face away from the queue; no windows to look into, no people to see. After what feels like hours we near the front. The prisoners ahead of us roll up their sleeves and stick out their arms. The guard at the door injects them with something, before moving them inside where another guard guides them to the buffet.

'I'm not getting anything injected in me,' I say in a panic. Flashbacks of Paisley's frail, shaky body hit me. 'What are they even giving them?' I bite the inside of my mouth, waiting for his answer, hoping it isn't what I fear. *Ichor.*

'Some vitamin concoction Le-Li came up with. They don't get any sun exposure here and Heda wants them to stay strong.'

She wants them to stay army-strong.

As we near the entrance, I glance into a room that resembles what you'd see on a show about American high schools – rectangular tables in rows, the walls painted a forced happy yellow, and a buffet on one end. I try to find my family but don't see them.

We get to the door and the guard instructs me to hold out my arm.

'She's with me,' Ben says, pushing me through. The guard doesn't stop us, most likely due to his grey uniform. The only difference is Ben isn't wearing a helmet. Suddenly it hits me why they wear them; everyone here is connected. We're all family and friends, and Hedonesses. The guards work for Heda who controls the Committee. They probably know the people they're incarcerating. And not only from their exchanges here as prisoners and guards – they're the friends of Hedonesses, or Hedonesses themselves. It makes me curious to know who's behind the helmets. Who would turn on their own like this and why? I glance at the ankle of the guard standing near the buffet line. Are they're being forced to betray their own or are they doing it of their own free will? Only one of those is forgivable.

140

I can't tell if they have anklets, so I scan the room for my family and follow the queue to the food. Even though I'm desperate to see them I'm also weak with hunger. I grab a tray and plate and start piling it on.

'Rachel?' someone calls.

I turn to see Sister Hannah Marie, my old teacher, standing at her table and waving.

'It is you,' she says.

The girls sitting next to her are students from St Valentine's – a lot of first years and even a couple from the year below mine. My chest constricts and all the feelings I had while I was in school come rushing back. I cling tighter to my tray and force a smile, pushing back the anger, resentment, shame, thinking I'm stupid for feeling these things about my old school when I have much bigger problems. But I can't help worrying that even now, after the Hedoness curse is broken and the school's closed, it isn't over. Even if I fight Heda to my dying breath, she's going to find a way to get the last of the power out of me and make all these people Hedonesses again.

Ben gives me a gentle nudge down the food line. I grab a few more items but my appetite isn't as big as it was. When I reach the end of the buffet, a guard directs me to an open seat at one of the tables. I turn to see if Ben is coming, only to find his hands empty. He didn't get any food, and he's standing beside another guard and they are speaking in hushed voices.

'To your seat,' the guard repeats.

I offer a half-smile to the Hedonesses sitting at my table and take my seat. I fork a roasted potato into my mouth and scan the room again for my family. I repeat this action until half of my plate is empty and many Hedonesses have come and gone from the room. On my next survey, I catch Ben's eye. He smiles and nods directly behind me. I turn, searching through the crowd for my family. I'm about to give up when Dad's bright orange hair catches my eye.

'Dad!' I scream, pushing out of my seat and manoeuvring around people. 'Dad!'

'Rachel?' He stands slowly and turns, his face lighting into a smile when he sees me. I half expect him to yell across the distance asking about Ma, but he doesn't, he just stands there, eyes pooling with tears, smiling. 'It's good to see you,' he says, half turning back – though his stare never leaves my face – to motion to my ma, Nani and Kyle sitting across from him. 'Look, it's Rachel!'

My heart races.

Ma glances up from her paper cup. Her eyes widen when they land on me. 'Rachel?' She drops her drink, tea spraying all over the table, and starts through the crowd towards me.

Kyle jumps up too, towering over the table. His dark hair is longer, the bleach blond tips hanging into his face. Still I'd recognise him by the way he holds himself. Even now, when forced into a blue tracksuit and under guards' surveillance, he has the same casual confidence of a celebrity on holiday. The girls seated at the tables around him notice it too. They blush and whisper among themselves, their eyes following his every move. No doubt they're experiencing that tongue-tied feeling I got when I first saw him exit his jacked-up truck carrying his baseball gear in Nashville. They'll be disappointed when they learn they're not his type.

'Cuz!' he shouts, offering a large grin. 'Good of you to finally show your face.'

Soon my whole family is standing and waving me over, and I smile my first real smile in days.

I make it around the last chair in my row.

'Return to your seat,' a guard says.

'I'm just going to sit with my family.'

'Return to your seat,' she repeats, her hand going for the electric bolt rod on her waistband.

'But . . .' I look for Ben to find him already heading over. 'Ben will explain—'

The guard grabs me, pushing me face first into the table. She holds down my neck, pins my hands behind my back.

'Rachel!' Ma cries.

A guard shouts at her.

My nose squishes painfully into the table.

My whole family is yelling.

More guards shout.

I manage to twist my head in time to see Kyle throw a punch at one of the guards.

Two more guards surge him, pinning his arms to the wall.

Soon everyone is standing, food and trays fly around the room. Guards dive into the chaos, bolt rods charged and raised. 'Sound the alarm!' one of them shouts.

People scream as they take the electric hits but they continue to swarm the guards, fighting for their lives. I struggle against the guard holding me, wanting to get loose and help my family.

Then someone blows a dog whistle and everyone in blue drops to the ground, lying prostrate and unmoving.

Everyone in blue but me.

Twenty

The guards pace the room. Rows of Hedonesses line the floor like prayer mats. I'm still pressed into the table, arms aching from the angle the guard's twisted them into. I'm the only one without an anklet, and it's a harsh reminder of Heda's plans for us.

Ben's beside me, trying to talk the guard into letting me go. But she doesn't, she presses me harder into the table.

'Heda's been notified. She'll be here soon,' she says.

'Great,' I groan, earning another shove to the head.

'Whoa, what are you doing?' Marissa's shrill voice registers in my ears. 'Let her go, she's Heda's guest.'

The guard relaxes her grip on me.

'Hand her to me, now,' Marissa orders.

With a grunt of frustration, the guard pushes me and lets go, leaving me bent over the table. Marissa slips her arm around my waist and helps me to my feet.

'My family,' I say softly.

'I know,' she replies.

Ben offers us a hand but she waves him away. 'I've got it,' she says. 'Get the rest of her family and Mrs Turner and meet us on the balcony.' Then she escorts me to a door on the far side of the room. She stops next to one of the guards, a larger woman, taller than Kyle by a good couple of inches. 'When Ben comes with the others, let them pass.'

The guard nods and holds open the door. As we step into a carpeted hallway I glance back to see Ben helping Nani to her feet, and a smile almost makes it to my face. But then I turn to find Marissa watching me.

'He's basically still in love with you, you know?' she says.

I can almost hear the steady rhythm of his heart and feel the warmth of his body against my cheek. 'I don't want to talk about this, Riss.' I pull away from her arm. 'I can walk on my own.'

'This morning, when she . . .' She pauses, choosing her words carefully. 'Something bad happened earlier today.'

Something bad? Is that what she calls Paisley's murder?

'No one could keep him from going to you,' she adds. 'Trust me, Heda tried.'

I remember the tenderness in his voice and touch when he found me on the bed, and how so many unspoken words passed between us in those moments. More and more my theory that he's only pretending to help Heda as a way to look after me seems right. But if that's true, I need to keep protecting him too. Which means letting them believe he's working for them. 'We have a history, nothing more,' I say.

I'm done with this conversation. I've never been in this part of the facility and I need to learn my way around. Paisley's death reinforces how dangerous Heda is. Now, having seen all those containers, and some of the prisoners up close, I can't help but wonder how many of them will survive her experiment and regain the Hedoness power. *And how many of them will die.*

Escaping isn't my only priority any more. I need to get the bow and arrows away from Heda. Without them she has no power.

Marissa takes me down a wide hallway similar to the one upstairs but the ceilings are lower, with a commercial-looking sprinkler system newly installed. The pipes are shiny and silver and the roof is dusty and water-stained. Instead of doors there are archways leading to all sorts of rooms, some with conference-like tables, others stacked with boxes of supplies. Unlike the hallway upstairs this one is warm, almost too warm, and smells strongly of sulphur.

I wipe the beads of sweat from my forehead. Marissa doesn't seem to be affected by the heat like I am. She barely even perspires, and the light glisten she has looks like she did it on purpose with shimmer powder. I roll my eyes and use my hand as a fan, trying to get a breeze.

'The air conditioning doesn't work very well in this part of the facility,' she tells me.

I find it hard to imagine that it's working at all. 'Where are we?'

'At the elevator,' she says stopping us at the next arch, which houses the elevator entrance. She pushes the button going up. 'I get the Ben stuff,' she continues, before I have the chance to clarify that I was asking about our location in the facility. Not to mention where the facility itself is located. It's a strange feeling of being lost, not knowing where I am. Marissa twirls a curl. 'I'd have a hard time forgiving him if he traded me too.'

Traded me?

'Like Heda can deliver reuniting him with his dead family.' Marissa's words flitter in and out of my mind. I don't know how to process what she's saying – Heda offered Ben the chance to see his family if he worked for her? It can't be that. It's impossible for people to return from Elysium. The doors to the otherworlds were sealed by the Committee years ago. Securing them was the only way to keep the gods from interfering with Earth and the demigods out of Olympus. Even *I* paid enough attention in school to learn that. If Heda could do it, I don't doubt Ben would want to be back with his family. It's all he's ever wanted. But I can't accept that he's willing to give away a love that was strong enough to end the Hedoness curse for a shallow promise from a disturbed old lady. Ben's smart enough to see through it.

Flashbacks of Ben holding me down while the red guard strapped me to the hard metal bed fill my mind, and suddenly I'm not so sure any more.

The elevator doors ding open and I rush in, trying to catch my breath and push Ben out of my mind so I can focus on coming up with a way of getting all the prisoners out. I can't let any more people become casualties of Heda's. I can't waste any more time waiting for Ben's help.

Twenty-One

The elevator rocks to a stop and the doors open. We exit on to the balcony near the stairwell door. Ben and my family sit on the edge of the paddle boat, surrounding Mrs Turner as she cries.

Marissa pulls me towards them, but my steps are sluggish and no matter how much I want to hold my family, Ben's there, and I don't know what to say to him.

'I can't believe him.' Marissa drops my arm when I don't keep up. Her heels click ahead with determination. She taps Ben on the shoulder, pulling him out of the circle. 'Why did you tell them Paisley died? You knew I wanted to be here.'

Just like that she blurts it out. It's a new kind of hurt to hear it spoken out loud. Until this moment I had bottled Paisley's death deep inside but now it's an airborne virus, floating around me, infecting the people I love.

'Marissa,' Ben hisses, turning to see if Mrs Turner heard. The circle parts, forming a clear path to her.

'Paisley . . . what? You're lying,' Mrs Turner says, taking a shaky step forward.

Kyle glares daggers at Marissa.

I catch my dad watching me with a deep curiosity. Before the cafeteria, the last time I saw him he was crumpled over my grave, mourning the relationship we never got. I haven't even had the chance to think of what I'll say to him. This will be our first time having a conversation when he's in control of his own will. All the fears and hopes for a normal father–daughter relationship come rushing back in. He smiles at me and raises his hand in hello. I return the hello, hoping he doesn't think my sadness over Paisley's death equates to a lack of interest in him. Because that couldn't be further from the truth.

Ben steps in Marissa's path, blocking her from the group. 'Mrs Turner was upset about the cafeteria fight,' he explains. 'A friend of hers got hurt bad. That's all.'

Marissa's eyes widen. 'I thought you'd told her . . . I—'

'You did whatever you wanted,' Kyle snaps. 'What's new? You don't care about anybody but yourself.'

Marissa looks like she's about to cry. I've never seen her so shaken. She hurries away in a rush of staccato heel clicks.

'It's a lie. I saw Paisley this morning,' Mrs Turner mumbles to herself.

Kyle and I share a quick look, wishing we could say more but knowing it isn't the time.

Ma rubs Mrs Turner's arms. 'Come, let's sit.'

Out of the corner of my eye I notice my dad weaving through the group and wonder what on earth he's doing. When he stops next to me, I almost jump in surprise.

'Hey,' he says, over Mrs Turner's cries.

Even though I heard him speak in the cafeteria, his voice seems so different I have to turn to make sure it's the same man that was there during my childhood. He looks the same: same freckles, pale skin, orange hair, same scar above his eyebrow. I can't get over how different he sounds – the British accent is still there, and so are the familiar notes of insecurity and confusion that come from being under the Hedoness power, but there are inflections of something that sounds like concern. I find myself taking fast breaths, my heart speeding.

'Hi,' I reply.

He kicks at the ground, his corkscrew-tight orange curls reflecting the sharp overhead lights and making them look like they're swirling. 'I'm sorry to hear about your friend. Were you two close?'

'Yes,' I reply. I've never felt so nervous to talk to anyone and I can't seem to form more words.

He smiles sadly. It's slightly crooked, and for the first time I realize we both share the same small gap between our front teeth. I have so much to ask him, so much I want to know. I can see the same glint of curiosity in his eyes and I want him to be the first to ask. I don't think I'm brave enough.

He leans closer. 'I know now is not the time but I'd really appreciate a chance to talk further with you,' he says, adding, 'If you would like, of course.'

I want to jump and scream, '*Of course, I've been waiting for this day all my life*,' but instead I say, 'Yes.'

'Very good then.' He nods, before swinging his leg and taking an awkward step away. I'm about to say something to stop him when approaching heel clicks cut me off. I spin towards the sound, surprised to see Marissa return with her duffle bag. I expected her to run away like she always does when things get too tough. But she sets her bag down and pulls out a folded blue uniform. Resting on top of it is Paisley's necklace – a spaceship with fangs.

A deep wail rises out of Mrs Turner as she pulls out of Ma's arms. If heartbreak has a sound, I've now heard it. She falls to the ground next to the paddle boat, crumples into a ball. Ma and Nani kneel beside her and rub her back.

Ma's tear-glazed eyes lock on me. Mrs Turner was her accountability partner through school. There isn't anything they wouldn't do for one another. Paisley was the closest thing to a niece Ma had. I can tell Ma's hurting for her friend, and herself, and for me too. She knows Paisley and I were close. But she doesn't know that my hurting is deeper than losing a friend. It's full of guilt that my blood, *my ichor*, couldn't heal Paisley.

After some time Mrs Turner dries her eyes and lifts her head. 'H-how did it happen?'

Ben starts to answer but Marissa cuts him off. 'They tried to give her Eros's blood.' Her eyes quickly find mine and she motions for me to stay quiet.

Both my ma and nani look over. I'm too stunned at Marissa's lie to respond. It wasn't Eros's blood. It was mine, she knows that. But she's covering for me.

'To heal her diabetes,' Marissa adds.

Paisley's ma starts to cry again.

Marissa folds her hands over her stomach. 'She was too weak at that point. She rejected his blood.'

'That's not possible,' Nani says. 'Eros is primordial. His blood is one of the most potent sources of immortality. It heals anything.'

'Heda has him in a collar made from the arrow of indifference.' Marissa flashes me a wary smile. 'It disables his power.'

Nani waves Marissa off like she's some kid trying to trade a broken toy. She doesn't realize now is not the time to debate the gods' abilities. But she's right about one thing: Eros's blood would have healed Paisley. I want to tell them all it was my blood they gave her but I can't bear to see what the truth will do to Mrs Turner. It's better she thinks her daughter's death was an accident than knowing that Paisley was experimented on to try to restore her Hedoness ability, then brutally murdered. It's the first time I can agree with Marissa about telling a lie.

Part of me wants to crawl on the floor next to Paisley's ma and cry too. But I'm done letting Heda rip pieces off my soul. My grief flickers into anger. It's time for answers.

I grab Marissa by the arm and drag her from the group, not stopping until we're out of ear range.

Marissa yanks her arm away, her face softening when she takes in the mix of anger and heartbreak on mine. 'I'm sorry about Paisley, Rach. I wish I could've done something.'

'Who is Bident?'

Marissa rolls her eyes. 'Like the one we learnt about in school?'

I blink long and slow.

She frowns at my irritation. 'Hades's weapon,' she clarifies, twirling a lock of her golden hair like she's ready to move on to the next conversation.

'Hades?' I repeat.

'The god of the Underworld, Zeus's brother—'

'I know who he is.'

'His weapon,' she repeats slowly. 'The sceptre with the two points. It's called a bident.'

'I didn't ask what is a bident. I asked who. Who is Bident?'

Marissa's face registers understanding then quickly twists into the one she makes when she's trying to find the most uncomplicated answer.

I step closer. 'Riss, just tell me. I need to know.'

'Why?'

'I just do.'

'OK.' She drops her curl and picks at her nails instead, watching me closely. I hold her stare until finally she says, 'It's the nickname of Heda's guard. The one that wears all red.'

My throat constricts with the memory of the leather straps being fastened again, so tight I couldn't breathe, and the rod being rammed for the first time into my body. The red guard did that. And the red guard killed Paisley.

'Where is she?' I ask, storming for the door.

'Rachel, stop.' She hurries to catch up, her heels clicking in sporadic beats.

'Not until I'm done with Bident.'

'What's got you so worked up about Bident?'

'She's the one who killed Paisley.'

'What?' Marissa gasps, grabbing my arm and spinning me to face her. 'Where did you hear that? I was told it was the treatment. It was too much for her. She couldn't take the ichor. Her body was too sick.'

Ice slinks up my spine. 'You mean she couldn't take *my* ichor.'

'Rachel, don't do this.'

I ignore her and continue to the containment room doors.

'Rachel, stop. I can't let you leave.'

'Why?'

'I . . . I, because I can't.'

I stop. It's too eerily similar to my nani's response about leaving her container. But Marissa's ankle is exposed, her grey trousers cuffed to show off her navy heels. Maybe there's a gold band there, hiding in the folded hem.

I glance around the balcony, trying to find something to make sense of this all, and my gaze lands on Ben in mid-conversation with Kyle and my dad. He catches my eye and frowns. 'Everything all right?' he yells, not waiting for an answer and instead jogs over.

'It will be. When I find Bident.' I take a step back and the large door opens behind me. I whip round, coming face to face with Heda and her guards, all of them wearing grey helmets and gear. Bident's not there. I shake with rage at the thought of her. I don't know what I'll do when I see her next. I once again imagine myself with the word *fighter* painted in red across my chest how I used to at St Valentine's – and I imagine running at her, hands wrapping round her throat, choking out her life like she cut out Paisley's. It's a gruesome but satisfying daydream.

And it scares me how much I want it.

Even though she's not there, I still find myself storming towards them. The guards pull their electric rods when I get too close. But Heda holds up her hand with the matt-black arrow wrapping over her wrist and they holster them again.

'Where's Bident?' I hiss, stumbling back when I realize her face looks years younger than the last time I saw it. She could pass for being in her early fifties now. I don't know what it is but that sense that I've met her before fills me again. It's probably because the younger she gets, the more she looks like Eros.

She smirks. 'Interesting question.'

'Just tell me.'

Heda lifts her chin and smiles, big and wide like Kali the demon. It's the type of smile you carve into jack-o'-lanterns on Halloween, and it makes me a new kind of scared.

'Bident's finishing up with Eros,' she says. 'She'll be here shortly.'

Twenty-Two

All I can picture is Bident skewering Eros with her swords. I tell myself he's immortal, he can't die. But then my eyes fall on the black and gold box being carried by the guard directly behind Heda and Eros's dull black collar comes to mind. She's found a way to keep Eros from his powers – with the arrow of indifference.

I don't know what that means for his immortality.

'Marissa?' Heda calls. 'Speed things along for us and go and get Bident. I can't wait to see what Rachel has planned for her. And while you're at it, arrange for another cot and some blankets to be brought here.' She pauses, making sure Marissa's listening. Marissa's expression is deadpan. Being bossed around was never something she responded well to. Marissa much prefers the bossing. 'Send Le-Li to me as well,' Heda adds. 'I missed our check-in this afternoon when someone started a fight in the mess hall.' She pauses. 'We'll also likely need his medical expertise after Bident is through here.' Her gaze lands on me and I cross my arms.

Marissa starts for the door. I don't feel like waiting around for Bident to come to us so I follow her.

Heda sighs. 'Ben, would you get Rachel, please?'

Heavy footsteps rush after me. I continue, ignoring them.

'Rachel, stop.'

With Mrs Turner crying in the background, and after what Marissa told me about his bargain with Heda, I'm really not in the mood to talk to Ben right now.

He closes the distance and grabs my arm.

I tear it away and whip round. The dam in me breaks and I don't hold back. 'Is it true?'

'Is what true?' he asks, tilting his head and pausing.

'You agreed to work for Heda for the chance to see your family again?'

'Oh my.' Heda's hand flutters to her heart. 'This should be interesting.'

Ben's gaze fixes on my sneakers. 'Yes.'

'But they're dead,' I blurt out, and instantly regret it when his eyes harden into a glare.

'You're dead to me.'

I take a step back. Ben's performance is too real to be an act for Heda. Maybe Marissa was telling the truth. I'm losing hope, fast. 'So I've seen.'

'What's that supposed to mean?'

I glance past him to Heda and the guards watching our fight. All they're missing is the popcorn.

'I don't know, Ben,' I say, my words bleeding sarcasm. 'Maybe my first clue was when you helped a murderer strap me to a machine that sucks my blood.'

'Oooh,' Heda says.

Ben's blue eyes ice over. I know it was a low blow – the Ben I cared for would never intentionally hurt anyone. But this is not that Ben. He starts to leave, then stops and turns back. 'At least I won't be alone,' he says with a mix of fear and anger. 'Thanks to Heda I'll see my family again. That's more than you've ever given me.'

I stagger a moment, trying to form my reply, and when I do manage, it's only a whisper. 'So, when you told me you loved me, and that we'd be together for ever in Elysium, what happened to that?' I lift my chin and shove down the urge to cry.

He glances at his boots and something seems to shifts in him, some sort of new resolve. His hands ball into fists and his body stiffens. 'What happened?' he snaps. 'What happened was that thanks to your decision to take ambrosia without considering me, we can't be together any more. Immortals don't go to Elysium. They don't die. Don't put this on me, Rachel. This was your choice.'

This is what he meant when he said we can't be together any more. My heart sinks all over again. 'But you know why I did what I did. I was trying to save everyone. I didn't know what the ambrosia—'

'But you were willing to forget me to do so, Rach. I didn't realize how much that hurt until . . .' He stops and glances up.

'You know I didn't want to leave you. How many times do I have to tell you I didn't know the ambrosia would make me immortal?'

Heda scoffs. 'Did no one tell you? Ambrosia is the food of the gods.'

I roll my eyes and glance to my family. They're busy consoling Mrs Turner and are missing this argument.

Ben waves for me to answer her.

'Yes, but –' I sigh – 'I didn't know that it was a source of their immortality.'

Ben throws up his hands, which only makes me madder.

'We could have found a way out of this together.' I force myself to lower my voice, not wanting anyone but him to hear my next fragile confession. 'You gave up. You gave up on us, Ben.'

'That's not fair!'

'Well, it's the truth.' I cross my arms and turn my back so he can't see the tears forming in my eyes.

'You want to talk about truth? OK, let's talk.' He clears his throat, less out of a need and more out of annoyance. 'So you didn't know about the ambrosia. But you did choose to leave me.'

I spin to face him. 'How can you even say that?'

'How can I . . . are you serious?' He runs a hand through his hair, his eyes wide with frustration. 'You knew that whatever you were taking was going to force the memory of me out of your head. Eros told you the cost of taking it.' He stops and flexes his jaw like the words hurt coming out. 'The cost of ending the Hedoness curse was forgetting me. You took it. Immortality or not, that sucks.'

My heart sinks to my stomach.

'It's worse than my family dying, Rachel. They didn't choose to leave me.'

'That's different,' I plead. 'I didn't know how you felt, and I thought I was doing what was best for you.' My words string together, I forget to breathe – my chest tightens into a knot. 'I was giving you back your dream—'

'It wasn't me who gave up, Rach. I would have gone to hell and back for you. But you didn't let me in. You decided what was best for me without even asking. You took the easy way out.'

'Just like you are now?' I wave in Heda's direction.

'Yeah, something like that.'

My dad steps between Ben and me. I didn't even see him approach. 'I think you two've "shared" enough.'

He escorts me past Heda and her guards who are finding way too much amusement in watching my heartbreak to want their entertainment interrupted, and leads us towards Ma and Nani, who are still trying to comfort a confused and inconsolable Mrs Turner. Kyle stands behind them, looking unsure if he should go and talk to Ben or come to me. I'm thankful when he catches my eyes and heads over.

It strikes me that he's changed since I last saw him at my fake funeral, and it's not just that he's no longer under the Hedoness influence or that his hair is grown out. His sharp brown eyes glint with the familiar mischief and something new. It takes me a while to realize that what I'm seeing is sadness. I glance at his hands, knuckles swollen and cut from punching the cafeteria guard. My stomach flips. It's because of knowing me that Kyle's been taken away from his ma, had his free will forced from him and is now imprisoned. *Because of me he's been put through hell.*

Kyle nods after Ben. 'That was a messy fight.' He leans down to wrap his arm around my shoulder. 'You going to be OK or should I go beat him up for you?'

The fact that after everything he's been through he still cares chokes me up. 'Can't I have both?' I ask, a forced smile on my face.

'Cheeky,' Dad interjects, giving me a little nudge.

Kyle laughs and Dad smiles for real, and it fills me with the same warmth as a clear summer day, lying on grass and soaking up sunlight.

I exhale, letting some of the disappointment from my conversation with Ben fall away. I like that my dad can calm me. He didn't used to do that. I can't help but wonder what else I'll like about him. I'm still not sure how to act around him. It's like my old dad is possessed by a more attentive man.

The guys walk me right past Ma and Nani. I half expected Dad to stop and check on Ma but he guides me to one of the containers and ushers us to take a seat in the doorway. I don't know whose it is but I'm curious because the inside walls are covered in fist-sized dents. I know what it feels like to want to take your emotions out on something. Today's been a horrible, wall-punching type of day. I lost a friend, *and a love*.

I glance at Kyle and Dad, sitting quietly beside me on the stoop. Both of them watching with concern-filled eyes.

Today hasn't been all bad. In the midst of all this pain I was reunited with my cousin and . . . I've finally gained a father.

Twenty-Three

Ma steps away from Mrs Turner and comes over to us. 'Rachel, can I talk to you?' She fiddles with the bottom of her shirt, her other hand absently rubbing her collarbone where her beaded necklace, the one she wore to honour her strange marriage to my father, used to be. Heda took it away along with every treasured item Ma chose to define herself: the neat way she pinned her hair from her face and the careful pleat of her sari. Now she's been assigned the same blue wardrobe as everyone else and her dark hair hangs loose. We look like cartoon characters in these clothes – the ones with white hats and blue skin. The name eludes me. If Paisley was here she'd know. She was the pop-culture queen. I fixate on the silver necklace lying on the pile of folded blue clothes an arm's reach from Mrs Turner before realising I've completely ignored Ma's question.

Thankfully, she's too busy watching my dad to notice. Dad smiles at her and a coy smile slips over her lips.

I stare back and forth between them, wondering what I'm missing. The next time my eyes connect with Ma's, I recognise the light gleam of embarrassment.

'Yes. Let's go,' I say, jumping up, smiling at the guys before following my ma to her container across the makeshift courtyard, passing Ben who's standing with Heda and her guards. I try to see if I can spot the black arrow shard I kicked there earlier but can't without making it obvious that I'm looking for something. We step around Nani and Mrs Turner. Nani looks up, her eyes pleading with someone to take over for her.

'I'll be back in a minute,' Ma tells her.

As we continue, she hooks arms with me and leans in, glancing at Heda and the guards who are watching from a distance, and whispers, 'I missed you, Rachel.'

'I missed you too, Ma.'

Her face hardens then, and it's not in the way it does when she's upset but rather when she's worried about upsetting me.

I stop in my tracks. Does she know about my ichor killing Paisley? 'What is it?'

'After what happened to Paisley, I don't want any secrets between us,' she says.

This comes as a shock. For one, I'm even more nervous now that Ma knows about my ichor. And two, Ma's always guarded her secrets. 'I want that too, Ma.'

'I need to tell you about how your father came under my Hedoness power. There's more to the story of his turning than you know.' Ma nods to Heda. 'But not out here.' She glances back at Dad as she guides us into her container. We sit on her cot and Ma tucks the loose fabric from her blue jogging bottoms into a pleat, securing it under her waistband. She catches me watching her and smiles. 'Old habits,' she says with a shrug.

When she looks back up, her eyes are full of a sadness I've never seen before. No, not sadness. Regret. 'Rachel.' She exhales my name, rushing into her next words like if she doesn't get it out now, she never will. 'It wasn't by chance that I chose your father. We were quite good friends once.'

My mouth opens and closes, breathing the questions I can't speak for fear of cutting her off and never hearing the story.

'We met when he was sent in to fix the computers at St Valentine's.' I try to picture Ma in the St Valentine's uniform and can't. Until coming here, I've never seen her in anything but a sari. And I don't know what's stranger: Ma in a sweatsuit or the fact that my dad was once at my school too. 'Somehow he managed to hack the school's servers,' she continues, 'and instead of getting rid of him, the Committee hired him to help keep them secure.' She stares at the container door as if the memories of that time were there, outside, an arm's reach away. 'He was always so smart. At nineteen he set up our Quiver system. I was one of the trial users, and we'd chat into the night about anything and everything. We always had great conversations,' she says.

So my dad's a genius. A smile flickers to my face. I kinda like knowing that.

'That was a hard time for me,' Ma says. 'Being away from your nani.' She glances back to the door. 'But he could always make me laugh. And when I was laughing I forgot how far from home I was.'

'Dad's funny?' I blurt. I can see the genius but I never got the funny vibe from him.

'Oh yes,' she says, 'but never on purpose.'

I smile, thinking about my fire-headed British father cracking a bad joke. Then my heart sinks with the realisation that for my whole life my dad's *existence* has been a bad joke. The time I'd begged Ma to release him from her Hedoness power and give him back his will plays in my mind. Her words that day were, 'It's not so simple.'

I can tell by her face that the answer is the same now.

'So then, why did you take his will?' I ask, pulling my knees into my stomach as I wait for her reply to the question I've been asking my whole life. The question I've never once got a straight answer to.

She plucks at the threadbare blanket that's spread carefully over the bed. It's not like Ma to get this serious.

I tuck in even tighter, waiting for an explanation that never comes. 'If you won't answer that, will you at least tell my why you kept him under your power all those years?'

Instead of answering she looks off to the door again, back at the memories of what Dad once was, and it gives me a chance to study her face.

'So, Dad?' I repeat. 'You stayed with him because you love him?'

Her deep brown eyes settle on mine and I realize how similar in shade they are to Paisley's. No wonder I always felt so comfortable around her.

'Of course,' Ma says. 'Mostly I love that he gave me you.'

Heaviness settles in my stomach. I wasn't expecting Ma to say that.

'But if you didn't love *him*, wasn't the right thing to let him go? I mean, he may not have been his full self, but he'd be a little bit him, right?'

'These are questions that no longer need answers. You ended the Hedoness ability.'

She doesn't know about the magic still in my blood. 'Ma, please, I need to hear your answer, it still matters to me.'

'All right.' Ma places her hand on my knee. 'I didn't want you to ever have to know this but when we were much younger, your father lost his brother.'

'Dad told me his brother died before I was born.'

'It was a tragedy and he couldn't handle it. Your dad became a shadow of the man he was and . . . well, he tried to kill himself.'

'What?'

She squeezes my knee and continues. 'Do you remember the painting of Eros at St Valentine's? The one with the bow and arrows?'

'Yeah, but what does that have to do with Dad?'

'A couple of years after I graduated, I thought I saw someone. He looked just like the painting. So I followed him and he led me to your dad's apartment. Well, I . . . I found him bleeding to death on his bathroom floor. I nursed him back to life, but my touch, you know . . . it changed him. By then in my life I wanted a child and I figured it was better to take the will of a man who did not have one then to take it from a man who did. It was the best way I could have you. I don't regret my choice. I justify it to myself because now there are two lives, where there would've been none. And I did care for him, truly.' Her hand slips from my knee and she hangs her head. 'It's not the way I wish it to be. But it is the best of the worst.'

All those years of thinking that my ma was part monster evaporate, and while I don't get how taking away Dad's choice, even in death, is okay, I now understand she did what she thought was good by my dad and me. I want to press Ma more about her decision to turn him, but the deep sadness returns to her eyes. I lean forward and brush the hair from Ma's face. 'What about now? Are you happy?'

'Yes, I'm happy.' She lifts her head, a tear escaping over her cheeks, and she smiles – a small but genuine smile. 'I have you.'

In that moment I know she means it. I grab her hand, holding it tight. 'What are we going to do?'

'About your father?' She crinkles her brow in confusion.

'Well, yes, about him and . . . everything else.' For the second time in my life I want to go all Joan of Arc for my family. Learning that all those years ago Dad wasn't plucked from his dreams to be a Hedoness pet makes me feel better about my ma. This new realisation lightens my heart more than anything. 'Ma, I need to tell you something.'

'What is it, Rachel?'

I squeeze her hand. 'It's Heda, Ma. She wants to use my blood to—'

The school-bell-sounding alarm goes off. Suddenly Ma's eyes glaze over and she stands and walks to the doorway.

'Ma?'

She doesn't answer and I know it's the damn anklet forcing her to obey.

I stand beside her and watch Mrs Turner and the rest of my family head for their containers. Kyle goes into the one with the dents in the walls and my heart breaks for him. His ma isn't here. He's basically all alone.

And it's all happening because I didn't want the Hedoness power. A power that is forever in me now anyway. Everything I chose led here, now, to this. My family's under Heda's control, and Paisley's dead. *If I'd only embraced my power then . . .*

Twenty-Four

'Oh my,' says Heda, as Mrs Turner passes her en route to her container. 'What dedication. It's like they have somewhere important to be.'

My family stands in their doorways, as still as Heinz's statues.

'This isn't fair.' I storm out of Ma's container and up to Heda.

'Fair is an illusion,' Heda replies.

I square my shoulders, lift my chin. 'You promised that my family would be together and that we wouldn't be harmed.' I wave to the question mark of five containers. 'Keeping us apart like this is harm.'

'I'm fairly certain I said I'd keep you *safe* and together,' she says. 'And that was dependent on your cooperation.'

'It's the same thing,' I tell her.

'Oh, is it?' asks Heda with a grin that reminds me too much of the one Marissa uses when she's purposely riling me. I know I shouldn't let her but I'm too emotionally shot to stop myself.

'I said, no one gets harmed . . . Paisley's dead.'

'An unfortunate accident.'

My fists clench. 'Let's not kid ourselves, Heda. You need me.'

'And?' she says, the humour slipping from her tone. She steps forward, her blue silk robe whips behind.

I wish I had time to find the black arrow shard. 'And as long as you honour our terms you will have access to my ichor.' I don't tell her I have no intention of honouring our terms myself. I want my family safe while I figure out how to get us out of here. Heda's armlet-clad hand rests stubbornly on the black box that she took from the guard at some point, and I worry there's no point trying to escape until I get the bow and arrows from her.

I wish Eros was here because he knows how to keep Heda's attention off me. My heart sinks at the thought of him – all this time he's been trapped with Bident. Anything could have happened to him by now.

There's a sudden stirring in me, a desire for the magic contained in the box only a few steps away. It's like the arrow's a magnet for the immortality spreading its disease through my body. *Spreading its power.* If I focus on it, like Eros said, I might be strong enough to overtake Heda's guards and grab the box before she can use the arrow to stop my abilities.

My eyes find Ben. He'd never forgive me for embracing this power. It bothers me that I even care about that now. I turn to the rest of my family, held motionless in their

175

doorways because of the anklets, eyes pleading for me to stay safe. I can't make them watch the guards put their rods on me and Heda use the arrow. They already buried me once.

Heda sees my turmoil and her mouth twists into a cold, calculated smile. 'When they said you can't draw blood from a stone they'd never met Le-Li.'

I'm done with these games. Le-Li told me he needed more blood because he didn't have the answers yet. I'm hoping that's still the case. 'A stone can only bleed so much before it goes dry. Are you willing to take the chance?'

'The chance?' She amuses me with her question.

'That you'll get your *answers* before you drain my last drop?'

'You best be careful who you threaten,' she says, her eyes landing on my dad in his doorway. She mimes slashing her throat. 'Hello again, Daniel.'

Before I can reply, Bident waltzes through the open door. A blood-red form, carrying a folded cot with the flair of someone using a silver-topped cane. I can almost feel the word *fighter* emblazoning itself on my chest. Ben catches my eyes and raises a hand, motioning for me to do nothing. The nothing I want to do is sprint the distance and rip that helmet off her head. I want to look into the eyes of the woman who killed my friend.

Heda follows my glare to Bident. 'Ah, finally,' she says.

176

'Let's up the stakes and see if you really are a girl of your word.'

My eyes stay glued on Bident.

'Well, are you?' Heda asks, amused.

'Yes,' I hiss.

'Then shall we?' Heda steps into the centre of the containers. 'Priya Patel, Anjali Patel, come here.'

At first I'm caught off guard by the use of my ma and nani's given names. Then the worry fills me. 'What are you doing? You don't need them.'

'Ah, see here,' says Heda, waving her arm in an arc. 'You promised not to give me any problems. This is feeling like problems.'

'Let them go.'

I'm shoved forward before I can blink. Bident holds down my neck and restrains my hands. It's the same move the guard in the cafeteria used. Either she's Bident or they all received the same training. I try to focus on what that guard looked like: did she wear a mask, did I see her face? But I can't picture anything past the red-heeled boots I'm forced to stare at now.

Heda bends down to talk to me, her hair hanging into my line of sight. It's blonder now but there are still patches of grey. 'Now,' she begins, in a tone one would use on a misbehaving child, 'rumour has it you were the one who started a fight in my mess hall. I was going to let bygones be bygones but then you went and got me mad.'

I yank my head away from Heda and catch a glimpse of the knife on Bident's belt before she shoves my head back down. A whisper of power blooms at my innermost core – if only I can summon it forth and control it somehow. Eros told me that whatever power I focus on manifests. Maybe with the powers I could even fight off the guards, remove the prisoners' anklets and get everyone out of here. I glance to Dad, watching nervously from his door. I need to ask Eros what will happen before I take chances that could get my family killed.

'OK,' I say, going limp in Bident's grasp. 'I didn't mean to cause a problem in the cafeteria. I saw my family and I got excited because I hadn't seen them in so long. I didn't realize how serious the guard's commands were. It won't happen again.'

'Good,' says Heda. 'Release her.'

Bident lets go of my hands and shoves me towards Ma and Nani, who are standing where instructed, awaiting their next orders. I put my arms out protectively, blocking them behind me, and stare back at Heda.

She tuts. 'I could just tell your mother and grandmother to come here and they will listen. But where's the fun in that?' Her eyes narrow into slits as she assesses me. 'Bident, get them.'

The red guard steps forward.

'You can't do this!'

'They will be safe, and when I'm done, they will be returned. I lost a valuable test subject today and I need to replace her immediately.'

'You didn't lose anything. She was killed by Bident!' I'm shaking, I'm so mad.

'I'm a fair woman, Rachel.' She holds up her hand, stopping Bident. 'Pick one of them. If you'd rather, I could use your father or cousin – anatomy is no longer an issue for me. But I require security so that I know you will obey.' She waves to them, then past the balcony to the stacks of containers. 'It's amazing how handy collateral comes in.'

What does she mean by anatomy is no longer an issue? I square my stance, keeping my arms raised. 'I had your word.'

'And I will keep it. With a few liberal interpretations. Are you going to choose or not?'

'You know I can't.'

She motions the red guard forward. 'Grab one, I don't care which.'

The red guard pounces.

My body erupts with white light.

In one sweeping motion I spin, grab Bident's knife – she tries to block me – and slam it into her hand.

Twenty-Five

Bident cries out. I drop the knife, watching it smear the floor with a streak of red, and stare down at my shaky, blood-tarnished hands. I did this. I stabbed someone.

The buzz comes before the rods. A wall of blue glow surrounds me once again. Heda has the black arrow around her wrist and is holding it ready to strike.

My ma grips on to Nani's arm. Her eyes fill with fear. It isn't the rods or the arrow that's causing it. It's me.

Heda motions to the closest guard. 'Go and see what's taking Le-Li so long and have him bring some of Eros's ichor with him.'

The guard sprints from the container room into the hall.

I turn to Ma. 'What happened?' I remember a deep rage taking over me and then light – blinding white light.

Bident presses her injured hand to her stomach, her blood darkening the red of her uniform.

'You snapped,' Heda answers for Ma. 'I had your word, then you attacked my favourite guard.' She tuts again. 'That wasn't really complying with my demands. Now I get to choose, and I'm taking them both.'

I open my mouth to protest but Nani pushes past me and Ma and walks herself into line behind Heda.

'Nani, no!'

'Don't argue, Rachel.' She waves me away. 'I go willingly.'

My ma looks equally worried. 'Ma?' she says, taking a hesitant step after Nani.

'I'm old,' Nani says. 'Being a Hedoness has been my life's work. If I can feel the power of immortality in me before I die, then I have truly lived.'

'But—'

'Don't argue with your nani.'

Now more than ever I need to speak to Eros. I can volunteer for another bloodletting. That would let me keep an eye on Nani. But I likely won't be left alone after the incident of Le-Li passing out, especially if Le-Li realizes Eros lied and he didn't slip on the ichor puddle but was struck over the head with chains and stabbed in the neck with sleeping medicine. I have to find a way to have them bring Eros here. Then it hits me. I turn to Heda.

'You promised my whole family would be together.'

She rolls her eyes. 'I will bring your grandmother back between treatments.'

'Then I can trust you will extend that courtesy to my entire family?'

'Yes,' Heda says, waving me off and turning to slip the armlet from her wrist and place it back in its box. She seems shakier, frailer, like she's aged five years. The black arrow sure works fast. I can't help wondering if she asked for Eros's blood specifically because she wants some of it for herself now too. I bet she takes a swig before she offers any to Bident.

'Then have Eros brought here,' I say. 'He's my family.'

She jerks her head up, hand still in the box, her face slowly twisting into a smile. 'You clever little wicked thing.' She closes the lid in her sanctimonious way and turns slowly to her line of guards. She smooths down her ever-greying hair, then the front of her blue robe, and yells, 'Why isn't Le-Li here?'

The guards look among themselves. Ben is particularly on edge.

'I don't care which of you morons goes, but go now!' She glances at me, her face hardening into a scowl. 'And have him bring my father.'

Two guards start for the door, hesitating when they see the other. 'Fools.' Heda throws up her hands and turns to Bident. 'Just go.'

As Bident jogs out of the container room clutching her injured hand, all I can think is that a stab to the palm isn't enough to make up for what she did. I'll find another way to make her pay for Paisley's death.

Heda leans over to Ben and whispers in his ear. His gaze flicks to me but he nods and heads to the panel by the door and enters a code. Soon a series of short bells goes off and Dad and Kyle and Mrs Turner exit their containers. Mrs Turner rushes to the pile of Paisley's things, gathering them in her arms and taking a long inhale before rushing back to her container and shutting the door.

My family stretches and regroups in the courtyard. On the other side of the balcony comes the sound of hundreds of doors opening and closing. I make my way to the railing. Heavy footsteps follow behind me but I don't stop until I'm at the edge, looking out at the containers.

Doors open and people climb down the ladders and gather in groups in the small aisle between the stacks.

'Heda sent me to keep an eye on you,' Ben says, coming up from behind and standing beside me, so close that our arms brush.

A familiar electric pulse rises in my blood. I slide down the rail, putting more distance between us. He keeps his eyes on the sea of containers but his body stiffens when I move away.

'*I wanted to come to you.*' His voice pushes into my thoughts.

I squeeze my head, focusing on watching a prisoner struggle down their ladder, helped by the group at the bottom.

'She lets them out for socialising once a day,' he explains.

I turn to see if he's talking or if I'm hearing his thoughts, but he nods to the containers waiting for me to reply. I don't, though. I look out over all the prisoners. There are so many Hedonesses from all over the world. I never realized how many there were. We were always kept separate in our families and schools, only able to connect to each other through Quiver. My dad's Quiver. It's so strange to think he built it and I never knew.

'Rach.' Ben says my name in a sigh, his eyes still looking away.

'Yeah?'

He puts his arms on the rail and rests his head on his fist, turning to look at me from under his dark floppy fringe. Even with the low lighting his blue eyes pop.

And when his gaze trails across my face, pausing on my mouth, the memory of his lips pressed against mine sends a shiver over my skin – my stupid, traitorous body refuses to remember the heartbreak.

'For what it's worth, I'm sorry I hurt you,' he says.

I drop my hands from my head and press my stomach instead.

The alarm goes off again and the people below us dart into their containers.

Ben cocks his ear to the sound and frowns. 'It's too soon,' he says, pushing off the railing and heading back round the containers on the balcony. Curiosity gets the best of me and I follow him.

I round Ma's container, stopping when I see Le-Li and Heda waiting for the elevator. They don't notice me in the container's shadows. He hands her a jar of bright blue liquid and she unscrews the lid and gulps it down. 'It's the transitioning,' he explains. 'I still can't isolate it when everything keeps changing.'

I press into the container, wanting to hear more. My heart's racing – they can't do it. They can't get an extract of Hedoness from my blood. It's the first piece of good news I've heard.

'Don't tell me what we can't do.' Heda throws the empty jar on the ground. It bounces in my direction, rolling to a stop just past my feet. 'What are our options?'

'Perhaps if we accelerate the plan—'

'Rachel?' Ben calls, turning towards me.

I give an awkward wave and step out from the container's shadow, making my way back. Heda and Le-Li ignore the elevator as it dings open and follow me over to Ben.

A loud grunt comes from the main doors and we turn to see Marissa, struggling to hold Eros, his weight hanging over her small frame. He looks even worse than when I left him.

Ben and I rush over, grab Eros and help him walk.

'Hey,' he says, wincing. The skin around the black collar peels from his neck like soggy onion. I try not to gag.

'Don't talk,' I tell him. 'You need to rest.'

I glare at Heda as we pass her en route to my ma, who's waving us into her container. Nani's eyes are wide and she bows in reverence as he passes.

Ma waves to Dad and Kyle. 'Keep an eye on my ma, I have to help.'

They head to Nani, who is in the line of guards waiting to be taken to the ichor room. We struggle to get Eros up the one step and over to Ma's bed. Every time we shift, the collar brushes another part of his skin and he hisses.

I look at Ben. 'We need to get this off him.'

He shakes his head and frowns down at the collar. 'It has to stay.' I know Ben never liked the gods but helping Heda do this seems cruel, even for him. That said, he doesn't like the collar, that's obvious by the frustration in his words. There's a salve that could help with the pain, but I don't trust Ben to get it for Eros. Maybe, just maybe . . .

I reach out and grab the collar.

A thousand bolts of fire shoot through my fingers. I lose my grip on Eros. He collapses sideways on the bed and I fall to the floor, clutching my hand and hissing like he did. 'How can you stand that?' I ask through clenched teeth.

His weight wavers on one shaky arm. Ben holds the rest of him up but it's a struggle. Eros bobs his head to look past me, out the door. 'For my daughter . . . I will endure anything.'

Twenty-Six

My hand is a blistered forest, skin swollen and peeling. Light blue ichor, a paler shade than it looks in the tubes, weeps out of the open wounds on my palm and drips down my fingers. I can't help wondering if the black arrow did that. If in that short burst of contact it diluted my blood.

Wherever ichor drips, touching my skin, the pain subsides. Soon it's enough for me to bear. I push off the floor with my good hand, scanning the room to find that Ben's gone. It's just me, Ma and Eros.

Dad and Kyle hover in the doorway but don't come in. Everyone watches quietly as Eros lies on the bed, snoring loud enough to drown out the air conditioning fans in the hall. His head hangs off one end of the mattress, his feet dangle off the other, showcasing how tall he is. I can't even imagine how long it's been since they let him lie down.

Ma kneels beside him, eyes wide. She reaches out to brush his curls but hesitates and pulls back. Then I realize it's probably the first time she's seen a god up close. My own reaction wasn't much different when he appeared out of nowhere among Heinz's statues.

She hears my steps and turns, sucking in a breath. 'Oh, Rachel, your poor hand. I should be helping you.' She glances back at Eros in a way that makes me think she's feeling ashamed of being enraptured by him instead of putting me first, like she always does.

'It's OK, Ma. There's nothing you could do.' It is strange how slowly it's healing.

I look over to Dad and Kyle, wondering why they didn't offer to help.

'We can't come in,' Kyle says, as if reading my mind.

'The anklets?' I ask.

Dad nods.

I sit on the bed next to Eros, supporting my damaged hand in my lap. My other hand tucks Ma's tattered blanket under my leg, securing it as I tear a loose piece off.

'Need me to help you wrap that?' Ma asks, nodding to my palm.

'This is for Eros,' I say, struggling to slip the cloth under his collar one-handed. This close I can hear Eros's skin sizzling as the anti-magic presses in. He needs it more than I do.

Ma helps me with the cloth and Eros takes easier breaths. But soon the cloth starts to smoke as the collar burns through it.

'We need another strip,' I say, struggling to pull something usable from Ma's blanket.

Eros opens his eyes a crack and smiles up at me. 'Don't worry about it . . . won't last.'

'Stop talking and it will last longer.' I try to slip a corner of a fresh strip under the thick black band. Up close, it looks like his neck opens into a dark void and I could reach into it all the way to the other side. But I know that's not true. My hand won't pass through the collar, it will only burn.

'Get lost, Marissa,' Kyle says from behind me. 'I'll do it. No one wants you here.'

'I'm just bringing the bed,' Marissa tells him. I turn in time to see Marissa knock on the container door and Kyle throw his hands up and storm off. 'Hey, you need this?' she asks, lifting the corner of the cot into the room. Dad helps her shove it in the rest of the way, his hands never crossing the boundary of the doorframe. Even though it isn't the full Hedoness powers, I hate seeing him controlled by the arrow of infatuation again.

'Put it over there,' Ma says, pointing to the far wall.

Marissa rolls the folded cot over and places two new blankets on top. 'I'll try to get you another bed,' she says.

'Thanks,' I say, turning from Eros. 'Any chance you could grab some plasters?' I hold up my hand and she gasps.

'What did you do?

I nod to his collar. 'Accidentally touched it.' I can't very well admit my real reason for doing it. As if summoned, Ben knocks on the door but doesn't wait for an invitation before passing Dad and stepping in. I guess he doesn't have an anklet after all. There goes that theory. *That hope.* He comes to the bedside, stares down at Eros's neck, then his eyes continue to my hand. His own clench into fists and his jaw flexes like it does when he's mad.

Ma leans over and lowers her voice. 'Do you wish him to leave?'

'It's OK,' I say, watching Ben, who's pretending not to eavesdrop.

Ma nods and turns back to Eros. 'I never thought we would meet,' she says, half to him and half to me. 'I have so many questions, so much to ask.'

'Ask,' says Eros, gasping through the pain.

Ma looks to me as if wanting my permission. I shrug and she slides closer to the bed. 'Was it you? Did you lead me to Daniel?'

'Yes,' he chokes.

'I knew it.' Ma whips around, eyes landing on Ben. 'We have to help Eros.'

'There's nothing I can do,' Ben says, glancing to his feet.

'You must find something. Rachel exists only because of Eros's help.'

I jerk back at this, never having made the connection. Maybe it's Ma's Hedoness loyalty or maybe it's something else, but it seems like she's giving him more credit than he's due. Sure, Eros helped her, but Ma said her feelings for my dad were a large part of her turning him, and it wasn't Eros who first introduced my parents. *Or was it?* My dad did work for the Committee. I push the thought out of my mind and watch Eros struggle to lift his arm and place it on Ma's shoulder, patting it twice, awkwardly, before dropping it back to the bed.

Ma smiles and sits straighter. I can't believe she's buying into this.

Ben leans over me. 'Remember when you saved me from getting shot?' his whisper stirs the hair by my ear and sends a shiver through me. 'Now we're even.'

Something lands in my lap. Ben leaves, passing Marissa as he steps out of the container. When I look down there's a little parcel no bigger than the size of a walnut. I shield it beside my leg, careful not to let Marissa or the camera see. I'm still not sure where Marissa fits into all this.

Ma's arms are crossed, eyebrows raised. I motion to Marissa, and Ma nods and gets up.

'Come, Marissa,' she says, taking her by the arm and walking her to the cot. 'Please, will you help me set this up?' As they struggle to unfold the bed, I unroll the paper, continuing to shield it from the camera with my hand. Inside is a tiny jar of gold dust and a note:

Shavings from the shield of Achilles.
It will block the arrow of indifference from siphoning power.
Add water and mix into a paste, then apply topically.

I smile. He delivered. I hoped he would. My emotions
are a bewildering mess, but right now I'm so happy I'm
tempted to run after him and hug him.

Twenty-Seven

The gold dust rests between my knees. I squeeze them tight, not wanting Ben's gift to be discovered. Out of nowhere, a grey guard appears, her tall form filling the doorframe. I jump and the container slips lower.

'Marissa,' the guard says, 'we're leaving. Heda wants everyone locked in their compartments.'

I lean forward, trying to slide my hand beneath my legs to keep the dust from dropping.

'See you later, Rach,' Marissa says, following the guard out the door.

When the coast is clear, I stick the container under Eros's leg and head after Marissa, marching straight up to Heda. 'What's this about locking us in?' I ask.

'Safety precautions,' Heda replies, her focus on waving the guards into line.

'Can you please let us leave the units and gather in the courtyard?' I ask.

'You call this a courtyard?' She points to the small space with an old paddle boat as a bench, surrounded by walls of weatherworn, perforated metal and illuminated by flickering overhead lights. She's right, it's not much to look at, but it's the only place we can be together.

'Please,' I repeat. 'Use the anklets, command them not to leave.'

She eyes me warily. 'You know about the anklets?'

'It's kinda obvious.'

'Is it?'

I glance at Nani, standing in line with Heda's guards. 'For one, my nani's not really into obeying other people's orders.' Nani gives me a glare that is really a smile.

'You know,' says Heda, 'I did notice that.'

'Haven't we earned your trust?' I say. 'I've gone willingly to the ichor room, and I will go willingly again tomorrow.'

She raises a brow. 'You'll go willingly when I tell you to, tomorrow or now.'

'Yes, that's what I meant.' It isn't. I don't want her having any more of my blood, but I don't tell her that. I open my mouth to threaten use of the black arrow shard, even though I'm not certain I know where it is, but I don't need to; Heda answers first.

'Fine,' she says. 'Gather around, Patel family, and Mrs Turner, and you, Kyle, whoever you are.'

They congregate before her in a line. She reaches her hand into the neck of her shirt and holds something as she gives them strict orders not to leave the balcony. They can only go to our courtyard and their containers. Her actions are strange but she gives me what I ask for so I don't question it.

We call goodbye to Nani as the guards push her out of the main door. I hate that there's nothing I can do to stop them, but I'll do whatever it takes to get her back. First things first, I have to help Eros. If anyone knows how to save Nani, it's him. I grab my ma's arm and pull her back into her container.

'Rachel? What's going on?'

'We need water,' I say.

She nods to the side that's curtained off. 'Why, what is it?'

I slide my hand under Eros's leg and retrieve the jar of dust. 'I have something to help the burn.'

Ma's jaw goes slack and she gives me a blank look.

'I'll explain in a moment,' I say, making my way to her makeshift bathroom and pulling the curtain back. There's a bucket and a small sink. I curl my nose in disgust and turn back to Ma. 'Do you have a cup or bowl or something for the water?'

'You have to scoop it in your hands,' she says.

'I only have one workable hand right now. Can I use you?'

She comes and cups her hand. I add a few drops of water before carefully uncorking the dust and sprinkling it in. I stir it with my little finger, feeling a tingle as it grips to my skin. It's a cooling sensation, and I resist the urge to scoop it on to my blistered palm as I add more gold and water until a paste forms.

'Turn over your hand,' Ma says. 'Let's put this on.'

'No.' I glance to Eros.

Ma pats my shoulder in understanding. 'You have a big heart, Rachel.'

Eros sits up, stretching his neck. 'You don't know how good this feels,' he says. His eyes land on my hand, cradled over my stomach. 'Thank you, love.'

'I'll be fine. My ichor is doing its thing.'

He nods. 'But it doesn't feel pretty while you wait.'

Ma stands before him now, hands twisted in front, shifting her weight from one foot to another, looking like a girl about to finally talk to her idol. It makes me smile until I remember what brought them together. I need her to know what's happening, all of it. I drag the new cot over and push it up to the wall opposite Eros, then take a seat and pat beside me for Ma to sit too.

'There's something we need to tell you, Ma.'

She glances between Eros and me then listens, sitting on the cot, refolding the pleat in her trousers out of habit or maybe nerves.

'Do you know how I survived being shot?'

Ma frowns. 'They told me you were immortal now. I never even thought of it much after that. I was just happy to learn you were alive.'

I hold her hand. 'It was Eros, Ma. He gave me ambrosia.'

196

'Ambrosia?' She looks to Eros and back to me. 'That explains things.'

'There's more,' I say.

Ma's grip tightens on my hand.

'When I took it, I was still a Hedoness. The power—'

She gasps, her free hand fluttering over her bare collarbone. 'It's still in you?'

'I think so, I don't know, but Heda—'

'She wants it out.'

It's not Ma who says it. It's Eros.

Ma helps Eros into the courtyard, even after his many protests that he can walk on his own – after being secured to the stool for the past week, his legs need a stretch. Kyle's already there, shirt off, doing push-ups and burpees. Dad's container door is closed and the light inside is on.

Ma catches my eye and nods to his container. 'It's time,' she says.

'It's time,' I repeat to myself, taking calming breaths as I walk over. Time to have my first real talk with my father. I'm determined to use more than one word this conversation. I take another deep breath and knock on his door.

'Hello?'

'It's me, hi, Rachel.' I wince at how awkward I sound.

'Come in,' he replies.

I glance back at Ma and she nods me forward with an encouraging smile. 'Dad?' I say, opening the door and stepping inside. He's sitting on his mattress on the floor, smoothing down the blanket for me to sit too.

'I'm glad you came,' he says. 'I've been worried about you.'

'Worried?' I mean, I know there's a lot going on, but I never in a million years expected my dad to tell me he's worried about me. I'm not sure if I should smile or cry.

Dad's face softens and he rubs his knees. 'I'm sorry, I'm new to this being-in-control-of-what-I-say thing,' he tells me. 'I don't want to make you feel uncomfortable.'

'It's OK,' I say, 'this is new for me too.'

He smiles and waves to the bed. 'Please sit.'

I lower myself to the far corner of his mattress, which feels like something far too familiar for our current relationship.

'What do you need?' he asks.

'Sorry?'

'Your visit? Can I help you with anything?'

'Yeah, uh, I have something I need to tell you.'

Dad leans back into the wall, his brow twisted as he processes what I said. He of all people knows how dangerous a Hedoness army would be.

'Rachel, may I speak freely?'

198

I nod.

'You don't really know me, but I know you enough to worry.'

I spin to face him, feeling uncomfortable when his eyes hold mine like it's me he's actually wanting to see. All my life I wanted him to look at me this way.

'I know something happened between you and Ben,' he says. 'And I know that must be painful for you.'

Of all the things to pick out of what I told him! To make matters worse, I never even got to the part about Ben betraying me. 'Yes,' I reply, not knowing what else to say.

We sit in silence for an uncomfortably long moment. I can tell he's giving me the space to feel safe enough to continue, but I can't bring myself to talk to him about Ben – the other guy to instil in me the feeling that I'm not enough.

Dad exhales a sharp breath and nods, accepting my silence. 'You should know Ben has been checking in on us, even before we were moved up here. He'd bring your ma and nani some of their favourite tea. He and Kyle would go for daily jogs, and I know that meant more to Kyle then he let on.'

'Why are you telling me this?'

He reaches out for me but pulls back and crosses his arms.

'Why do you think?'

The walls in this container feel like they're encroaching and the air's so stuffy my lungs burn. All this talk of Ben, here with my dad, makes my head spin. I shrug.

Dad rolls his blanket and tucks it behind his back. 'Did your ma ever tell you how she saved my life?'

'Yeah, she said she found you, that you . . .'

'Tried to commit suicide,' he finishes.

'Yeah.' I glance at my partially healed, blistered hand, not knowing what else to focus on.

'That's not exactly true,' he says.

'What?' I stare up at him.

'It was Hedone,' he says. 'She wanted me to recruit your ma, she wanted me to lead her on and convince her to come to headquarters along with the most powerful of your kind.'

My kind. 'What?' My heart slows, the room seems to spin.

Dad lets out a long exhale. 'The problem was I didn't need to pretend to like her. I'd already fallen for your ma. I was mesmerised by her strength and beauty and love for tradition.' He pauses and holds my stare. 'You remind me so much of her, you know.'

Heat rises to my cheeks. I always thought my ma was the most beautiful woman I'd ever met, and Dad compared me to her. 'What happened?' I ask.

'I refused and quit my job. By time that time Hedone and her supporters had completely taken over the Committee.

She ordered my death to clean up any loose ends and had it staged to look like I killed myself. I think she did that to hurt your ma.'

'Does Ma know?'

He shakes his head, making his red curls bounce. 'I've been waiting for the right time to tell her.'

'We need to tell her now!' I say, standing and heading for the door. 'Come on.'

'Rachel, sit back down.'

'But Ma—'

'Your ma has waited this long, she can wait a little longer. Right now I'm more concerned about you. Please come back,' he says, patting the bed.

My legs are shaky as they return me to him. Never in my life has Dad put me before Ma. I don't know what I'm even feeling. The one clear thing is that Dad's story demonstrates things aren't always what they seem.

I thought the little kindnesses Ben had shown me were signs. But after learning he abandoned us for a chance to see his family again, I don't know any more.

Does Ben still care?

'Rachel,' Dad repeats. 'Tell me about Ben.'

And for some reason I do, starting with how he saved me, like how Ma saved Dad with her love. When I finish I turn to Dad. 'And now he works for Heda. How are we supposed to find the bow and arrows or break out of here when he's always there, a reminder of what's lost and—' I start to hyperventilate, all the heartbreak squeezing the air from my lungs. Dad slides down the bed and puts his arm around my shoulder. I stay rigid, not knowing how to respond to his touch.

'Rachel,' he says, rubbing my hair. 'You don't need him to save you this time. All you need is yourself.'

At that I let go. I fall into my dad's arms. And I cry.

Twenty-Eight

I search all around outside Ma's container for the piece of the black arrow but can't see it anywhere. I'm worried Heda found it, or it got caught in the boot treads of one of the guards and is now lost for ever. After my fifth loop I give up and go to see if either of the doors or the elevator will open for me. My family watches from the paddle boat, confined to the small area by their anklets. I realize quickly that everything requires a key card. The elevator won't even let me push a button without one.

I sigh and return to the courtyard, resolved to look again for the shard later. We sit, legs straddling the wooden pew-style seats, knees knocking, heads together, and I fill them in on everything I know.

Mrs Turner clutches Paisley's sweater; the alien necklace hangs around her neck. 'A Hedoness army?' she repeats, not sure she understands our situation correctly. She glances behind her to Dad's container, gazing thoughtfully like she can see past it to the hundreds of containers below the balcony.

I nod. 'This is why we must get the bow and arrows from Heda. I know she carries the black one, the arrow of indifference, in a box. But I don't know where she keeps the bow, or the arrow of infatuation – that's the one responsible for the anklets,' I say.

Kyle raises his trouser leg and spins the gold band. 'One thing I don't understand. Marissa told me only girls are Hedonesses and Hedonesses can't turn other girls.'

'Yes,' Ma says. 'The power doesn't work the same on them, it just renders them unconscious for a little while.'

'But didn't Hedonesses come from this arrow of – whatever the anklet is?'

'Infatuation. They did,' says Ma.

'Then how is it making you do things and not just me and Mr Patel?'

'Call me uncle, or Daniel, please,' Dad says.

I glance at Dad. It seems strange now hearing him called Mr Patel and not his surname Groundwater. Especially since I don't even know where he and my ma stand.

'The arrow works on everyone,' Ma explains.

'I still don't get it,' Kyle says.

I lean forward. 'The arrow of infatuation fused with Heda's DNA when she was an embryo, creating its own kind of magic, something different from the golden arrow. It only seemed to work in girls. That's what Heda wants to take out of me now.'

Dad puts his hand on my knee. 'And we're not going to let that happen.'

Ma smiles.

'So,' Dad continues, 'our plan. We talk to people at meals. I know someone who works in Le-Li's lab. And we try to find where they keep the bow and arrows.'

'Then what?' Kyle asks.

'Then we figure out a way to get them,' Dad says.

'How?' Kyle asks, waving to the wall of containers.

Dad glances around the room, his eyes coming to rest on the key card system next to the main doors. 'If I can get access to a laptop I can hack that.'

Kyle crosses his arms. 'And what good would that do?'

'I'll be able to access the alarms, cause some ruckus with the prisoners. And I should be able to reverse their door-locking systems by deactivating the need for key cards.'

Kyle opens his mouth to ask another question and I cut him off. 'We gain information and we find a laptop.'

'Then what?' Kyle asks. 'They'll attack us, we're outnumbered. Maybe we should ask Eros what he thinks.'

'He's sleeping,' Ma replies. 'And we're not outnumbered. There are hundreds of us.'

Kyle crosses his arms. 'They have weapons and we don't.'

That reminds me of my stash in the vent. 'I know where there are enough sleeping meds to bring down a couple of guards. It's a start, but maybe we can use them to access a laptop.'

'Excellent.' Dad clasps his hands. 'If you can get to a computer you should be able to bring up a facilities map. There may be a weapons locker somewhere.'

'No,' says Ma, and her eyes fix on the sweatshirt in Mrs Turner's grasp. 'It's too risky. We can't have Rachel running around out there alone.'

I don't tell her I've already been, that that's how I learned about Paisley. 'I'm the only one without an anklet, Ma. We don't have another option. Besides, she won't hurt me, not excessively anyway. She needs my ichor.'

'But if she catches you, we'll be screwed,' Kyle says.

'If we work together, I won't get caught.' I glance down at my palm, wondering when it will finally heal, and thinking about what damage will be done if Heda does catch me.

'Rachel's right,' Dad says. 'We'll be smart. We'll take it one day and one task at a time.'

'Assuming there are computers here, we get into one and get a map?' Kyle repeats.

'That's the first step,' says Dad. 'We need a map, supplies and weapons, and to find out where she keeps the bow and arrows. Then and only then do we get them and get out of here.'

I pick a piece of wood from the paddle boat. 'And where are we?' I ask, suddenly desperate for a proper answer. 'What's outside these walls?'

'We don't know,' Ma tells me. 'We think we're somewhere in Greece.'

'Greece?' I've always wanted to see Greece, but not this way.

She nods to Kyle. 'Show her.'

Kyle jumps up, rocking the small wooden paddle boat, and goes to his container. He returns carrying a worn piece of paper and hands it to me. 'I found this in my container.'

I unfold it to see what looks to be a shipping invoice in the same language as all the facility signs. In the header is a picture of an island with a volcano and a ferryboat in the water, and the words *Lemnos, Greece*.

My eyes lock on the volcano, my mind niggling that there's something here I should be connecting but I can't quite get there.

'How's it going?' comes Marissa's voice from behind us. I didn't hear the main doors squeak open. She must have come from the elevator or the stairwell.

I fold the invoice and hand it back to Kyle, then turn to face her. She's still wearing her customised grey uniform and carrying a clipboard and pencil.

'What do you want?' I ask. Her face drops, and I have a sinking feeling something isn't right. 'How're Nani's treatments going?'

She eyes my family over my shoulder. 'Can I talk to you privately?' she asks.

'Just answer me, Riss.'

'That's why I'm here,' she says, her voice wavering. 'It's not looking good. She's too old and the treatments are making her sick.'

'What?' Ma says, stepping out of the paddle boat and going to her. 'Tell me what's happening. Where is she?'

'I don't know,' Marissa says. 'When they leave the lab, they take them to a place I'm not authorised to go.' She glances up, her eyes full of fear. 'I didn't want to keep this from you guys,' Marissa says. 'Heda would kill me if she knew I was here.'

'Then why are you here?' Kyle asks, his tone dripping with contempt – there's a lot unresolved between them.

'I want to help,' she says. 'I've been trying to convince Heda to use someone else but she's got it in her head that the only way to control Rachel is with your family.' She looks at me and holds up the clipboard. 'I thought maybe if you wrote Heda a letter committing to your bleedings or something, but I don't even know. What should I do?'

I imagine my nani in a black body bag being trolleyed to the incinerator like Paisley. 'We need to stop this,' I say, turning to my family. 'Our plan was good but we don't have the luxury to take our time any more. Nani depends on us. If Marissa's offering to help we should probably take it.'

'Plan?' Marissa asks.

'I don't know,' Dad says, eyeing her warily.

'No way in hell!' Kyle says.

'I want to,' Marissa says. 'Tell me what I can do.'

Kyle shakes his head. 'We're not stupid. You don't care about anything but yourself.'

She takes a step closer. 'I deserve that, especially from you. What I did to you was unforgivable.'

'You forced me to change my sexuality. Damn right it's unforgivable!'

Marissa's grip on her clipboard shakes. 'That was wrong. I regret it. I will never stop trying to earn back your forgiveness,' she says.

Kyle glares. 'Prove it with actions. Your words mean nothing to me.'

'Anything,' she says in a whisper.

Dad shakes his head, unsure. Ma gives me her warning look. But Nani's life depends on it. All our lives do.

I turn to Marissa. 'We need a map of this facility, so we can find and rescue Nani.'

'How?' she says.

'Well, can you draw one from memory?' I ask.

'I can draw a little, but I'm not allowed in most of the facility. You've seen basically everywhere I can go.'

Dad stands from his seat on the paddle boat's edge. 'Can you get me a laptop?'

'Ha! I don't even have access to a phone to check my socials. We're cut off here.'

'OK,' Dad says, probably unsure why checking social media is so important. 'Well, is there a room anywhere with access to a computer system?'

Marissa frowns and takes a step back.

'Riss, please, do you know where we can access a computer?' I repeat.

'I don't think I can help. I couldn't print off a map without raising flags.'

'Then copy one.'

'The only place I know that has anything like that is Heda's office. But that's a high-traffic area. If they see me copying the map, they'll ask questions.' She nervously taps the pencil on the clipboard and takes another step back. 'Plus, I don't even know how to access a map once we get to the computer.'

'Any computer will do,' Dad says. 'There are usually facility maps hardwired into every system for emergency reasons. Shouldn't be much more than a few simple hacks to bring it up.'

Marissa shakes her head. 'I don't know. I can't draw, and I'd need someone to keep watch. But there's no one I can trust not to tell Heda.'

I grab her hand. 'Then take me with you and give me your clipboard. I'll draw it.'

'Rachel, no,' Ma says.

Marissa pulls back. 'If we get caught she'll—'

'All talk,' Kyle scoffs from behind us.

Marissa's lip quivers.

I give her hand a squeeze. 'Do you want to help or not? This is what we need. This is what we're asking.'

'I do, but . . .'

Everything in me hopes that she's on our side and I can trust her. The entire plan rests on her decision. But history tells me to listen to Kyle. That Marissa isn't as innocent as she lets on.

I position myself behind her, arms raised, ready to grab her in the event she says no. Because if she won't help us, we can't let her leave this place. She'll just tell Heda everything. I really don't want to have to hurt the last friend I have. But I have to protect my family.

Marissa glances at Kyle. 'OK,' she says, 'I'll do it.'

I drop my fists and hug her, feeling relief that she's still in my corner after everything we've been through. 'Thank you!'

'Don't trust her,' Kyle scoffs. 'She hasn't earned it.'

He doesn't understand that we have no other choice right now. We need the info. We need to know the layout of the building. It's the only way we can figure out how to get the bow and arrows, rescue everyone and escape. Mostly he doesn't understand that I won't let my guard down around her, not for one minute.

Twenty-Nine

Ma grips my arm like she's afraid I'm going to float away. She sees my decision before even I do. And she's right. 'We need to go now.'

'Rachel, please,' Ma says.

'Now?' Marissa whips around. 'This isn't something we can rush.'

'My nani needs us. We'll be careful. We won't get caught,' I say.

Kyle lets out an exasperated sigh. 'Save your breath, Rach. She's not going to help.'

Marissa glares at him, arms crossed. 'I said I'll do it and I'll do it.' She marches her clipboard over to my dad and holds it out. 'Write down your hacks, or whatever. And try to keep it in normal-people speak so I can follow them.'

Dad takes it from her, sits on the edge of the paddle boat and begins jotting notes.

Ma's grip on my hand tightens even more. 'This isn't wise, Rachel,' she says.

I walk her away from the group. She stops suddenly and I realize her anklet won't let her go any further.

'Ma, staying here and letting Heda do whatever she wants to us isn't wise either. Nani needs us.'

'I've already lost you once,' Ma continues. 'And while we might not like Hedone's way of doing things, maybe she has a point. The Hedoness powers do help the world.'

'Ma! Seriously?' I can't believe she's even suggesting this, though to be honest I've been wondering the same thing – if I embrace my powers it would solve a lot of our problems. 'You know she has to drain me of my blood and hurt people to get the Hedoness ability back, right?'

Ma's face drops when she realizes what she suggested. 'I'm sorry, I feel so helpless. I don't know what I can do. When I had my powers I never felt like this.'

It's not like her to be so discouraged, and it's hard to watch.

Kyle claps, loud and slow. 'Idiots,' he says. 'The lot of you.'

Dad looks up from his work long enough to mouth a shocked 'wow'.

'Don't talk that way,' Ma yells back at Kyle. 'We're doing the best we can.'

Marissa shifts in the doorway of Ma's container as she watches Eros sleep. The look on her face lets me know she feels like my ma does without her powers.

'Enough!' I say in a sharp voice. 'Everyone just stop!' They listen, except Kyle, who mumbles one last insult before stomping over to his container and taking a seat in his doorway.

'Like it or not, we are prisoners,' I continue. 'And even if Heda's plan with the Hedonesses was for the good, the way she's going about everything is appalling. We can all agree on that, right?'

There's a collective muttering of acceptance.

'Then please stop this. Let Marissa and me try to get this map. It's the only way I'll know where Heda is keeping the arr— Nani,' I quickly correct. Dad flashes me a nervous look before checking to see if Marissa caught my slip.

She picks her nails and kicks at the floor, and I'm hoping that means we're OK.

'Maybe I should go too,' Kyle shouts from his container door. 'No offence, but I have a better chance of fighting off the guards, and I'm fast.'

I shake my bare ankle and he glances down at the gold band around his. 'Right, this damn thing.'

'I'll be safe, and I'm fast too.'

'She got a trophy in running track in school,' Ma says, her maternal pride temporarily outweighing her desire to keep me from this plan.

It's cute seeing how proud she is of me, especially since it was just a participation trophy. And besides, I am a good runner. It's the only thing I was allowed to have just for myself back in New York, so I spent a lot of my time doing it.

'Then what?' Marissa cuts in.

'What do you mean?'

'I still don't understand what happens once we have the map. Like what good is it to know where your Nani is being kept with no way of getting to where you want to go?'

I don't tell her about how I have what I need to sneak out of the ichor room hidden in the vent. I can't, because no matter how much I want to trust Marissa, she's let me down before. This excursion will be my answer. If she goes through with this and we pull it off, then I will know she means what she says.

'I'll figure that out then. First things first. How are we doing this?'

She sighs. 'Fine. I guess I'm supposed to say something cheesy like follow my lead.'

'Follow my lead will do.' I smile and give a quick goodbye hug to my ma, afraid if I let it go any longer that I'll listen to her and stay. Still, I have to drag myself from her arms. 'I'll be fine, Ma.' She's too busy trying not to cry to respond. When I turn around, Dad's there.

'Here,' he says, handing me the pencil and clipboard.

'Thanks.' I take it from him and hold it to my chest, unsure whether I should initiate a hug or not.

He begins to step away and stops himself, turning back and pulling me into a quick embrace. 'Be careful.'

'I will, Dad.'

He smiles.

Marissa's at the main doors. She cracks one side open and pops her head out, then glances back at me and motions it's not safe.

'You there,' she says to whoever's in the hall. Silence falls over us as we wait to see if the escape is foiled before it starts. 'Go get Le-Li, tell him Rachel's ready for the ichor room.'

I slink over to her, listening as the person replies.

'I'm not supposed to leave this post until a replacement comes.'

'I'm here, she won't be unattended.'

'Still,' the guard says, unease filling her voice.

I bite my lip and Marissa's back stiffens in her cat-ready-to-pounce way. 'Darla, is it?'

'Yeah, why?'

'Oh, I just wanted to tell Heda who kept her from getting an early next dose.' She steps back into the balcony and turns to me. When the guard doesn't respond, my mood drops. She didn't buy Marissa's lie and now we're stuck waiting here until she leaves. Marissa shrugs. 'I tried,' she mouths, pulling the door the rest of the way. It stops, inches from closing, a grey glove wedged in the gap.

My heart skips a beat.

Marissa grins, then puts on a fairly convincing stern face before popping her head back out. 'Yes?' she says, sounding annoyed.

'I'll get him,' Darla tells her.

'Good. Thank you.' She watches until the hall is clear, before turning back. 'We have to go quick. It will take her a while to find Le-Li since he left the facility to get more medical supplies. It should buy us enough time to get the map before he returns.' When I don't reply she adds, 'You sure you want to do this?'

Ma, Dad, and Kyle are standing as far away from the containers as their anklets will allow, watching me. It's the quietest they've been all day.

'I'm sure.'

'Be careful,' Dad says.

'Kick ass,' Kyle says.

'I love you,' Ma says.

I nod, my mouth seemingly unable to form words.

Marissa glances at Kyle and lifts her chin. 'I'm doing this for you. It's my first sorry in action.'

He grunts and she turns to the door, propping it open and waving me before her into the hall. I smile one last goodbye to my family, ignoring the rush of fear that tells me what I'm about to do is dangerous and, worse, that I'm risking never seeing them again. And I step into the hall.

Thirty

The large vents blow their sulphur-tinged cold air at my legs. The blue track bottoms do very little to keep the cold out.

Marissa leads me towards the ichor room. When we come upon my vent, I hang back and pop the corner of the cover out. Paisley's face fills my mind and I fight back the urge to cry as I slide my hand inside, reaching around until I brush the glass vials and syringes. They're hard to grab because of the awkward angle and the condensation that's built up thanks to the air conditioning. I manage to grab the syringes, the refill vials rolling out of reach. I could pop the grate off and get them, but that's sure to draw Marissa's attention. The syringes will have to do. It's two chances, if needed. I shove them in my bra, click the grate back in place and jog to catch up to her.

'Stop breathing so loud,' she turns to say. I smile and nod her forward.

We pass the ichor room door with no troubles and walk into the section of the hall I haven't explored yet. My hand darts in and out so fast Marissa doesn't notice any of the small pencil marks I'm making on the walls at every new turn. I still don't know if I trust her. Lies come too quickly, just like the one she told the guard to make her go and get Le-Li, and like the ones she's been telling Heda to make her believe she's on Heda's side. *Or the ones she's telling me.*

'We're close,' Marissa says as we take another turn.

Footsteps come up the hall. Marissa grabs my hand and runs us to the next alcove, shoving me into a short entrance and using her body to shield mine. She holds a finger to her lips. We're so close it nearly brushes my mouth. I roll my eyes.

'Behind you,' she mouths. 'The door.'

'Yeah, I kinda feel it pressing into my back.'

She cocks her head and glares. 'It's not where we were headed but I'm pretty sure there's a control panel in there. Do you think you could bring up your map?'

I shrug. 'My dad said they should be in every system.'

Marissa nods, pulls a key card out of her front pocket and holds it to the pad. The red light flashes green and the door clicks open. I'm about to step in when the air exits Marissa's lungs with force.

Someone clears their throat.

'What do we have here?' a deep voice says.

I turn slowly, taking in a beastly woman so big her shoulders nearly touch both sides of the alcove. She has Marissa in her grip like she's a doll.

Marissa tries to yank free then gives up and lifts her chin. 'I was escorting her to Heda.'

I'm impressed at how fast she thinks under pressure but the guard doesn't buy it. 'This isn't the way to Heda.' She looks at me, her grip tightening on Marissa's arms. 'Don't run, or your friend gets hurt.'

'Stop this right now,' Marissa says, wriggling in the guard's grasp.

While she's focused on Marissa I slip my hand down my shirt, pulling out the syringes.

'Do you know who I am?' Marissa continues. 'I work with Le-Li.'

It takes me two tries to get the first needle uncapped behind my back. Some of the drug spills on to my fingers.

The guard ignores Marissa and reaches for her radio. Before her hand touches the receiver, I pull out the syringe and stab her in the arm.

'What the—?' She stumbles back. Marissa uses the opportunity to untwist from her grip and kick her in the shin. I uncap the next syringe and lunge, needle out. She swings for me but Marissa blocks her arm and I manage to get the needle between her ribs. Her eyes roll back and her grip on the radio loosens. She topples to the ground, swinging her arms in slow motion.

'Grab a leg,' I say, sliding the clipboard and pencil under my arm and picking up her foot. Marissa does so grudgingly, letting me know with every grunt that she isn't impressed as we drag the guard's large form into the control-panel room and out of sight.

'What happens when it wears off and she radios this in?' she asks.

'We'll take it with us,' I say.

I bend to grab it, but Marissa slams her heel into the radio then kicks it into the corner.

'There. It's not a problem.'

'It's not a help either,' I say, wishing we could've kept it to listen to the guards talking.

'What about her?' She points to the large woman.

'She'll be confused when she first comes to, probably won't remember a thing.' At least Le-Li didn't seem to.

'Hopefully she won't check whose key card opened the door.'

'Like I said, confused.'

Marissa finishes dragging the body into the room and the door clicks shut after her. She drops the foot and turns to me, crossing her arms. 'So, you carry that stuff around with you?'

'Something like that.'

I glance around the room, spotting a computer screen newly mounted to a wall – its clean black cables not yet covered in a blanket of filth like everything else in this room. I rush to it, resting my dad's instructions on top of a thick line of cables. Marissa breathes down my neck, making it hard to concentrate. I glance over my shoulder at her.

'Shouldn't you stand watch outside the door?'

'So another thug can bruise my arm? No thank you. I'm staying right here.' She goes to the door and puts her ear to it like that's enough of a compromise, and I don't have the time to argue.

I read over my dad's handwriting. It's shockingly similar to mine, just a little more slanted and messy. I've never seen it look like this – before it was always neatly printed and in all caps. It makes me wonder how much of him was twisted up into the Hedoness power. How much of him will I still discover?

I plug in his first command, relieved when no alarms go off, and a screen opens with English prompts. His instructions are easy and soon there's a map of the facilities before me. I try to make out where the ventilation system and the corridors overlap, thinking I can use the vents when needed. I hold the paper up and trace on it the way from the ichor room to the room marked as Heda's office. If I'm reading the map right, it's not too far from where we are now. Just down the hall and through a door.

'Have you been in Heda's office?' I ask, wondering if that's where she keeps the bow and arrows.

'Yeah, why?'

'What's it like?'

'I dunno.' Marissa turns from the door and glares at me like I'm wasting her time. 'Like every other office, with a desk and a filing cabinet.'

Probably not there, then.

I complete outlining the route on my paper and am about to fold it and stick it in my shirt when I notice the last note from my father. It reads: *Internal Communications, Facial Recognition Software, select and hold down the following keys until the search screen pops up: Command, Shift, F3.* I should be going, I got what I came for, but my dad wrote that message for a reason. So I push the buttons. Instantly a screen pops up: *Scan facility*, with a search box that instructs me to type a name. I type in *Hedone*. A staff directory, with her picture and a button asking me to confirm my selection.

'What's taking so long?' Marissa asks, keeping her ear glued to the door.

'Almost done,' I say, pressing *Accept target* and watching as the cameras search through all the faces in the facility until they find Heda's and zoom in.

Orange light moves over her face like she's standing before a glowing ocean. Everything else is too dark to make out. I push the sound icon in the corner of the screen and her voice fills our small room.

'Shut that off!' Marissa shrieks, diving across to my side. 'Are you dense? They'll hear us in here.' Then she looks at the screen and her eyes get even wider. 'How did you get this?'

I hold up a finger. 'Shh.'

'We've had a minor setback,' Heda tells someone.

'Our timeline does not allow for setbacks. We'll need our armies.' The voice is gravelly and low.

'Lord Hades, if you would listen—'

Hades? She can't possibly be referring to *the* Hades. 'It can't be,' I say, turning to Marissa. She flicks her eyes to the ground and that only confirms my worst fear. Somehow Heda is working with the god of the Underworld.

'I expect better upon my return,' Hades says.

'And when is that, my Lord?'

'Tonight, eight hours.'

Chills cover my entire body. If the god of the Underworld is a part of Heda's plan, we're in worse trouble than we thought.

A leg shoots out – startling us – and Marissa and I screech, jumping out of the way as the guard begins to stir.

I wish I had more of Paisley's sleeping serum to give her. I don't want to leave yet, not until I've heard everything.

Heda's still speaking. 'That gives us plenty of time with the new subject –' Marissa reaches for the button to disconnect the screen – 'she's taking to the treatments better than the others have.'

'Just a second,' I say, batting her hand away. 'Heda's saying something.'

Marissa shoves into me, knocking me aside, and closes the window. 'We don't have a second. We need to leave.'

'She said Nani was doing good.'

'She's lying, Rach. She doesn't want Hades to know she's failing him.'

'Marissa?'

She ignores me and points to the guard. 'We have to go. Now!'

'Fine.' I grab the paper and twist my hair up using the pencil. I leave the clipboard. It'll only slow me down if we need to run. There's a digital clock resting on one of the exposed pipes near the door. I slip it into my top next to the map and step over the guard, pulling the syringes from her body in case I need them later. I wait as Marissa slides her key card out, rescans it and pulls the door. It opens only a crack, blocked by the giant woman's body. I have to suck my stomach in to squeeze through.

We rush down the corridors, stopping at every turn to make sure it's clear. When we pass my vent I toss the empty syringes back in and continue, following my pencil marks more than Marissa. My mind replays the conversation between Heda and the man she called Hades. He wants an army of Hedonesses, and he wants them soon.

An image fills my mind – hundreds of black body bags lined up ready to be incinerated, one after another, until I see their faces: my friends, my teachers, my family. I can't let this happen to them.

Hades said he'll return in eight hours and I'm going to be waiting in that room. I don't care what it takes to get there. I need to know the rest of their plan.

Marissa stops and I ram right into her. We topple to the ground, a knot of limbs, the pencil flying from my hair and skidding down the hall.

She huffs, rising to her feet and dusting off her clothes. 'What the hell?' she whispers.

'Sorry, I was distracted.'

'Get out of your head, Rach. We're here.' She waves me to the container-room door.

As I stand up, I debate going for the pencil but something else a few feet away reflects the overhead light and catches my eye. It takes me a moment to realize it's Marissa's key card. I quickly step on it, hoping she doesn't realize it's fallen out of her pocket. Marissa's been weird ever since seeing Heda on the screen and I don't fully trust that she'll help me get back into the control room tonight.

This little accident is the lucky break I need. When she can't find the card, I'll suggest she use a code, like Ben did. HUM-something. She has to have that as a backup too.

I bend down, pretending to tie my shoes, fingers slipping round the plastic square. Marissa gasps. She stares down the hall, rocking back and forth on her feet like she doesn't know what to do. I follow her gaze to see Ben and a handful of guards standing in a circle, a short way away.

Ben's eyes lock on mine. He squares his shoulders. His hand rushes to the Taser on his hip.

Thirty-One

Our fate is in his hands. He can sound the alarm, let the other guards know I'm outside of the container room, then who knows what Heda will do to me? I shake my head, mouthing the word *please*, pleading with him to let this go.

Marissa takes off down the hall. Her heavy footsteps seal my fate – the other guards start to turn.

I'm frozen, key card in hand, the door on one side and Ben and the guards on the other. My eyes are on Ben's hand as it wraps around his Taser and my heart sinks all over again.

So this is his answer then. He really is on Heda's side.

Defeat pours through me, erasing any hope that was there. The urge to fall to the ground and hug my knees is strong. But that solves nothing. The guards will catch me, and I won't be able to save my friends and family.

Dad's words flicker in my head. 'You don't need him to save you this time. All you need is yourself.' And even though I don't feel it, I know he's right.

I square my body, ready to use what little fighting experience I have. I'm going to run. If I can evade the guards long enough to make it back to the control-panel room, I can buy enough time to learn more about Heda and find another way out. I'm about to turn and start after Marissa when something loud shatters on the ground near the guards. They crouch, picking up the pieces. Ben stays upright, eyes on me, his Taser not in his hand or on his belt. That's when I realize what he's done. He dropped it hard enough to break, and loud enough to cause a distraction.

He bought my escape.

I nod my thanks and fight back the desire to linger there with our eyes locked. I swipe the key card and shoulder into the room, careful to close the doors quietly behind me. I stay there, leaning against them, catching my breath and settling my hammering heart.

'Rachel?' It's my dad. He stands at the furthest distance he can from the containers. Ma and Kyle are quick to flank him. 'You OK?' he asks.

'Yeah,' I say, and my mind fills with Ben.

Thirty-Two

I take a seat beside my dad in the paddle boat. He looks up from the map. 'So the facial recognition software, how did you know about that?' I ask.

'It worked, then!' He smiles and straightens his slouch. 'I installed it as a security measure in the system at their Athens headquarters years ago. I was hoping it was transferred here too.'

I twist the corner of my sweatshirt and think again about how much of my dad I don't know, that I missed out on. If he installed this system before becoming a victim of the Hedoness curse, what would he be capable of now?

'Did you see anything?' he asks.

I look up. 'Yeah, it showed me Heda. She was talking to Hades.'

'Hades?' He places the map in his lap and stares at me, like he's trying to look into my mind and see what it was I saw. But only one of us here can read minds.

Before I answer him, Kyle hops in the boat, taking his favourite seat at the helm, and Ma joins us, stepping delicately in. Nani still hasn't been returned. After what Heda told Hades, I worry if she ever will be.

'Eros isn't coming out,' Ma tells us. 'He thinks the balm is wearing off and wants to take advantage of the pain-free time to catch up on sleep. We'll have to finish the conversation without his help.'

'Should we check on Mrs Turner?' I ask. 'She's been in her container a long while.'

'She'll be fine. She needs some time,' Ma says, glancing warily over to the container. I know she's worried about her friend but she's giving her the space to grieve.

'Just the four of us then,' I say, nodding to the map. Dad holds it out and we each take one corner. It's a strange sight to see all our hands so close, and our hope literally in our grasp.

Dad leans forward, nose inches from the map, as he inspects it. 'I've been trying to figure out your sketch. Is this the ventilation system?'

'Yeah.'

His eyes light up. 'Good job, thinking to incorporate that.' He returns to examining the map. 'I should've had you draw the electrical system too. Then I could see where they're routing all their power. They'll likely have a high-input security system on the arrows. Did Marissa tell you anything?'

I make a mental note to look at the electrical system later tonight. 'Marissa didn't know where they took Nani and she said Heda's office was a normal office.'

231

'That doesn't mean anything coming from her. The bow and arrows could be there,' Kyle says.

'Yeah, maybe,' I reply.

Kyle sits back hard, making the boat rock. 'So, we didn't get anything useful?'

'We at least know where not to look, and I do know a bit more of where we are.'

'What did Heda say to Hades?' Dad asks.

'Hades?' Ma's attention fixates on me, her eyes wide. 'What about Hades?'

'I was able to pull up video surveillance and found Heda. She was with someone she called Hades, and she told him her subject was taking to the treatments. I assume that's Nani.'

'So Nani is OK?' Ma asks, letting go of her corner of the map to clasp her hands under her chin like she's about to say a prayer.

'I don't know,' I say, watching the hopefulness slip off Ma's face. 'Marissa said Heda was lying.'

Kyle narrows his eyes. 'She'd recognise a liar.'

Ma's knee starts to bounce and the paddle boat rocks again.

Dad reaches out, resting his hand on Ma's arm. 'We'll get her back, Priya. Don't worry.'

Ma's shaking stops. It's the most natural interaction I've seen between them and for a moment I almost forget how my parents came to be together. Ma nods and tucks her hands under her legs before returning her attention to me. 'Tell me what Hades said.'

I don't tell Ma that Hades is coming again tonight because she'll know that means I'm going to try to get back to the control panel so I can watch them. It's also why I don't tell them that I have Marissa's key card. Even though this card is the tool we need to see our plan through – come and go undetected, collect the weapons and supplies needed to get the bow and arrows, and get out of here. But there's no point adding to their stress and worry right now, after all the uncertainty about Nani. I'll sneak out when they're sleeping.

I look at her. 'He said they need the army—'

There's a bang. We stand alert, the sudden movement rocking the paddle boat. I hold out my arms to balance. The main doors slam open and a handful of guards enter, weapons raised. Ben and Marissa follow after them.

Dad quickly tucks the map up his sleeve.

The guards march over and circle the paddle boat. 'You're not in your containers,' one of them says.

'We're stretching our legs,' I lie.

'You're standing in a boat.' She frowns and turns to Ben.

'They're permitted to be in their area,' he says.

I bite my lip to contain the impulse to thank him for saving me earlier, and the need to ask what that means

233

for us. Despite everything, a part of me still hopes for an *us*. Now that I know Ben's on our side, I don't feel bad about admitting that any more. But no matter what happens, having an inside guy makes this all a lot easier. I have to find a way to tell him about my plan. Maybe he even knows where the bow and arrows are kept. And maybe he can help us get them.

'Can I have a moment alone with Ben?' I ask, hoping that for some unknown reason they'll let me.

'I'll look things over,' Ben says with a nod, dismissing the guards. A smile escapes my lips. I motion my family to leave too and watch as they go sit on the stoops of their containers. When I turn back, Marissa's still here.

'Alone,' I say.

She ignores me and stays next to Ben. My frown returns.

The guards wait by the door, pausing in the entrance.

'I'll finish up in here then meet you in the hall,' Ben says.

'Rach—' Marissa starts.

'Do you have an update on my nani?' I ask before she says anything further.

'No.'

'Then I have nothing to say to you.' I lift my chin and turn to Ben. 'Thanks for earlier.' The words leave my lips before the doors even close after the guards.

Marissa wrinkles her nose and glances between us. 'Thanks? What did I miss?'

'After you ditched me —' the cattiness in my tone catches me by surprise but I'm so mad at her for running off that I don't try to hide it — 'Ben caused a distraction so I wouldn't get caught.'

Kyle was right. Even if she is on our side she can't be trusted to care about anyone but herself. I look at Ben and my breath exits my lungs like a punch. He stands rigid, arms crossed, glaring at me.

'Distraction?' he asks, like he has no clue what I'm talking about.

I frown. 'W-when you dropped your Taser so I could get back in the container room.' My eyes scan down his body to the new Taser resting in the holster on his hip.

'Dropped my Taser? Some loser bumped me. Don't thank me for that,' he says. 'If I'd seen you, I'd have alerted the other guards.'

If he had seen me? But he was looking right at me? I'm sure of it, but then again, what if I just thought . . .

'She's confused,' Marissa cuts in. 'They drained too much ichor yesterday and she hasn't eaten a proper meal yet with the whole cafeteria incident. It makes her say things that don't make sense. What she meant is that she was out of her ma's container, in the common area, here.' She turns to me and puts her hand on my shoulder, leaning down so that we're at eye level. 'That's what you meant, wasn't it?'

She doesn't wait for me to answer. 'Remember when I told you it's OK for you to be in the common area? You don't have to worry about the guards catching you here.' She pats my head like one would a little child, and I'm too confused to stop her. Is she protecting me, from Ben? The Ben that moments ago I was certain had protected me from the guards? I don't even know what's happening any more. Can I trust either of them?

'Why are you here?' I ask her.

'I've lost my key card,' she says, slowly, emphasising the severity of the situation. 'Ben and his crew were tasked to help me find it.' Her eyes widen, and I know she's trying to warn me that we could both get in a lot of trouble if it's found by the wrong person. I don't tell her the wrong person already has it.

'Marissa, have you been in here recently?' Ben asks her.

'No,' she says. Another quick lie.

'We should keep looking then. We have to find it before Heda makes us reprogram the system.'

'Reprogram?' I blurt.

Marissa steps between us. 'I need to talk to Rachel for a moment. I'll meet you in the hall.'

He looks at us. Questions fill his eyes. 'Don't be long,' he says, leaving for the door. I raise my arm to stop him but stop myself instead. I have a bigger problem on my hands.

As soon as the door closes behind him, Marissa starts. 'I'm sorry I had to run like that. I wouldn't be able to help you if I was caught. It was the only thing I could do.'

I don't know what to say, what to believe. Was she seriously looking out for my best interests back there?

'Yeah, I, well—'

'I know you're planning on escaping,' she says. 'All your questions and the need for the map, it isn't just about getting back your nani.'

I try to think of something clever to say to throw her off.

'It's OK, Rach. I want to help.'

Ben knocks on the main door, before propping it open and sticking his head in and calling over, 'How much longer? We've got orders to start the reprogramming. Heda wants it completed in the next twenty-four hours.'

I gulp. 'Twenty-four hours?'

'I gotta go, Rach. I'll check in as soon as I can.' She doesn't wait for me to answer, and heads for the door.

When they're gone, I turn back to my family, watching from their stoops as our well-thought-out plan crumbles under a new deadline. Reprogramming the system means the key card we have won't work any more and that means doing a week's worth of work in hours.

My family wanders back to our gathering place at the paddle boat. It takes everything in me not to scream for them to hurry. My hands perspire, my throat tightens.

'I told you we couldn't trust her,' Kyle says, breaking the silence before I can. 'She probably set you up with the guards and is pretending to have lost her card. Now they'll have everything on lockdown until they find it. That means no more exploring for you.'

'I don't know if we can trust her or not either.' I don't know if we can trust Ben for that matter, but I cannot let myself dwell on that now. Not when I have only twenty-four hours to get what we need and figure out what Heda and Hades have planned. I look back at Kyle. 'But she didn't set me up.'

Ma grips my arms, registering something's wrong, and Kyle crosses his. 'How do you know?' he says.

I pull the key card out of my top, and he grins.

Thirty-Three

Ma paces beside the boat. 'No way. We can't let you do this on your own.'

Dad watches her, his head rocking back and forth. 'I'm with your ma on this, Rachel.'

Kyle leans back into the paddle boat, tossing a balled sock in the air and catching it. He's about to say something but I cut him off.

'I can get out. I don't have the anklet, and for now the key card will open the doors.'

'I'm coming with you,' says Ma.

'How do you plan to leave with the anklet?' I ask.

'I'll saw my foot off if I have to. You need me.'

'Remember when I would complain about going to St Valentine's and you'd tell me I was being melodramatic?' Ma doesn't smile at my attempt to lighten the mood. Instead she looks down at her hands and I know she's wishing she could touch the next guard that walks in here and force them to take off her anklet. But she can't. Her powers are gone, and she hates that.

'Ma, I'll be OK.'

'You can't know that. It's not just Hedone any more, Hades is somehow involved.'

Kyle lobs the sock ball too high and it arcs out of his reach, landing in Dad's lap. Dad sighs and hands it back before turning to me. 'But what if you come across a guard?'

No matter how much my family protests, I'm going to find out Heda and Hades' plan. I have to.

'Rachel, answer your father,' Ma says. 'What will you do if you cross the guards?'

I almost want to laugh. After at all the times I wished they'd scold me like real parents, now that it's finally happening it's the worst timing. 'I'll hide in the vent until they pass,' I tell them, though it's not really the best of plans.

'The vent!' Ma throws up her hands.

'That's not practical,' Dad says.

'Smart,' Kyle adds.

'I've done it before,' I tell them. Paisley fills my mind and my stomach flips.

Ma's gaze shoots to me. 'What?'

I take a deep breath. 'I have to make it back to the control panel. I'll figure out where the power is routing, search the directory for anything that can help, weapons locker room, whatever. Then I'll be back for you all.'

Kyle shakes his leg. 'And what about these? Even if you get all that, we still can't leave the room.'

Crap, he's right. There's only one person I can think of who might know how to get them off. And Kyle isn't going to like it.

'We use Marissa. Have her ask around about removing the anklets.'

'No way,' says Kyle.

Dad leans forward, folding and unfolding the map. 'And if it works, we leave without saving everyone else?'

Kyle waves his finger in a circle. 'You all heard her say she wants to bring Marissa in, right? I'm not hallucinating that?'

'We'll get help and come back for the others,' I say, ignoring Kyle. 'Without the bow and arrows, Heda can't do much damage.'

Kyle slaps his lap and crosses his arms.

'I know it's not ideal,' I say, glaring at him. 'But the key card was reported missing so that gives me only tonight to take advantage of having it. I have to get the information and tools we need. Like it or not, this is our best shot.'

'I dunno, Rach.' Kyle tosses his sock in the air and catches it with one hand. 'It's too easy,' he says.

'What?' I ask.

'Explain,' Ma says.

'Well,' he starts, 'they didn't even search us. If they knew the card was missing, and after what you said to Ben about being out of the container room, why wouldn't they search us? Ben's not stupid.'

Dad crosses his arms. 'He's right. This could be a set-up.'

'A set-up? They have to want something in order to set us up. What could they possibly want that they don't already have?'

Everyone goes quiet while we think it all over. Dad stares at the ground, then suddenly his head jerks up, his eyes going from my ankle to his. 'You don't have an anklet, that's the only thing different about us. Why? Why didn't they put one on you? Even Eros has a collar.'

'Well,' I think out loud, 'the anklet controls you with the arrow of infatuation.'

'But you already overpowered that once,' Dad says.

'Yeah, I guess I kinda did. Plus, it's technically still in me.'

'And the collar?' he asks.

'The collar stunts magic,' I say, repeating what Heda once told me. 'She needs to access the immortality growing in my blood so she's less likely to put me in that.'

'So the collar would stop your transition to becoming immortal?' Ma clarifies.

'Yeah, I think so.' I remember what Eros told me about his blood being darker without the collar. 'At least it slows it.'

Kyle catches his sock ball and holds it. 'Is that why Eros has a collar but she still uses his blood?'

'That's a good point,' Dad says. 'It stops him from being able to use his powers, but it does not stop his blood from providing healing and immortality, is this right?' He glances at me. 'If so, what does this mean for you, Rachel?'

'I'm not really sure. Eros mentioned the first part of the transition is immortality, so I'm not sure if the collar affects that.'

'That's it then,' Ma says.

We turn to look at her, wondering what her conclusion is and why it's making her look so depressed.

'Your transformation,' she says. 'Heda wants you to use your powers. She wants you to complete the transformation.'

'But why?' Kyle asks.

Then it all comes rushing back: the conversation I overheard between Heda and Le-Li. 'Le-Li,' I say, a breathy whisper. But all eyes and ears are tuned in. I lift my chin. 'Le-Li can't isolate the Hedoness gene while I'm in transition.'

Thirty-Four

A voice drifts over from behind us. 'So then don't transition, and she won't be able to take the Hedoness gene out of you,' Eros says, standing in the door to Ma's container, trailing his fingers over the skin around the collar.

'Don't transition?' Ma asks. 'Is that an option?'

'How much did you hear?' I say.

'Enough to get my ass out of bed and help you, love.'

'About time,' says Kyle.

Eros shifts in the doorway like he's unable to get comfortable and nods to my dad. 'Did you ask him?'

My body goes stiff and my cheeks heat. I shake my head no.

'Ask me what?' Dad asks.

'Nothing,' I blurt.

Ma cocks her head, reading my soul how she always does. 'It's not nothing.'

'It has to be nothing because I'm not willing to have this conversation.'

'Rachel?' Dad says.

I turn my back.

'Eros, tell me,' Dad presses.

'I'm sorry, love.'

My body stiffens and my lungs contract. I can't bear to turn around and watch Eros tell my dad.

'I'm a father,' he continues. 'If there was any way to save my daughter's life, I'd want to know.'

'Save her life?' Ma gasps.

'She can reverse the immortality,' Eros says in one sweeping blow.

I could, but not any more.

'How?' Dad asks, sceptical.

Eros hesitates. I know he's waiting for me to join the conversation but I refuse to turn around. He sighs. 'She'll have to consume the life force of a mortal relative.'

'Mortal relative?' Kyle asks. 'Like me?'

'No,' Dad says. 'Like me.'

I glare over my shoulder to see Eros offer me a sad smile, one that says he wishes it wasn't this way. Dad stands alone in the boat watching me. What Eros doesn't know is why I didn't want to have this conversation with my dad.

Ma continues to pace, firing glances at Eros, Dad and me. I turn back to staring at the floor. 'What exactly does "consume a life force" mean?' she asks.

'She'll need to drink a cup or so of his blood,' says Eros.

I've used my abilities already, I feel it. It's too late for this fix.

The group of us go quiet, me not sure how to stop this conversation before I have to confess I've been hearing voices, and the rest of them processing what this means.

'It's weird and I don't understand it,' Dad says after some time. 'The whole blood-drinking thing seems hocus-pocus, but if it will help Rachel, of course I'll do it.'

I can hear Eros shift in the doorway. 'It shouldn't take much, right, love?'

I whip around to find his blue eyes burrowing into mine. I know what he's asking. He's asking if I've used any of my abilities.

My heart sinks. 'It might take more than we think,' I say under my breath. But he hears me.

'How much more?'

I drop my eyes to the floor.

'How many times?' he asks. 'Two?'

I kick at a piece of dirt.

'Three?'

I count them: the multiple times hearing voices, the guards that mysteriously ended up on the floor, the white-light hand-stabbing incident. Definitely more than three.

My silence is all the answer he needs.

'That fast? I didn't know. I'm sorry.'

'What does this mean?' Dad asks.

'It means,' says Eros, filling the door with his large frame, his voice low and commanding – it's the first time he's appeared godly in a while – 'that Rachel is too far along in her transition. She'd have to eat your heart to reverse the immortality now.'

Ma gasps, her hand flying to her chest.

Dad retakes his seat, alone in the boat. He folds and unfolds the map before stuffing it under his leg and leaning on his knees. 'OK,' he says. 'How do we do this?'

'No! It's not OK,' I say. 'It's not even funny to pretend. I get a say in this, and unless you plan on holding me down and forcing your heart down my throat, I am not doing it.'

Dad's eyes lock on me. 'We should at least try the blood drinking. It will be saving so many people. If she can't take the power from your blood, then she can't make Hedonesses. If it takes more than my blood then I'll do it.'

I know how much he hates what Hedonesses can do, and it's sickening that I can't stop it.

'I won't—' I look at Dad and I can see in his eyes he knows what I mean.

He rubs his face then stands and comes to me, leaving the map behind, alone in the empty boat, a sad

247

symbol of our attempt at escape. He puts his hands on my shoulders. 'I wasn't there for your childhood, not really. And I hate that, Rachel. I can see an absence when I look into your eyes. You carry a lot of pain, and I was a part of that. If there's a way I can make up for it and give you back a life where you know beyond a shadow of doubt that you have a ma and dad who love you, then I will do it. No hesitation, no matter the cost.'

A sob escapes Ma's throat, but for a second I thought it was coming from me. Ma presses her stomach like it will make the pain go away. And I wonder if I should press mine too.

'And what if she embraces her immortality?' Kyle asks.

I snap my head to him and Dad drops his arms.

'She can't,' Dad says, looking right at me. 'If she completes it, she'll be everything she hates.' He uses the same words I have so many times in conversations with Ma, and I'm shocked he actually listened. Something about that makes the words sit even heavier in my chest. *Everything I hate.*

Whether it's weakness or love, I know in this moment that I would exchange outliving my family a thousand times over for one life getting to know my real dad. All I can do now is hold off my transition for as long as possible so that Heda can't get her cure.

'I won't,' I say. 'I just got you, and I won't lose you.'

'You could never lose me.' Dad smiles.

Kyle hops to his feet and tosses his sock into his container, getting it right through the propped-open door first try. 'I guess we're holding her down for the blood-sampling thing, then.'

Eros takes a hobbled step forward and stops, clinging to the metal doorframe for support. 'While that is an interesting proposition, it won't work. She needs an item of spare magic to help the blood into her.'

'Spare magic?' I ask. The last time he told me about spare magic we were in Heinz and Frieda's statue garden and he gave me a vial of ambrosia to drink.

'Something like the goblet of Kronos, Poseidon's Trident . . . my arrows.'

I glance back up at the mention of arrows. A caution alarm blaring inside me. It seems pretty convenient that his arrows are what's needed to help reverse my looming immortality. But no matter how I look at it, we're back to my plan – I sneak out and gather info, try to find the keys and where Heda keeps the arrows.

A small voice deep inside whispers:

Maybe there's still hope.

Maybe you didn't use too much of your abilities.

Maybe you can still drink the blood.

Eros waves to his neck. 'I know where they keep the keys to undo this.'

I ball my fists. 'You're only telling me this now?'

Eros shrugs. 'It never came up, and I wasn't really in the talking mood.' He coughs, further driving in his point.

'Does it work on the anklet?' Kyle asks.

'It does.' His words are raspier, like he can't catch his breath.

I snatch the map from the boat and march it to him. 'Show me.'

He points to a spot under Heda's office. 'Two floors down, the basement, there's a vault. I'd guess she keeps the bow and arrows there too when they're not with her.'

'How do you know this?' Dad says.

'When are they not with her?' I ask.

Eros looks at Dad and then at me. 'During the prisoners' meal times, when she's getting her infusions.'

'Your ichor?' I ask.

He nods. 'And yours too.'

'Why are you telling us?'

Eros looks to Ma and smiles. 'Because I know you are good people. And I feel responsible for what's happening. And believe it or not, family means a lot to me, too.' He winces and leans over, sucking mouthfuls of air.

'You're hurting yourself,' Ma says. 'Go and lie down.'

Eros grips the door for support and struggles to stand. 'It's guarded –' he coughs – 'you'll need help.'

The key card burns in reminder against my skin. I reach into my top and pull it out, squeezing it in my fist like a lifeline. I shoulder past Eros and into Ma's container, looking for my clock. I find it, and it's just as I thought. I have two hours before Hades returns. Two hours is more than enough time to make it to the control-panel room but I have so much more to do than make it to the room.

I storm past Eros in Ma's doorway, and past my family, and head for the exit.

'Where are you going?' Ma asks. 'It's the middle of the night.'

'You know where I'm going.'

'Rachel,' Dad calls. 'Stop.'

'We've wasted enough time,' I shout back.

'Let her go,' Kyle says. 'As much as it sucks, we need her to.'

I turn back and smile, taking a moment to really look at each one, before scanning the card and opening the door. The long hallway looms like a throat ready to swallow me in its shadows. I take a breath, ignoring the urge to turn and run back to my loved ones, and step out into the dark.

Thirty-Five

It doesn't take long for the computer to locate Heda, and I'm surprised when that disappoints me. A small part of me wished for a few more stolen moments alone in this control room. It's been so long since I've had a chance to catch my breath and think without Marissa or my family hovering.

The camera locks on Heda's face. She looks tired, the lines on her eyes heavier than usual. She walks forward, the harsh orange glow illuminating her face, then she stops and a flash of green light fills the room and something reflects in her eyes. Not something, someone.

If only I could see past her face. My gaze lands on a settings button in the top corner of the screen. I push it and a small window pops open. The words *Camera zoom* catch my eye. I smile and select it, moving the camera as far out as I can. From the new angle I make out the back of a tall man dressed in a green Halloween-ish costume. His large form fills an elaborate, freestanding doorway with big scrolling patterns cut into the wooden frame. He wears a fitted suit and a gold helmet with bull horns that elongates his height, and he grips a gold sceptre with matching horns.

My heart races when I realize it's not a sceptre, it's a bident.

So this is Hades.

I should feel more fear than I do. His outfit is what you'd expect of the god of the Underworld, so much so that it seems cartoonish, right down to the crow perched on his shoulder. At first I think the crow is part of a costume, a prop like the helmet and bident, but then it ruffles its feathers and nuzzles deeper into Hades' neck.

Something about that drives me to turn the volume on my screen down a few notches. I lean in low, ear almost to the speaker.

'My lord,' Heda says with a bow.

'I have no time for pleasantries. Where do we stand?'

'The arrow is breaking the door's seal,' she says without hesitation. 'It shouldn't be much longer.'

He scoffs. 'Use something more than the speck of indifference you've offered and time will be a non-issue.'

'My lord,' she says out of politeness, though it's obvious from her forced smile that the words sting coming out, 'you know I need the majority of the arrow—'

'Yes, yes, to control your hordes, how pitiful.' He cocks his head, the horns nearly scraping the

253

doorframe. 'Perhaps the delay is an attempt to buy time. I still have not seen proof that you can isolate the Hedoness gene.'

'To control my hordes, yes. But if you'll recall, we are opening the remaining gateways, not just yours. And I've already told you that the first girl lacked fortitude.' Heda lifts her chin, refusing to cower to him.

The first girl. Does she mean Paisley? My vision fills with blood – the blood-red uniform of the guard who killed her. I ball my fists, trying to keep from punching the screen.

'As mentioned earlier today, the new subject is responding to the doses better,' she continues. 'I'm certain we'll get the answers needed. We'll be strong enough in numbers by the time you're through.'

'She is not ready now?'

'Soon,' Heda replies, cementing her stance.

The crow cackles something in his ear and Hades raises a hand, thick silver rings on each finger, to slowly stroke the bird. He nods, as if understanding what the crow is saying, then turns his attention back to Heda. 'Soon is not enough.'

'We can't accelerate any faster without—'

'*Cant's* are for fools. There is possibility in everything. Get it done.' He waves his bident around the doorway.

'If we go any faster, there will be many casualties,' Heda tells him.

'When are there not?'

'Hm,' she says, as if in complaint.

'If you do not deliver—'

'We will,' Heda says. 'And I trust you will maintain your side of the bargain.'

'Yes,' he hisses, twisting one of the bident's horns, making the whole sceptre spin. 'Once we have the armies at our control, we'll be unstoppable.'

Something about what he says makes me replay his words from earlier today: 'We need our armies'. . . 'our armies' . . . 'armies.'

My heart sinks to my stomach.

Not army, but plural.

I pace the small room, glancing back at the screen every few steps. My body shakes as I think about the Hedonesses in their shipping containers – Heda's army. The pieces start to click into place. Marissa told me that Heda promised to reunite Ben with his family. His dead family. She can only do that if Hades isn't the only one leaving the Underworld.

Armies.

Hades and Heda are combining forces.

With all the people that ever died – Hades' army is colossal.

The room gets so stuffy I take in big gulping breaths, glancing back at the table I dragged in front of the door for added security. I don't feel very safe.

An army of the Undead and an army of Hedonesses. What will they do with them? The answer comes to me like a fist to the gut.

Olympus. That's what Heda meant when she said she'd break down their door and make them bow. They're going to destroy Olympus.

'Good,' says Heda, pulling me back to the screen. I grip the sides and focus on stilling my heavy breathing so I can hear.

'How much longer do I have to stay in this hellhole?' Hades punches the doorframe and looks back up. 'Pun intended,' he adds in a monotone.

'We estimate one week before the arrow—'

'The sliver.'

She clears her throat. 'The available portion of the arrow takes down the seal. Unfortunately, we are unable to reproduce the arrow of indifference with Eros's bow, the same way we can reproduce the arrow of infatuation. There is only one and it is in high demand.'

'Well when we cross over, there can be no delays. My presence will trigger notice.'

'We will be ready for you,' she says, though she doesn't sound confident about it.

'I am a man of my word.' He pauses, tilting his head to his crow as the bird rattles something in his ear.

'Curious,' Hades says. He turns, slowly, until he's fully around and I see his face – it's a mirror of Eros's, but his hair and eyes are black and his skin a warm brown. Eros's face is strikingly beautiful with darker colouring and I find myself drawn to the familiarity of Hades. He shifts his stance and the shadows of the door silhouette him in deep obsidian reminding me that Hades is very different from Eros.

He looks up and I gasp when his stare locks through the camera as if looking right at me.

Thirty-Six

I make it back to the container room to find the lights are off. Everyone must be asleep. I'm exhausted and worried about everything but thankful that this time I didn't run into any guards on my way back. After the look Hades gave me, I was sure Heda would have ordered them after me. The last thing she needs is me trying to stop her. There's only one week until Hades is here; one week for Heda to make an army out of my friends and family – an army from my blood.

I don't even know how Nani's doing. The last person experimented on with my ichor ended up dead.

I shudder as Paisley's frozen face floods my mind: her lips, pale and flaky around the edges, her marble eyes, shiny and lifelike, but stone.

Dread fills me with more force than anything I've ever felt. More than the electricity that once moved through my blood. More than the sensation of my first kiss with Ben. If I don't do something my whole family could end up like Paisley. Or worse.

They could become Hedonesses again.

There's a rustle in my ma's container and the inside lamp flicks on. Ma comes to the door, a blanket around her shoulders and her hand over her throat. 'Rachel? Thank the gods you're back.'

I flinch at her words. The gods had very little to do with my return. 'I think I got everything we needed,' I say, hoping my ma doesn't hear the emotion in my voice.

She smiles and holds out her hand, waving for me to join her. 'Come, let's meditate together. It'll help you make it through the day.'

I would need a whole lot more than meditation to help me through my day now that I know there's another, bigger clock over my head counting down. Today is day one of seven before Hades arrives, and hour ten of twenty-four with the key card.

'Ma, I actually need to talk to you. To all of you, it's important. Can you wake Eros?'

She frowns as she takes me in. Her eyes soften when they land on mine, like she somehow can look through into my brain, into the mess and torment that fills it.

'I'll wake him,' Ma says without question.

I head to Dad's container and knock on the door before opening it and stepping in. Dad sleeps on a mattress that he's pushed into the corner, perfectly still and fully clothed like someone who'd lain on top of the bed for a quick nap. He registers something's different and jolts upright.

'Just me, Dad,' I say.

'Oh, Rachel, hi. Is everything OK?'

'I need to talk to you all. It's important.'

'I can see that,' he says. 'You look like you saw a ghost.'

'No, not a ghost.' Though Paisley is below every thought waiting for moments she can slip in and remind me what Heda's done. 'Worse,' I say.

'Well, in that case.' Dad stands and heads to his sink, splashes water on his face and then turns to me. 'You better go wake Kyle. It can take a while.'

I nod and spill out of his container, making my way into Kyle's. Unlike my dad, who sleeps fully clothed, still and organised, Kyle's in his boxers and splayed all over the place, legs and blanket a twisted mess. I nudge his leg with my foot. He grumbles and rolls over.

I tap it harder. Same thing. My eyes fall on the sink in the far corner. I go to it, fill my hands with water, thankful when my wounded palm no longer stings, and I toss the water in Kyle's face.

He jolts upright, batting at the air. 'What the hell?'

I shudder at his choice of words. *What the hell, indeed.*

He rubs his eyes and holds up his blanket, confused that it's wet. When he's awake enough to focus on me, he frowns. 'What's going on?'

'I need to talk to everyone. You should put some clothes on.'

'Less fun that way,' he says with a grin.

260

When I don't smile he realizes how serious I am and hops up and grabs his blue shirt. As Kyle gets dressed, I make my way out of the container to the courtyard and climb into the paddle boat, sitting beside Dad who's already there and busy spreading out the hand-drawn map.

♥

Kyle slumps in the boat. 'So in order to see my mum again, I have to take on the god of the Underworld?'

'All we need to do is get Eros's bow and arrows before they figure out how to take the power from my blood,' I say. 'It's getting them that's the tricky part.' If we manage that, we'll at least stop Heda's army.

Eros waves to his collar. 'And the key.'

Kyle exhales loudly and nods to him. 'You seem pretty chill, having learned your daughter is working with Hades.'

Eros doesn't reply and that gives us all the answer we need. He already knew.

Dad leans forward, not wasting more time. 'One week, right? That doesn't leave a lot of options here.'

I shake my head, flicking the key card between my fingers. 'We have to stop them. We just have to. We can't let the Hedoness power come back.'

'Yes,' says Eros, his voice croakier than when he last spoke, and I wonder if it's because he's tired or because his pain is back. 'Once we get the bow and arrows and key, this collar is coming off and I can use my powers to stop her, and if Heda cannot control the Hedonesses it will be a much easier fight.'

Ma's back stiffens. 'What if I volunteer—'

'No,' I say, cutting her off.

'Listen,' she says, 'if I do, and my power is restored, then I can use it to help fight.'

'I didn't come to you with this to save your powers. I'm trying to save your life. Paisley died because of what they did to her. There's no telling what will happen to you. Because they *will* come for you.'

'Likely sooner than later,' Dad adds. 'Heda will use you as leverage to get Rachel to do whatever she needs. She already took your mother.' His eyes light up, like he's thought of something new. 'She said the experiments are working with the new subject, right?' I cringe at his use of the word *subject*. But it would be even worse if he said Nani's name. 'Even if that is a lie, it's only a matter of time before they start on others.'

'Then I will volunteer,' says Ma. 'It is our duty to protect the Hedoness power.'

'Ma, stop!' I slam my hand on my knee. 'This is bigger than us, and the Hedoness way.'

Ma squares her shoulders and points a long finger at me. 'If the Hedoness power was not ripped from us, Heda would not go to such measures to get it back. Our ways are all we have.'

'Ma,' I say, exasperated, 'it is more than that. Don't you see? Heda's been controlling the Committee for years. Our ways have long been under attack, our kind manipulated for her game.'

Ma opens her mouth then closes it, her entire face dropping. Finally, she says, 'I've suspected for a while that something was wrong with the Committee.' She sighs. 'I don't like feeling useless. We must do something.'

'We must do what is right,' Dad says, flipping a corner of the hand-drawn map in his fingers. 'And in this case what is right is stopping Heda and Hades from getting control of us. The gods only know what he will do with an army of Hedonesses at his beck and call. Rachel is right, our plan should be to get the bow and arrows.'

Kyle holds out his ankle. 'How we going to do that?'

I glance up. 'With Marissa's help.'

He doesn't argue but he doesn't look happy about it either.

'We'll have to start immediately,' says Dad. 'How do we get in touch with Marissa?' He glances around the room. 'I bet we could trigger an alarm on the keypad by the door,' he mumbles to himself.

Kyle takes off his shoe and throws it – it rockets in a straight line, smacking into the keypad first try.

It's an impressive throw, even if unnecessary. 'You know I could have walked over there and pressed it, right?'

'That's less fun.' He grins, and I'm not sure if I should be mad at him for making jokes right now or thankful that someone is still finding time for humour in this mess.

'Speaking of,' Kyle adds, 'can you grab my shoe for me?' He holds out his anklet leg and wiggles his toes. 'Can't leave our courtyard.'

Before I can answer, the door to the container room flies open and a group of guards armed with Tasers and rods, storms in. Sauntering in behind them is Ben, and next to Ben is the guard dressed in red.

'We're too late,' whispers Ma.

Thirty-Seven

Ben motions for Bident and the guards to hang back. They obey, except one of the grey guards, who follows behind him as he approaches us. I'm thankful Bident stays back because last time we were this close I stabbed her. Right now, I need to control my anger. Eros told us that Heda locks the bow and arrows up during the prisoners' meal times. Which will be any moment. I can't risk causing a scene and missing this window to search for them.

'The alarm on our radios went off,' Ben says, his face twisted into a frown. 'Is everything all right in here?'

The guard behind him squares her shoulders, one hand resting on the Taser holster.

I nod to Kyle. 'We were playing catch with his shoe and it accidentally hit the panel.'

'That would explain this,' someone says from behind us, and Kyle's shoe comes skittering across the floor, stopping when it hits the boat.

The guard beside Ben scoffs. 'Find something else to occupy your time, so you don't waste ours.'

Kyle slips his shoe back on and flashes her a cheeky grin. 'Not a lot to do around here. There's only so much pirate ship we can play in this thing.' He smacks the paddle boat and I fight back a laugh.

The guard unhooks her Taser and Ben grabs her arm. 'Go and check the prisoner command alarms. See if they're still working.'

She turns around, facing the guards by the door. Two are bent over the panel, pulling pieces apart and reconnecting wires. 'Is it working?' she yells.

Ben sighs, his eyes wide in annoyance.

'No,' one of them shouts back. 'Bident's going to get the tech.'

I watch Bident slip out of the large steel doors and feel my tension lessen immediately. My fists unfurl, and I realize I was squeezing them so tight I left crescent-moon nail marks on my palms. Bident isn't even gone a minute when Marissa storms into the container room and right over to us, bypassing the guards by the door and stopping by the one next to Ben.

'What's going on? I just saw Bident in the hall.' Marissa looks genuinely worried for us, her eyes darting around the room as if checking to see if we're all OK.

'Alarms went off,' Ben says. 'Everyone's fine.'

She lets out a heavy breath. 'Thank goodness. I was worried it was your nani, Rach.'

Ma's head shoots up at the mention of Nani and my heart sinks. But getting the bow and arrows needs to be our priority, then we save Nani.

I hope she makes it that long.

The guard next to Ben starts to beep. She unclips her radio and holds it to her ear. The volume is too low for me to hear anything but static. After a few nods she pushes the button and speaks into the receiver, 'Right away.' She turns back to my family. 'Since the alarms aren't working we'll have to escort you down to breakfast ourselves.'

'I'm not very hungry,' Ma says. 'If it's all the same I'll stay here.'

'No can do,' says the guard. 'You'll miss your injection.'

Kyle grumbles. 'I hate those things. They make me nauseated.'

'Large doses of vitamins will do that,' Ben says, 'but they keep you from getting sick. With so many people in such close proximity, even the common flu could cause an epidemic.'

'Whatever, I'm not taking it,' Kyle says.

'I'll see what I can do,' Ben replies. 'But you have to come with me.'

Kyle sighs and gets out of the paddle boat. Dad steps out too, offering Ma his hand. She takes it and smiles, but then her eyes land on mine and she gives me a sad shrug. She knows my plans are spoiled now.

'You too.' The guard waves at me. 'They want you fed so you have strength for another bleeding.'

The guard holds up her radio and the school-bell alarm blasts out. 'To the door,' she orders, and my family listens, heading single file to the stairwell. Ben takes a step towards them and stops when he realizes I don't move. 'Come on,' he says.

'I'm going to stay with Marissa. We'll catch up.'

Ben looks at Marissa and I hold my breath, waiting to see if there's still a chance, if she'll follow through on her offer and help me.

'Yeah, go ahead,' she tells him. 'We'll be right there.'

With the guards guiding everyone to the cafeteria the halls are empty. We worry less about making noise and more about getting there fast. As we jog towards the stairwell Eros showed me on the map, my shoes slap the floor in rhythm to my breaths.

Marissa glances over. 'I can't believe you talked me into this, again,' she says, panting.

I can't believe you agreed. 'I'm just glad you want to help.'

'Of course I do.' She stops, bending over to catch her breath, hands on her knees. 'I wasn't joking when I said I regret what I did to Kyle – that especially was really wrong of me. And selfish. And you deserve a better friend than that.'

I take a step back, bumping into the cold metal of one of the hall's vent grates. The air conditioning feels nice after the jog. 'So, if you mean that, then why have you been helping Heda this whole time?'

'I'm a survivor, Rachel. I practically raised myself while my mom gallivanted around the world. The first thing you learn in survival is take the path of least resistance. It was easy for Heda to believe that I wanted to restore the Hedoness powers. It's an easy lie to tell, because it's not a lie. But when hurting you became a part of it, I knew I had to do something. You've been the only one who ever . . .' She pauses, trying to find the words. 'What was that thing you always said?' Soon her eyes light up with an answer. 'You said you wanted someone to see your worst and still choose to love you. Well, you're the only person who does that for me. And if I'm being honest, the pathway of least resistance is going along with your hair-brained scheme. So here we are. Alone, in the hallway and in desperate need of manicures.'

She's telling the truth about lying and maybe even caring about me, which confuses me enough that I find myself agreeing to needing the manicure.

'We should get going.'

She nods, and we start down the hall again, speed walking instead of jogging, and soon pass the ichor room. I scan the wall for my pencil markings.

'It seems full circle from our days at St Valentine's,' she says. 'Like this was always the path we were destined for.'

'Huh?' I glance over.

'One of the most powerful –' she points to me – 'and one of the most eager Hedonesses –' she points to herself – 'fighting injustice together. It's like that shirt you always used to wear.'

'My Wonder Woman shirt?'

'That's the one.'

I quicken the pace and in no time we pass the control room and the last of my pencil directions. It's just plain grey walls and cement floors, illuminated in the yellow wash of the flickering overhead lights. The stairwell Eros pointed out is up ahead.

I catch a whiff of her familiar shampoo and a warning goes off in me, in Kyle's voice, *We can't trust her. No matter how convincing she is.* I know Marissa better than anyone, and if she's helping us, I'm not naïve: I know it's because it serves her own desire. What I don't know is what she wants. What does she get out of helping us?

Unfortunately, I don't have the luxury of time to find out. All I can do is continue blindly after her towards the room Eros thinks contains the weapons.

We come across a stairwell and I pull out the map.

She snatches it from me. 'This is the one?' she asks, pointing to the marked spot on the paper.

'I think so.'

She nods, tucks the map under her arm, smooths her hair, straightens her belt, then steps into the industrial stairwell. I fight the urge to ask for the map back and follow her down two flights, the light getting duller as we descend. At the bottom, she waves me after her and we head down another hall with poor lighting, lower ceilings and no vents. The combination of sweatsuit and running makes me miss the cool air on the upper floors. Soon the corridor widens into a lobby style room with matching office chairs, and Marissa stops to catch her breath. So far we've managed to avoid the guards.

Kyle's voice pushes back in. *'It's too easy.'*

He's right. It is. Marissa showing up when I needed the help, empty sheltered hallways because the guards are escorting prisoners. If there's one thing I've learned it's that easy means we need to be careful.

There's a niggle deep inside that tells me I can know her intention. I can open my mind to her thoughts and let her truth slip in. But then the other voice, the one buried much deeper, whispers that I've already risked too much, will require too much of my dad's blood. Any further use of power means that's it. No going back. Heda will have what she needs and I'll spend an eternity alone – when everyone I love dies of old age and I'm still a teenager.

I keep my mind closed and follow Marissa deeper into the dark lower level.

Lights flicker to life as they sense us moving through the shadows and turn off again when we pass. Even though Marissa leads us with the map, I wish I'd brought a pencil to mark our way. We're so close to the room where Heda keeps the arrows, I can feel the faint pull stirring the abilities in me and beckoning me to the right. I follow Marissa, my body tense with desire for the arrows.

I remind myself why I'm here, who I'm fighting for, replaying the faces of my family, my friends, Paisley, over and over, trying to push the need for power out of me. It only helps a little. Paisley's face helps most of all. I don't want to let her down. Saving her mother and our school friends won't bring her back but at least it won't mean she died for nothing.

Marissa holds up her hand, stopping me, then leans round the next corner. 'Six guards,' she whispers, pulling me into a crouch behind the wall. 'We need to find somewhere to hide.'

Six of them, armed and trained, and only two of us.

Thirty-Eight

When Eros said it was guarded, I was expecting there to be more guards than six. Still, six will be a fight I'm not trained for. The self-defence classes at St Valentine's taught us how to manoeuvre our attacker into a kiss position. I don't think that will help either of us here.

'What do we do?' I ask, clenching my fists. I can't help my body's reaction. I know what the bolt rods feel like and I definitely don't want to get hit with one again. A familiar warmth floods my arms and chest, and my eyes start to see the white light, like before I stabbed Bident. I unclench my fists and shake my arms, blinking to clear my vision. It could be from the looming fight or the siren call of the arrows, but I don't like that my powers are rearing up in me.

'You know what you need to do.' Marissa's face is shaded in the dimly lit hall. Still, even in the dark it's hard to miss her smug *I told you so* look.

She's right. The easy way through all this would be to embrace my immortality, to unleash the powers I've been holding back. But if I let them out, I know I won't be able

273

to go back. I'll be immortal. And if I'm immortal, not only will I be forced into an eternity without my family, but Ben will truly never forgive me.

My heart sinks, remembering my first time talking to Ben, in jail. It struck me right away that he was sad, with his frayed cuffs and lonely eyes. It wasn't until later, at our van camping trip in Little Tokyo, that he told me he was an orphan. He knows what it feels like to be left behind.

'It's worse than my family dying, Rachel. They didn't choose to leave me.' As Ben's words push to the front of my mind, I'm starting to understand why he left me before I could leave him. He couldn't bear a lifetime together only to face an eternity apart.

If I embrace this power, I'll be doing it to him all over again. And this time, it really will be my choice to say goodbye. My entire body shakes at the thought.

It isn't until Marissa glares at me and says 'Shh!' that I realize I'm hyperventilating.

I can't use my powers, I just can't. 'I'm not going to do it, Rissa. I won't.' I shudder at the thought of six rods slamming into my back, stomach, sides. I can almost feel the burn and taste the metallic ichor filling my mouth.

'Don't be stupid, Rach,' she says. 'When you got it, flaunt it.' She flicks her hair over her shoulder like she used to when we were tourist-watching in Times Square and she'd flirt with the boys who passed by.

'No,' I say, a little too loud.

Her eyes widen and she glances around the corner again. I half expect the lights to click on as the guards charge towards my voice, but luckily we remain in the dark.

'We have one shot,' she whispers, her words sharp staccato beats that slice into my heart. 'If they notify the other guards, the whole facility will be on alert. We need to be quick.'

We need you to use your powers. Her thought forces itself into my mind and I fight it, squeezing my eyes shut and pressing my head, trying to push it out.

What a diva. She can't go five minutes without being the centre of attention. What does she think she's—

'What are you doing?' she asks.

I open an eye to find her watching me and realize she spoke the last question out loud. 'Oh, thank the gods,' I say in an exhale.

'Thank them? They're kinda what put us here.' She frowns, placing a hand on her hip. 'You're losing your mind.'

Actually, I'm fighting to keep it.

'Your plan?' I ask, hoping to change the subject and distract myself from the anxiety swishing in my chest and pressing into every corner of me.

'Remember when you viciously attacked me?'

I frown, trying to figure out when she means. 'When you wouldn't give us the keys to look in the surveillance SUV?'

'No,' she sighs. 'The other time.'

'When you insulted my clothes and I pushed you.'

'I don't think it happened quite like that, but yes,' she says, unimpressed. 'Anyways, when I was on the ground, I knocked your knees out.'

'You want to crawl up to them and knock out their knees?'

'Don't be stupid. The lights will go on, they'll see us coming.'

'Then?'

'Then we'll walk up to them in the lights.'

'OK, now you're the one being—'

She sighs. 'I'll act like you're my prisoner, shove you down, and while they're distracted you knock out their knees and I grab a Taser. If we're fast enough—'

I think of my family, wrapped in black body bags, lined up next to Paisley. 'We have to be fast enough,' I say.

She gently squeezes my arm, and I imagine her eyes would soften if they knew how. 'Are you sure you're not willing to use your powers?'

Ben's frayed denim cuffs fill my mind. 'I'm sure.'

'Fine,' she sighs. 'Let's do this. Then she grabs my arm, the gentleness from before gone, and marches me towards the guards.

The lights spring to life around us.

The guards grab their weapons and step into our path.

Thirty-Nine

All six guards point their Tasers as we approach. I flinch, fighting the white fire that fills me as Marissa shoves me forward.

'Caught this one wandering the halls,' she says.

'Oh yeah?' the guard closest to me asks. 'And how'd you get out?' She takes a solid step forward. As she does so, I recognise her gait and the way she leans casually to the left. She's the guard who attacked Marissa and me in the control-panel room. She'll be the first I knock out.

Marissa nudges me a step closer, not realising that our cover might be blown. 'She doesn't have an anklet so she can move around. This is Heda's valued guest.' She says valued like it's some inside joke they all have and it makes a shudder go down my back. The group eyes me curiously.

'I recognise you,' the large guard says, taking another wavering step. Her eyes suddenly widen.

Marissa gives a quick double-squeeze on my arm. It's time.

My eyes find my mark – her weapon belt. Her hand rests on the empty holster and I realize it isn't a Taser she's holding, it's a gun. I quickly glance around the group. They all have guns; they're the first guards I've seen to carry them. I don't have time to panic. I have to find a weapon, and fast. Marissa's fingers dig into my shoulders. She'll push me down any second. I glance at the holster on the other side of the guard's belt, thankful to find she has a bolt rod and that the security strap is unfastened. I take a deep breath and everything I have to do fills my mind like a map.

Marissa shoves me to the ground. I use the momentum to dive for the rod. Fear slips away; the room becomes razor clear. My fingers wrap around the hilt and pull it free in one clean move. I press the activation button. The bolt rod bursts out before the guards even register what's happening.

I'm on my knees by the time they jump back, but not fast enough. I circle, rod raised like I'm wielding Joan of Arc or Athena's sword – whacking and slicing at their knees. It's like watching from outside my body as they crumple into a pile of twisted bodies and I spin through them.

There's no white light, no sting of powers. And yet I know this fighter's intuition, and the way my body moves, is not natural. I can't seem to make it stop. I push the feeling aside and credit my newfound skill to all the first-hand experience I've been given each time I fought the guards. Unfortunately, I've never been one to believe my own lies.

Behind me, Marissa wrestles the large guard out of the circle. Their movements, though slow and cumbersome, sound crisp to my ear. It's like I know she manages to grab the gun – but the large woman doesn't let go. I knock the last of the guards down and spin, eyes closed, bolt rod raised. I stop mid-swing, holding the weapon firm in my hands, and open my eyes. The rod's inches from the woman's throat.

My heart starts to race into a panic.

Deep down I know the truth. *I like how this makes me feel.*

Marissa helps me drag the last guard into the supply room, dumping her body against one of the many stocked shelves. After we bind their hands and ankles together with cable ties Marissa found, we remove their weapons, helmets and walkie-talkie radios, and pile them on the table in the centre of the room. Marissa finds a roll of duct tape and proceeds down the line of guards, putting strip after strip over their mouths. When she finishes, she stands back and looks over her work, the six of them staring up at her, eyes wide.

'Not quite finished,' she says, heading to the table and grabbing an armful of the bolt rods. She turns them all on and places them one by one around the guards. 'There. Now if any of you try to move, you'll be reminded not to.'

The guards squirm as far away from them as they can. Marissa's dedication to help me has me wondering if maybe I've been wrong all along. I can't wait to tell Kyle about this.

'So,' she says, dusting her hands and standing, 'let's find those arrows.' She brushes hair out of her eyes and heads towards a thick steel door on the far side of the room. Glancing over her shoulder she adds, 'You coming?'

'Shouldn't we search all this first?' I wave to the rows of shelves lined with boxes and trunks and other supplies.

'This is a glorified janitor's closet. There's nothing valuable here. Look if you want, but my money is on a vault behind that steel door.'

I step over a guard and follow her to the room. She has a key card in hand, most likely belonging to one of the people she tied up, because her real key card is burning a hole in my top. I didn't notice her pull it off anyone though. I'm about to ask who she took it from when she scans the card. The light above the door flashes red and a screen lowers from the ceiling.

'Seriously? A retinal scanner!' She turns back to the group struggling to get out of their cable ties. 'Which one of you has clearance?'

They shrug, replies muffled by their gags.

'We can do this the hard way, one by one with an extra bolt shock for good measure,' she says.

I feel helpless. We shouldn't stay here long, wasting time until we're caught. Every second we spend is a second Heda has to do gods-know-what to Nani. But we're too close to the bow and arrows to turn back. I know because my body buzzes with need.

I have the ability to find out who can help us, the ability to read their minds. But I've already used it so much. One of the voices inside tells me that I'm already past the point of return and into having to accept that I'll live for ever while everyone I love dies.

They'll die a lot sooner, and a lot more painfully, if we don't get into this room.

We've come so far and are so close.

Just this once, I tell myself. *Mind reading doesn't require much power.* I'll open my mind quickly and as soon as I know who it is, I'll shut it off. But then one of the guards rocks on to her knees. She's saying something that's muffled by her gag.

It's obvious the others don't want her to give herself up by the way they struggle to get in front of her, eyes wide with fear. I can only image what Heda promised to do to them if they didn't protect those arrows at all cost.

'Good,' Marissa says, heading to the girl. She undoes the guard's legs and pulls the girl to her feet, shoves her to the door and holds her face to the scanner. Marissa is so determined to get those arrows, I feel like I'm the one who's helping *her*.

The light above the door blinks yellow now. I step back when a wide beam shoots from the screen, scanning up and down as it examines the girl's stern features until an exact replica of the girl's eye is mirrored on the screen. The light flashes green and the door clicks open.

Forty

Marissa lifts the handle to the vault door and a blast of hot steam spurts through the cracks. I'm instantly soaked through, half from sweat and half from the moisture in the vapour. We shield our faces and wait for it to settle before opening the door all the way. Marissa's hair is limp and wet and mascara runs down her cheek. She'd never let anyone see her like this. Anyone but me.

Our friendship feels real for the first time ever. 'Hey, Riss?'

'Yeah?'

'Thanks.' I smile. 'For everything, you're a good friend.'

Her eyes fill with tears and she nods, too choked up to answer.

The steam finally settles enough for us to go in. My heart races. Anything could be through the door. We're so close to ending this thing with Heda and getting out of here. 'Shall we?'

'Let's do this.' She pulls it all the way open, struggling against the weight. I reach round to help and soon we're side by side, entering a cavern of treasure. It's unlike anything I could ever have imagined. The room is a giant bedrock dome with intricate designs carved into the walls and ceiling. Steam swirls across the ground and down a gleaming gold wall. All around us are marble stands with velvet pillows on which rest everything from ruby-encrusted weapons to jewellery and art, and they're all under glass domes.

Marissa stops by a case containing turquoise stones strung in long lines resembling a shawl. 'I want it all,' she says. 'Who knew this was here?'

We explore the cases nearest us. I pass a goblet, some porcelain shoes and a bow – it's not Eros's bow, unfortunately. This one is sleek and simple. It doesn't have any of the carvings or amethyst that Eros's has, and it's tarnished a turquoise colour. I notice a small plaque inside: *The Bow of Heracles*.

'Marissa,' I call. 'You have to see this!'

There's a rustle and the next thing I see is Marissa wearing a brass-coloured dress over her guard uniform, which hangs on one shoulder and cascades to the floor like liquid. She has a bright blue diamond necklace on and a tiara that looks like it's made of stars.

'Take that off!' I say. 'You have no clue whose that is.'

'Actually, this dress belonged to Harmonia, and the jewellery was Hippolyta's. How wild is this?'

'This bow was Heracles'.' I wave to the case.

'The one he used to kill the Hydra? That was my favourite story in school,' she says.

'It's so bizarre seeing all this. We could explore for days.'

'We should,' Marissa says, straightening her tiara. 'There's so much for me to plunder.'

'Let's just find Eros's bow and arrows. We can come back for this stuff later.'

'Come back for it? There might be something in here that's even more powerful. We would be doing our cause a disservice by not looking for it.'

'We told Ben we'd be in the cafeteria soon. He's probably noticed we're a no-show by now and has gone looking for us.'

'What *doesn't* he notice?' she says, unimpressed.

'Right! It's kinda creepy.'

She laughs. 'Look at us getting along. Who would have thought? Now to plunder.'

The pull in my body is telling me to head to the left. 'No. First we find—'

'Yeah, yeah, the arrows.' She spins, letting the metallic fabric pour around her. When she stops suddenly, it continues to move in waves. Marissa raises her arm and points left. Sparkling gemstones adorn each of her fingers. 'Look,' she says.

I follow her gaze to an opening in the displays near the solid-gold wall. A single beam of light pours out from the top of the dome and falls on to a platform that's bigger and more distinguished from the others. Whatever it is, it's a focal piece of this collection.

We look at each other, both hoping it is what we think it is. The pull inside me tells me we're right.

'Race you there,' Marissa says, kicking off her heels and running.

I make it there before her. It's exactly what we thought – the bow, though unstrung; the box containing the black twisting bangle and the arrow, its lid open so it is displayed, and next to it on a large red silk pillow the tail feathers of the gold arrow. The rest of it must've been melted for the anklets. I wipe the sweat from my forehead. I can't even remember how many times I looked at the painting of Eros and his golden bow with its white gold and amethyst handle with carvings of a celestial battle scene. Now it's right here, and soon it will be in my hands.

I glance up to see Marissa's palms planted on the glass, her eyes as wide as I imagine mine being.

'It's strange seeing them, isn't it?' I ask.

Marissa looks up. 'Kinda heartbreaking to see what she's done to them.'

I never thought of it like that, but then again, I never carried the love of their power in my heart like Marissa does.

'Help me lift this,' I say, reaching my fingers under the glass dome.

'What if there's an alarm system?' she asks, stepping back.

'We've come this far. If there's an alarm, we use the arrows against whoever comes to stop us.'

'Or,' comes a voice from behind, 'you can step away before you get hurt.'

We spin to see Heda and the guards we left tied up in the supply room step out from the mist and shadows, weapons raised. Heda is even younger now, maybe in her thirties, with bouncing golden curls. She looks so much like Eros. She's beautiful, strong and deadly, and she has us surrounded.

I shove my body into the glass.

'Stop her,' Heda yells.

'Marissa, look out!' I throw all my weight into another run. The case slips over the side, crashing to the floor, the bow and arrows landing in the shattered glass by Marissa. 'Grab the arrows!' I scream.

The guards rush me from behind. I crawl over the podium and drop to the ground next to Marissa. She's holding the bow and is headed for the armlet, so I scrape through the blanket of glass looking for the golden tail feathers. My fingers dig into the shards, ichor dripping everywhere, but I don't slow down.

Marissa screams and is yanked to her feet by two guards. They hold their bolt rods to her throat and strip her of the bow. Another guard carefully retrieves the black armlet.

'Don't move,' Heda says to me, 'or your friend dies.'

I stand slowly, arms raised, trying to decide if I can take this fight – six guards and Heda against me. Even if I turn my powers on, that won't be easy. But I've done it once before. I can do it again. Next to my foot is a shard of glass large enough to use as a dagger.

I clench my fists, ready to pounce for the weapon.

'Get it,' Heda commands.

Le-Li steps out from behind her, his black coat swaying in the steam, his purple hair out of the bun and slicked back. He approaches me, but not as a threat, as something else. I keep my eyes on the shard, waiting for the moment to dive for it and take Le-Li hostage. But he stops a good distance away and picks up a piece of blue glass. No, not blue glass, glass with my ichor on it.

'Test it,' Heda says, holding out her arm as one of the guards slips the black armlet on to her wrist. She flinches in pain and grits her teeth, but still she keeps it on. As she moves, I notice an IV stand behind her – two bags of dark blue ichor and one bag of my light blue ichor mixing together in a tube and travelling under the neckline of her robe. No wonder she looks younger and stronger. She's absorbing years and getting her fix at the same time.

Le-Li rushes out of view. I slither towards the glass shard and notice a speck of gold glisten under a nearby pile. I slide a little closer, glass tinkling with my movement. Heda whips around to face me. 'Do you not care if I kill Marissa?'

I lift my chin.

'You're running out of friends,' she adds.

I glance at Marissa; her eyes are wide and pleading for me not to do anything foolish. But no matter what we do, Heda will kill us when she's done anyway. Before I can act, Le-Li returns and Heda twists to face him.

'So?'

He shakes his head. 'Closer though.'

She exhales, loud and annoyed. 'Bring them.'

The guards charge at me and I don't hesitate. I grab the shard of glass, clutching it like a dagger, and I rush Heda, aiming for her heart. Her eyes widen, death looming in them. The guards are behind me. They can't save her now. The sharp edge slices into my palm, my ichor making it slick, but I squeeze tighter. I won't let it drop.

She holds her black-arrow-clad arm out. I don't care if it stabs me, as long as I stab her first. I'm an arm's-length away from finishing this.

There's a blur as someone jumps out from behind a display and steps in front of her. I'm about to ram this shard into their heart until I look up into those familiar blue eyes and the shard drops through my fingers.

Ben.

Ben saved Heda.

Forty-One

I'm shoved down, face into the glass. Shards stabbing like dozens of bee stings. Someone's knee jams into my spine.

'Stop!' Marissa yells. She squeaks in pain, then goes silent.

Heda crouches, her blue robe swishing through the steam like a ship parting waves. She grabs a handful of my hair, yanks my head back and holds her bangle to my throat – the sharp tip of the black arrow breaking my skin.

'The arrow of indifference feeds off magic and when there's no magic left it takes away your emotions. One little touch of this and you won't care about anyone or anything again. Sounds like a dream, doesn't it?'

I grit my teeth and stare back at her. This is the woman who tried to kill my father, who killed my friend, and is threatening to turn everyone I love into a Hedoness again.

'Let me go!' I hiss.

She smirks. 'Or what?'

'I'll make sure you never see Olympus.'

'Will you? And how's that?'

My hands scrape through the glass as I struggle to push up. I search my body for new powers but feel only a low vibration coming from the black arrow.

Heda laughs. 'There really is no point fighting. You've played perfectly into my plan every step of the way. When you scanned Sarah's eye –' she looks over her shoulder, yanking my head to face the guard standing behind her, the one Marissa held to the retinal scanner. The girl waves, gun in hand – 'it notified me that you were here,' Heda finishes.

'No!' Marissa gasps.

My worst fears are realized – Ben not searching for the key card, the lack of guards patrolling the halls, how quickly the two of us fought off six of them. No wonder it was easy. Heda was leading me here all along.

But that leaves the question . . .

. . . how did she know I was coming for the arrows?

'Lift her,' Heda says. 'If she gives you trouble, shock her.'

They yank me to my feet – a bolt rod rests on my stomach, ready to deploy with a click of a button. A guard's chest rises and falls, pushing into my back. Heda keeps the black arrow inches from my throat. My attention flicks to Ben, his face absent of any emotion as he watches, our eyes never connecting.

I have so many questions for him; like how he can just stand there and do nothing, or why he would risk his life for *her*.

Heda walks in a sweeping circle, towing the ichor blood-drip stand behind her. The guard holding me spins us after her so that the arrow tip never leaves its place, hovering over my skin.

I roll my eyes. The black arrow is a hollow threat. She won't use it. She needs the magic in my blood.

Heda points to the gilded wall, staring up at it with reverence. It's then I follow her gaze and realize it isn't solid gold like I first thought, but a floor-to-ceiling stack of gold-painted skulls.

'Impressive, right?' She forces her words, sarcasm evident in each note. 'They are all that's left of the Committee's demigod murder spree. The weapons and garments you two were so rudely meddling with belong to them.' She weaves us through the glass display stands and over to the wall. The guard holds my head, forcing me to watch as Heda runs her free hand over the skulls. 'Sometimes I come here and wonder which skull belongs to which friend.' She buffs a golden jawbone with her sleeve. 'Is this my dear friend Polydeuces, who died saving me from the Committee?' She slides her hand to another skull. 'Is this his brother Castor?'

I know she's trying to make me sympathetic to her cause. The Committee hunting down and killing her friends and family must've been scarring. But from where I'm standing, she's turned into the very monster she hated.

Heda's hard eyes return to me. 'Very few of us got away, and the ones that did were used by the Committee. But not me. I do not like being told my value rests in serving others, so I showed them what I'm worth and infiltrated, turning and taking over one by one until the Committee was under my control.' Her eyes go distant like she's returning to that time and a tiny smile forms on her lips. It disappears immediately. 'Then you went and annihilated the Hedoness power,' she says. 'You took away my ability to protect myself.'

She shoves the arrow closer into my throat. Though I feel a physical pull to its power, I press further into the guard out of instinct, trying to get away from it.

Heda grips my arm. 'Thankfully I can undo your mistake, and just like a broken bone that needs to be re-broken and reset in order to heal better, it will be stronger.' She squeezes harder. I yank my arm away and she motions to Le-Li. 'Le-Li has insured biology will no longer restrict the Hedoness power. I will build an army that is tied to my blood and big enough to take down Olympus.' She grins, wicked and conniving. 'I won't only control the Committee. I will rule all.'

'Sired?' I ask, struggling to keep my lips from shaking and hoping fear isn't evident in my voice.

She smiles a dreadful smile that shows a sliver of teeth. 'You think isolating the Hedoness gene is the only thing Le-Li's been working on?'

I try to hide the panic from my eyes, but Heda's half-smile turns full.

'You didn't really think the injections my guests received were vitamins, did you?'

My mind fills with the image of the long queue of blue-clad Hedonesses, cuffs rolled and arms held out for the guard to shove a needle into. I swallow the sneaker-sized knot in my throat.

'Oh darling, so naive.' She clicks her tongue then slips a necklace out from under her blouse and holds it up – I feel its power almost instantly.

'Do you know what this is?' Heda asks.

I flick my eyes to a looped gold cord tied to an arrowhead carved in the same style as Eros's bow, but instead of depicting a battle scene, the golden arrowhead has an engraved garden with lovers' mid-embrace.

It's such a beautiful thing that the feeling of hate I have for it almost seems strange. 'The arrow of infatuation,' I say.

She nods. 'Do you know what it does?'

'Forces people to love.'

'It forces them to obey,' Heda corrects. 'And this –' she twists the cord, making the arrowhead spin – 'this string is from Eros's bow.' She leans in even closer. 'Let me spell it out for you: whoever has the string and the original arrowhead can make unlimited copies of the golden arrow. The anklets are—'

'The arrows.'

'Phew,' she says. 'I was beginning to worry you'd never figure it out.'

'And the injections?' I ask, still unsure why they need them if she can control everyone by their anklets with the arrowhead.

'Le-Li's found a way to inject indifference without it defusing the anklet's magic. Sadly, there's no permanent fix yet, so daily injections it is. You see, I can't have them falling in love and breaking the power of their anklets.' She pauses. 'A big thank-you to you and Benjamin for pointing out that flaw, by the way. Love is the most powerful magic, yada yada yada.' She leans into the ichor drip, holding the pole like one would a staff. 'Here's a history lesson they don't teach in school: the arrow of infatuation works by *giving* love and the arrow of indifference works by *removing* love, and thus removing magic. As long as they get their injections, they won't be able to love without the help of magic. Without the ability to love, they will never break their hold on my anklets.'

I turn my head as much as I can with the arrow at my throat. There's Ben, a blurry grey mass in the far reaches of my vision.

Is this what she did to him?

Did she stop his ability to love?

Something pierces my throat. Warm liquid trickles down my neck. I lift my chin, expecting the black arrow, but the armlet is on the hand that holds the ichor-drip. She has something else pressed to me now.

I step closer, even though it only pushes me deeper into the sharp edge. I know what I have to do. I have to stop her at all costs. 'You can't control them if you're dead,' I tell her.

For a split second the edge shakes into my neck, like she's afraid I'll use my powers and stop her.

She's right, I will.

Ben isn't a good enough reason not to any more. Nor is an eternity without my family. If I don't stop her, everyone will pay.

The trick will be doing it before she takes any more of my ichor.

She grabs my hair again, turning my head back to the wall of skulls.

'When you die, I'll put you next to Polydeuces.' She taps the skull she'd been buffing earlier. 'Or was this one Castor? I can never remember which is which.'

'Neither,' I say, careful not to move and hit the bolt rod at my stomach. Still, the risk of further pain is worth it. She needs to understand she's every bit as evil as the Committee who hunted down and killed her friends. 'That's probably Paisley,' I finish.

'Paisley?' She whips to face me, leans in and smiles. The skin around her eyes begins to pull, and I swear there are fine lines and wrinkles slowly forming. She either needs more ichor or the arrow armlet is doing that to her. Or both.

The blood bags she's dragging are almost drained too.

A grin spreads on Heda's face. 'No dear, that's not Paisley. I'll take you to Paisley.'

She grabs my arm, fingers digging in, securing the sharp object to my throat before pulling us away from the wall. I feel the bolt rod leave my stomach and the warmth of the guard leave my back. It's just the two of us now.

I assume we're headed to wherever the incinerator is, the one they threw Paisley into after they killed her. But Le-Li joins us, carrying a box of medical supplies and folded red fabric the same blood-red shade as Bident's uniform, and the only thing I'm sure of is that whatever it's for can't be good.

I strain to see if Ben and Marissa are coming too, but I can't twist my head enough.

Le-Li leads us past many cases filled with treasures, memories of the demigods that once roamed Earth. It's heartbreaking to think they were forced out of Olympus for not being fully immortal, only to be hunted down and killed for being too godly here. I know what it's like to exist between two worlds, never belonging in either. Not black or white but the grey between. It's lonely at times, living in that shadow.

Though Heda and I are different in so many ways, I see that loneliness in her too. She lost her friends; she was abandoned by her family. I couldn't even imagine what that feels like. My family is the most important part of my life.

And I need to find a way to save them now.

I remember what Marissa told me – take the path of least resistance; a lie is easier to tell if it's partially true. It's worth a try.

'I'm sorry they did this to you,' I tell her.

Heda stops dead and the momentum jerks my head down to see the steam swirling at our feet and a knife at my throat. It's exactly the response I was hoping for. 'The Committee was wrong to kill them,' I add, choking into the blade. 'It wasn't their fault they were born demigods. They didn't choose it.' All the feelings of being a Hedoness, and being linked to that monstrous power, come flooding back.

She takes another step forward, yanking me with her. I need Heda's head out of her game. I need to fluster her so she slips up and I can find a way to attack. With Heda and that armlet gone, no one will be able to force the blood from my veins.

So I say the one thing I know would most fluster me. 'I'm sorry your father cared more about breaking the curse than getting you back home where you belong.'

She jerks to a stop again, her grip on my arm tightening. 'Keep your mouth shut.'

So, her father *is* her weakness. I try not to smile.

Now to find a way to exploit it.

Forty-Two

We descend a narrow passage in the rock. Le-Li leads the way and Heda's behind me, her arrow-clad arm wrapped around my shoulder, a blade pressing into my neck. Steam pushes up the slope, heating the tight corridor and making it feel like we're heading into an oven. My sweatsuit sticks to my legs. It's hard to walk with Heda's knees bumping into me and the tight grip on my arm. But I manage, one foot after another, following them into the unknown.

Lining the walls are long glass cases, fogged from the heat. Though blurry, I make out the skeletal remains inside them: bony fingers gripping dagger hilts, arms strapped on to shields, spines and ribs draped in chainmail, shin bones jutting out of a boot. It's like a battle was fought and lost in this very passage, the dead covered in glass and left to rot.

Heda notices my curiosity. 'These,' she says, waving the arm not pressed into my neck, 'are the ones I killed.'

I clench my fists, fighting the urge to attack her right here in the middle of this slaughterhouse display. My resolve to embrace my abilities has never been more clear. Heda is dangerous. She must be stopped.

I try again to find the electrical stir in me, but the black arrow being so near is blocking any connection. It's like I'm hollow. All I feel is pain.

She slows her steps, forcing me to slow too. I'm not sure if it's because the slope is getting steeper or because she's tiring. Her breathing is deep and loud, but all of us are struggling in this heat.

She unhooks the IV, leaving the stand and empty ichor bags behind.

Though slower, we keep going down, past more cases with the glass so fogged I can't see in. The steam is boiling and all of me is now slick with perspiration. Heavy footsteps continue behind us. I haven't heard Marissa. I hope she's OK.

The slope starts to level out and Le-Li stops. The steam mixes with smoke and it's so high it covers the path before us, making it hard to breathe. 'We're here,' he says, balancing the box and waving at the air so Heda can see his face. He shifts his load higher, bumping the button over his heart and the baseball game broadcasts into the tunnel, '*and we're set to go . . . down the middle . . . strike one.*'

Heda leans around me, her body pressing uncomfortably into mine. 'Turn that off and turn on the fans.'

Le-Li sets his box on the ground, smacks his chest off and pulls a tablet out of his lab coat pocket. He pushes a strand of sweat-slicked purple hair behind his ear and punches in a command. The electrical whirl of industrial fans fills the small corridor. Soon the wall of smoke moves back, clearing enough for me to see we're at the mouth of the passageway leading into another cave, and it glows a strange orange. This is where I watched Heda and Hades plot.

The area without smoke seems even larger than the cavern with the demigods. Other than the odd few glass display cases lining the wall near the entrance, this one is not decorated with carvings and gold. Sharp stalactites hang like icicles from the ceiling and it's so hot the air is thick in my throat.

Heda leads me past Le-Li and out of the passage to the row of large industrial fans, each blade the size of me. She puts her head back and lets the fans whip her robe and long blonde hair about as we dry off. The fans help with the heat, though only a little.

She turns me round. The smoke recedes enough to see the source of the orange. I gasp, stepping back, but Heda holds me at her side.

'Beautiful, isn't it?' She pushes us forward and waves down to a river of molten lava, flames licking up the high rocky edge like waves on a windy day. 'Rachel, meet Phlegethon. One of the five rivers that guard the passage to the Underworld.'

The whirl of fans drowns out my racing heart. The wall of smoke shifts further back, revealing a rocky

301

outcrop that forms a little island in the middle of the river, with a bridge made up of three steel cables connecting to this side of the riverbank. On the rock isle are two doors. The first is the very same carved wooden frame I saw Hades standing in. Shadows fill it again now but I'm not close enough to see who it is. Still, a shiver runs down my spine, even in this heat.

The other doorway is made entirely of gold, more intricately carved than Hades' door, with big looping spheres that spin on its top. That door is shut, but a laser rig blasts light at both frames, the larger of the rays directed at Hades' door. It must be another of Le-Li's inventions. I'm guessing it's what's bringing down the seals so Hades and his army can exit the Underworld and march into Olympus with Heda and her army of Hedonesses.

Heda pushes me forward until I'm close enough to the edge to make out a pile of painted stone remnants between the two doors. There must've once been a third doorway – if the gold leads to Olympus and the wooden to the Underworld, the only other place in the otherworlds you can go to is Elysium.

I yank around looking for Ben. If the doorway to Elysium is gone, he's never seeing his family again, no matter what Heda told him.

'Stop moving,' Heda says. 'You're going to want to see this.' She points to the wall of smoke but I ignore her and keep searching for Ben.

Heda spins around me, keeping the blade to my skin and the black arrow close. Her eyes flick over my shoulder. 'Secure her,' she tells someone behind me.

The buzz of the bolt rod carries over the noise of the fans, hovering inches from my back. The black-arrow-clad hand slips from my shoulder, the blade from my throat. Heda's just made her first mistake.

With the arrow of indifference further from my body, the powers stir in me again. I turn to face the guard holding the rod, scanning the group behind her in hopes of finding Ben. I need to see him one last time, as I am, before I fully embrace my immortality.

In a heartbeat, I spot him with the other guards. He has his arm around Marissa, a bolt rod to her throat. He whispers something in her ear and she nods.

My heart sinks. He isn't Ben, not my Ben, any more. Whether Heda forced him to be this way by removing his ability to love or whether it was his choice all along, I can't wait for him any more. I need to act now. Tears flood my eyes as I let down the internal walls and summon my powers. All of them, every forgotten or forbidden tremor.

Suddenly white light erupts from me, forming a protective dome around my body and sending the guard holding the rod rocketing back. She struggles to her feet and charges, only to get knocked down again by the light. I reach out and touch the edge of the dome, feeling the sensation of fingers brushing against my own skin. I can't believe my powers made this.

More of them come for me. More of them are blasted back. They get up and try again, my electric dome knocking them down every time.

The light surrounding me flickers. I'm unpractised and my energy's being sucked dry, much like how my body felt when the ichor machine took my blood. The dome wavers. I focus on keeping it whole and spin in time to see Heda marching towards me, black armlet raised like a shield, slicing through the dome with ease. My legs shake; my arms are too weak to lift. The power takes everything from me.

Le-Li and a handful of guards follow Heda. My body surrenders, dropping to the ground and landing with a smack. I'm hit with rods and something stabs into my arm. I ignore it all – all the pain, all the fear, and try to find my electricity so I can fight back.

Somehow I manage to get on to my knees and am grabbed and lifted the rest of the way. Heda slams me into a glass case. It rocks on the stand, cracking from the force, a sharp edge cutting into my back. The black arrow is once again at my throat, and this time she presses it into me, breaking skin.

'Thank you,' she says. 'You've given us exactly what we needed.' She glances at Le-Li. Watching us, standing with his back to the wall of smoke, he's cradling a small vial of bright blue liquid. Not pastel, not light blue – this is what Eros told me of: the royal blue blood of immortals.

'Now you watch,' Heda continues.

My lips tremble as another set of fans comes on and the smoke is pushed further back to reveal a set of stairs leading to a glass room, suspended above the fiery river, about a football field's length back from the island with the doors. Le-Li turns and heads for the room, flicking on a light to illuminate what looks like a lab you'd find in a hospital or university. Inside, Nani is strapped to a bed.

'Nani!' I call, jerking in Heda's arms. 'Nani, I'm here!'

Heda pushes me further into the broken display case.

'Rachel?' Ma's voice floats over Heda's heavy breathing and the fans and the cackling river of fire – it's so faint I'm not sure I'm hearing right. Maybe it's the voices in my mind. Maybe they're clearer now that I've embraced the powers in me. I search wildly for her but other than the river, the suspended glass room and the rocky island with the doors, all I see is the wall of haze.

'Rachel?' she calls again.

'Ma? Ma, I'm here!'

'Keep watching,' Heda says, holding my face towards the smoky barrier.

It inches back like a slow-motion tsunami. Soon the other side of the river comes into view. The cavern is twice as big as I imagined and lining the far riverbank is a sea of blue-clad prisoners. Hundreds of them, maybe thousands, lined up like an army ready to march. Standing at the front of the pack, at the edge of the cliff, is my family – Ma, Dad, Kyle, Mrs Turner, even Aunt Joyce is there, clinging to Kyle's arm like she's afraid at any second she'll fall into the fire. I didn't even know Heda had her.

'Ma!' I wave. 'Head for Nani!' I point to the glass room suspended between us, but Heda shoves the arrow deeper into me and I drop my arm and become quiet.

Forty-Three

Heda presses the arrow so hard into my throat that I choke. Ben's in my line of sight and I catch him flick his eyes to the glass case I'm pressed into. I reach behind my back, slide my hand across the glass until it comes upon a large gap and follow the broken edge down. My fingers brush what feels like a sword hilt. My heart races. With the black arrow at my throat I can't use my powers, but I can use a weapon.

I inch the hilt up the crack. I almost have it close enough to pull through the gap but I can't get a good enough grip. I stretch as far into it as I can without alerting Heda. My fingers slip off the handle.

I grunt in frustration and Heda smiles, thinking my irritation is directed at her. She presses further into me, my back jamming deeper into the case. Her extra shove moves me the distance I need and in no time the handle is up the side of the container and sticking through the larger gap in the glass. My fingers wrap tightly around the hilt. One move, one chance to get that arrow off me.

I throw my body into it, knocking her back and pulling the sword free. But it sticks in the crack and I'm jerked on my feet. Heda struggles to regain her grip on me. Ben lets go of Marissa and charges to Heda's rescue, slamming his body into the display and toppling the three of us before the guards even realize what's happening.

He scrambles through the broken glass, finding another sword, larger and more decorative than the one in my grasp. I spin on to my back, holding my sword out as I try to summon my powers again.

He swings his sword around. I tighten the grip on mine, waiting for impact.

But his blade isn't pointed at me.

He's holding it to Heda.

Ben reaches over and offers me his hand. I hesitate to take it, unsure if this is another trick, another time he's pretending to care, but when I do and our fingers wrap together, the electricity in me fires every nerve, like a cool wave washing over my body. He pulls me to my feet and positions himself between Heda and me.

I missed this, him. Us, fighting side by side.

Heda slowly backs away, arms raised. 'The swords of my grandfather, Ares, the god of war. Some of my most prized possessions. It's said they cut through anything.' It's obvious she's stalling for the guards who are encircling us, bolt rods in hand.

Ben raises his sword. 'I heard.'

Next thing I know, Ben brings it down in one sweeping

blow. Heda moves to block his strike with the armlet. The blade slices though flesh and bone like water.

An ear-piercing scream echoes off the cavern walls. Heda clutches her severed wrist. Ben lunges forward, pulling out the arrowhead necklace and cutting it from her neck. Then he picks up her severed hand, shakes off the bangle and loops the golden arrowhead around the black arrow. I stand there, clutching my sword and shaking.

His eyes are so cold, his actions so dark, I worry that whatever he's been through with Heda has taken him far away from the kind and gentle guy I loved. Ben holds the tip of his sword to Heda's throat with one arm and with the other tosses the cord and arrows to me but, before he can let go, Heda lunges and the arrows release at a weird angle and skitter across the ground towards the guards. Marissa dives forward, grabbing them and looking at us.

'The fire!' Ben yells.

I hold my breath, waiting for her response, but when she sprints for the river's edge and holds them out over the lava, I know my accountability partner truly has my back.

'Tell your guards to back down,' Ben says, pulling away from Heda and stepping protectively in front of me. 'Or I'll tell her to drop them.'

Heda starts to laugh. She stands, ignoring the sword at her throat and wrapping her amputated wrist with her blue silk robe.

Confused glances dance through the guards but they hesitantly lower their weapons.

'You stupid cocky boy,' she says, walking confidently towards us, forcing Ben and me to step back closer to the fiery edge. 'Did you think you had me fooled? When we brought you here you woke up swinging your fists and threatened to kill anyone who kept you from Rachel. You even broke Le-Li's nose.'

I glance at Le-Li up in the glass box with Nani. He's injecting her with something and I hope it's not my blood.

'No!' I cry, glancing back to the rubble – all that's left of the doorway to Elysium. If Nani dies, where will she go?

Le-Li catches Heda's eye and nods, then pushes something on his tablet.

'Then,' Heda continues, ignoring me, 'when we offered to reconnect you with your family you were so quick to follow me and put Rachel behind you.'

'It was a lie,' I say. 'The door to Elysium is gone, Ben. She can't give you back your family.'

'I know,' Ben says, turning to face me, his blue eyes telling so much more than his words can. 'I always knew.'

My heart flutters.

Heda smirks. 'Regrettably, Elysium is gone. The Committee destroyed or put their damn seals on all the doorways years ago. Now the dead have only the Underworld. Unfortunate, isn't it?'

Ben and I share a worried glance.

She turns back to Ben. 'Where were we? Yes, the beginning. I'm not a fool. Anyone could see then, Benjamin, what we see now – that you'd give up everything for Rachel, even after she chose immortality over you. You'd even give up them.' Heda points behind us to the island with the doors.

We turn to see that Hades' doorway has expanded in size in the few seconds we weren't looking at it. Now a number of people wait inside for the seal to drop. In their centre is Paisley. I'd recognise her anywhere. I push past the confused guards to the river's edge, still clutching the sword.

'Don't move,' Ben calls to Marissa before he leaves Heda behind and comes to my side. The cable bridge is only a few steps away and I'm tempted to rush over to Paisley. My heart hammers at my ribs. I never thought I'd see her again.

'Paisley?' I call, my voice wavering, afraid to believe my eyes.

'Mom?' Ben says.

I look at him. 'Mom?' Then I look over to the woman he's staring at. She has long dark hair and the same ever-watchful eyes as him. She stands beside Paisley, and from the shadows behind her appear an elderly gentleman and a teenage boy who is a mini version of Ben, maybe my age or a year or so younger. They flank her as another man comes and stands behind her, wrapping his arms around her shoulders.

'Dad? Luca? Gramps?' Ben chokes out.

More people cram in the freestanding doorway to the Underworld, waiting to get out. Hades' horned shadow fills the space behind. It's strange to see them all and know that I could walk all around that door and not touch them – like one of those three-dimensional optical illusions. They're here, but not really.

The Hedonesses on the far riverbank see them too, and some start to call to their loved ones. They press closer, pushing my family nearer to the edge. My dad tries to calm them, holding Ma's hand to keep her safe.

Ben's family watches me. They heard Heda say Ben would choose me over them.

'Bring me the arrows,' Heda calls to Marissa. 'The only way to let your loved ones out is with my armlet; the laser needs more fuel. Don't be foolish. Think about the people you love.'

Marissa stands a few feet away, the arrows dangling over the edge of the lava, unsure what to do. Ben looks from her to his family. I look from Nani to the blue-clad prisoners.

What *do* we do? If we drop the arrows, we'll be forced to say goodbye all over again. If we give them to Heda she'll make an army with my blood and control everyone we love.

'We can't let her have them,' I whisper, lip trembling.

Ben's shoulders droop and he steps towards them. 'Mom, I'm—'

'It's OK,' she says. Her lips quiver but they stretch into a smile, tears running over her cheeks. 'I'm glad you found love. It's everything I dreamed of for you.' Her eyes peel off him and her smile redirects at me for a brief moment before returning to her son. 'She looks lovely.'

Mr Blake rubs her arms and pulls her closer, wiping away his own tears. 'We're proud of you, son.'

A hollow cry, like something from a wounded animal, rises up from Ben and he collapses on to his hands and knees, his entire body shaking with grief. It's hard to see him this broken. I gently touch his shoulder and he stands up, tilting his head back, and taking a deep calming breath before facing his family again. He looks slowly at each of them. 'I'm sorry,' he chokes out.

'It's the right thing,' his mother says. His grandfather nods once in agreement.

'I miss you,' Ben says to his brother, Luca.

'We miss you, too,' Luca says, wiping his face with his arm.

'I'm sorry,' Ben says again, eyes lingering on each of them one last time before turning to Marissa. 'Do it. Drop the arrows.'

Forty-Four

Marissa holds the arrows over the lava.

'What are you waiting for? Drop them!' Ben yells.

The large fans blow our hair about. I push it out of my face and watch Marissa, waiting for her to let go.

Heda smacks her stomach in an attempt to clap and takes a slow step forward, injured arm raised. 'You're forgetting the part of our little talk when I told you I'm no fool.'

'What?' Ben says, glancing from her to Marissa.

'What's happening?' Ben's dad shouts from the doorway.

Ben glances back. 'I don't know.'

Heda steps closer still and I lift my sword and face her.

'You didn't actually think I believed you trustworthy?' she asks Ben with a laugh. 'I knew you only obeyed me so you could help Rachel when the time came.' She waves her severed arm in an arc. The blue silk wrap is soaked through, a purple hue. 'This is that time, is it not?'

Ben glares at her then turns back to Marissa. 'Drop them already.'

'Actually don't, my darling. Bring them here.' She waves Marissa over.

'Rissa?' I ask, sword shaking in my grip as I watch her blonde hair whip about to form a halo in a backdrop of flames. She looks fierce. My stomach twists – something isn't right.

Marissa smiles at me and lowers the arrows to the ground by her feet, bare of the blue heels she kicked off in the demigod cavern. She steps out of the dress and her grey guard pants and whips off her grey top to reveal the red leather uniform of Bident.

'No!' I gasp, the sword slipping through my fingers, my legs wobbling. She's Bident. She killed Paisley. She set me up. I force back the urge to cry and choke out, 'Please say this is a joke.'

'It was you!' comes Paisley's voice from the outcrop doorway.

Ben grabs my shoulders, keeping me steady. But even he can't calm me now. All those years, our friendship, every 'second chance' I've given her, it all comes down to heartbreaking betrayal. It feels similar to what it felt like to lose Paisley, but with much, much more anger.

'Ahh, this is better,' Marissa says, tossing the grey uniform into the flames. 'I hated having to wear that crap.' She runs her hands down her body, then grabs the arrows and heads to Heda's side.

'W-why?' I manage, fists clenched, legs so wobbly the large fans push me from side to side.

Heda holds out her undamaged hand and Marissa places the golden arrowhead and string in her palm and slips the black armlet up her arm. Then she glances back at me. 'You're probably the only friend I've ever had,' Marissa says. 'But you stand counter to everything I believe in.' She glances across the river to my family. 'I can't have you interfering. We've worked too hard for this.'

'But you killed her. You killed Paisley!' I lift my sword. It shakes in my arms. I'm ready to run at her and ram her through, but Ben holds me tight.

'Rach, don't let her get to you,' he says, his lips pressed into my hair. 'It's what they want.'

'Paisley's death was strategic,' Marissa says. 'We needed to learn how to restore our power. Besides, I knew I'd see her again soon.' She nods behind us to the doorway, where Paisley and the Blake family stand.

Heda rests her injured hand on Marissa's shoulder. 'You've known my daughter a long time. Is it really that much of a surprise?'

'Daughter?' Ben and I say in unison.

Seeing them side by side, the same tall frame, the same blue eyes and blonde hair – though Heda's is turning grey fast. Her injury is causing her to lose years in seconds. It's no wonder Heda seemed familiar. I feel stupid for not seeing it earlier. It wasn't because she's Eros's daughter, it was because she's Marissa's ma.

316

My entire stomach flips. I use the sword as a crutch and squeeze my gut to keep my insides in.

'Do you remember now?' Heda asks me. 'We met once before.'

I do remember, but her hair was cut into a bob and dyed black and she wore a gold fitted suit. We only met in passing, once when Marissa and I were first assigned accountability partners. No wonder Marissa was always alone, making excuses for her mother's absence. I hate myself for forgetting Heda's face. If I had remembered, I'd never have trusted Marissa and let her lead me into this trap.

Heda turns to one of the guards and points to her severed hand lying on the stone in a puddle of sticky blood. 'Grab that, will you? I need some ichor to heal this and something tells me Rachel won't cooperate.'

'I'd rather cut off your other hand,' I say.

Heda smiles. 'See.'

She and Marissa start for the stairs leading into the glass room, then Heda stops, turning back to her guards. 'Oh, and kill them,' she orders.

They pick up their weapons, and more guards pour out of the passage. There are at least twenty of them against us.

Ben and I stand side by side, swords raised. I focus on my rage, trying to turn it into electricity, to call it out of me and into light, but it bounces through my body and I can't seem to grab on to it.

He leans over to me. 'This would be a good time for that dome light thingy.'

'I'm trying,' I say. 'It's not as easy as it looks.'

The guards press in and we step back, feeling the river's heat claw at our calves. Ben's boot slides over the edge.

'Careful,' our families cry in unison.

I grab his sleeve and help him balance, half pulling him up. The formation of guards nears, bolt rods raised. Ben glances to the cable bridge of the rock outcrop, a couple of metres to our right.

I nod, and we run for it.

He makes it there seconds before me, balancing his sword and holding a wire. The cable bounces with the weight. It's obviously a one-person-at-a-time sort of bridge, but the guards are almost here.

I step on behind him and it swings so low that fire licks at our feet.

Ben hisses and takes another step forward.

The cable cuts into my hands, leaving a trail of bright blue blood on the steel. I struggle to hold on and not drop the sword. The electricity inside me stirs, a little late, but I'm thankful it's back. The next time the cable bounces us up, I use the momentum and toss the sword to the outcrop. It lands on the rock mere feet from the bridge.

Ben twists around. 'Nice!' He holds his like a spear, struggling to balance against the bridge's sway, and lobs it forward. It hits the side of the rock and falls into the molten lava. 'Damn.'

'It's OK,' I say, 'just hurry.'

Being able to grip with both hands helps us move faster, but the bridge bounces more with the added weight of the guards. Each new step drops us closer to the flames. The electricity starts to burn beneath my skin.

When Ben makes it to the other side, his family cheers from the doorway.

'Rachel, look out!' Paisley calls. I twist as a bolt rod zips past my face, inches away.

'Oh hell, no,' I say. With Ben out of danger, I cement my grip on the wire cable and let the electricity free. White light blasts into a dome around me, knocking the guard behind me into the fiery river – a plume of smoke rises from where the lava sucks her under. Two others dangle, trying to hang on as I rush the rest of the way, cable bouncing in my wake.

Ben helps me off and I grab Ares's sword. More guards file on, hoisting their comrades back on to the bridge, and another dozen or so wait at the mouth ready to cross.

I wave the sword, remembering what Heda told us. 'This can cut through flesh and bone. Should we test it on the cables?'

'You'll be stuck,' Ben's dad says from behind me.

'So will they,' I add.

'I like her,' his brother replies.

'She's awesome, isn't she?' Paisley says. 'We're best friends. Partners in crime!' She winks at me.

I smile back at her then bring the sword down on one of the cable handrails. It whips up, twisting the whole bridge. Guards shout warnings, clinging to each other as the cables sway.

'Back up!' the one closest to me shouts.

They do, and when they reach the other side they form a line, waiting for when we try to leave.

'If one of you steps back on, I'll cut the other rail. Got it?'

They nod.

'Got it,' Heda says, her voice faint but amused. 'But I don't see how keeping yourself detained benefits anyone but me.'

I whip round to find her in an open metal lift, being lowered from the glass room down to the crowd of blue-clad Hedonesses on the far bank. Marissa, a grey guard, Le-Li and my nani are next to her.

'Nani!' I call. 'Nani!'

'Can't she hear you?' Paisley asks.

'I'm not sure.' The way she clings to the railing, moving in small circles like she's trying to keep her balance, is worrisome. I don't know if it's the jerky movements of the lift or whatever Le-Li injected her with that's causing it.

When the lift hits the ground, the grey guard opens the gate and wheels out another IV drip. The bags are full of royal blue blood – I have no clue if it's mine or Eros's, and that sends a shiver down my spine. Heda follows. Her injured hand is somehow reattached and in a splint, the IV tube sticking out of her arm. Her hair's already returning to its golden blonde hue.

'Give us room,' Heda says, and the crowd backs up, forming a circle around my family. Heda waves Le-Li forward. 'Take off Priya's anklet. I need to make sure it works.'

Ma and Dad exchange looks before turning to me.

'When it's off, you run,' I mouth.

Le-Li bends at Ma's feet and unhooks it. Before the gold band even hits the floor Ma starts for the lift and jumps in, turning the lever to make it rise.

Heda stands still, watching until the platform gets a couple of inches off the ground, then she leans over to my nani standing beside her. 'Take her will, and make her return to me.'

'No!' I cry as Nani dives on to the metal platform and grabs Ma by the leg, her lips finding my ma's bare skin.

They both scream from the pain of the Hedoness power slicing out of Nani and tearing through Ma. Dad tries to get to them but Marissa uses her bolt rod to keep him back.

Ma shakes into the metal railing, then slumps over the edge like a rag doll.

'Come to Heda,' Nani says.

Ma instantly stands, stops the lift, jumps out and marches to Heda.

'Isn't this fun?' Heda says. 'So much more can be accomplished when anyone can turn anyone.'

'You're a monster!' I shout.

'Am I? Well, if you say so.' She grins at me then turns to Nani. 'Command her to jump into the flames.'

'Don't you dare!' I head for the bridge as a dozen or so guards pour out of the glass room and join the ones on the other side.

'Obey her,' Nani says.

'Ma, no! Don't listen to Nani, look at me, Ma. Ma!' I wave my sword, trying to get her attention, then head to the side of the island nearest her, jumping over the ray shooting out of Le-Li's device on route. Ma steps up to the corner of the riverbank. Flames lick up the edge, like arms trying to grab her feet.

'Ma, please! Focus on me.' I search my mind for Ma's voice, hoping I can use my powers to push into her head and make her stop. But the only voice I hear is Dad's as he screams her name, and the only voice Ma hears is Nani's.

She glances back, and Nani nods for her to do it. Then Ma looks at me, her eyes saying everything the Hedoness power in her restrains.

She hesitates, but steps over the edge.

Forty-Five

Dad pushes past Marissa, getting the bolt rod in his back. He cries out in pain and stumbles forward from the blow, somehow managing to catch Heda's arm for balance. He hangs on to her and reaches out, grabbing Ma before she falls. It all happens so fast. One second Ma's stepping off, the next Dad's wobbling on the edge, a hand holding on to Heda and another holding Ma in place by her sweatshirt – they form a chain with Heda as the anchor. If she shakes him loose, both my ma and dad will die.

Marissa runs for them, and Heda manoeuvres the rolling portable IV pole ready to use it as a club to pry Dad away.

'Stop!' I yell.

Heda holds up her splinted hand, making Marissa slow her pace. 'Or what?'

'Or—' I glance around for something, anything I can do to make it stop. Dad manages to drag Ma in and they teeter on the edge of the riverbank, trying to keep their balance.

'It's opening!' Paisley shouts.

We turn to see a small fissure forming in the Underworld's doorway, like a crack on an iced-over pond. Paisley sticks her hand through its centre, wiggling her fingers out past the frame. 'It's hot in there,' she says, pulling it back.

Hades pushes forward from the shadows and shoves her to the side. He sticks his bident through. A crooked smile spreads on his face. 'Our time is near,' he tells them. 'Ready the next step, Hedone.'

The laser contraption is propped up by rocks, the ray beam shining at the doorframes. Heda's arm is the only thing keeping my parents alive. The sword in my hand suddenly burns with the need to smash something.

'If you let them fall, I'll make sure Hades never gets out.' I position myself over the laser, sword raised and ready. It's then I notice a black metal shard, the same colour as Eros's collar and Heda's armlet, with cables hooked onto it like it's a battery powering the machine. This is what Heda and Hades meant when they were discussing the sliver of arrow Heda had allotted to open the doorways. Of course she's using the black arrow to undo the Committee's magic seals.

Ben glances between his family and me, eyes wide. He knows I have to stop Heda but he isn't happy about it.

Heda glares daggers at me as she pulls my parents in from the edge and they collapse to the ground. She steps over them, her blue robe slicing through the air. 'Rachel,

324

move back!' Her words are slow and deep, and a shiver flits through my gut. Ma and Dad scramble into the crowd with Kyle and Joyce, out of Heda's reach.

'Listen to her, step away, little girl,' Hades says from the doorway. The crow on his shoulder caws in agreement.

My grip on the hilt tightens.

Ben lets out an airy laugh. 'I wouldn't call her that if I were you,' he says.

'Little girl with her little knife, making big threats,' Hades says.

'Rachel, don't,' Heda adds in warning.

I glance to my family, weaving away from Heda, then back at the doorway, to Paisley and the Blakes.

Hades' bident is through the opening. It glows an eerie green, starting at the base then moving to the two tips as if it's charging.

'Rachel, look out!' Paisley warns.

'Don't even try,' I tell him, bringing the sword closer.

'If I see that little knife move towards that laser I will blast you into the Phlegethon's fire.'

'Do it, Rachel!' Paisley shouts.

Hades pulls his bident from the gap and turns around, blasting her instead. The green energy surrounds her body like a web and she starts to have a seizure, foaming at the mouth and falling to the ground.

I fight back my tears and the urge to run to her, because even if I did, I wouldn't be able to get there. It's just a freestanding doorframe in a cavern, no matter which way I approach it. The only way to Paisley is letting this laser rig bring down the seal, and I can't do that.

Hades' bident begins charging again. He presses it back into the opening.

'Yes,' I tell Hades. 'With this little knife.' And I slam the sword down.

The black arrow shard arcs through the air and over the rocky edge into the fiery river. The beams sputter out.

'No!' Heda cries, running towards the lift with Marissa and Le-Li.

'You little fool,' Hades says, opening fire. Green webbing blasts from the door. I dive to the side, only to realize it wasn't aimed at me.

Ben convulses on the ground, his body covered in the glowing web.

I crawl to him as Hades recharges his bident.

'That was only a taste of what I'll do to you,' he says.

Another blast comes rocketing out and I ignite my energy dome.

'It can't be,' Hades says. 'The only person who can do that is the god of war.'

'Well, we're technically related,' I say, grabbing Ben and pulling him into my arms as the last of the green webbing fades out around his feet. He doesn't wake up.

326

'Ben?' I pat his cheek and shake him. 'Don't you dare leave me now. There's so much I still have to yell at you for.' I shake him again, harder.

He opens one eye. 'When you say "so much" do you have an estimate of the amount of trouble I'm in? Because I'm seeing the white light at the end of the tunnel, and maybe it's safer to go that route.'

Somehow, in the midst of this chaos, he makes me smile. I slap his arm. 'That's not funny.'

Another green blast hits the dome and it starts to flicker.

'Can you stand?' I ask. 'We need to get out of his range.'

He nods. I help him to his feet and support him, using the sword as a crutch, as we circle around to the back of the freestanding doorways. When we get there, we see a mirror image of the front. The Blakes are crouched around Paisley, and Hades is in the frame, his bident sticking out of the opening. It's almost recharged.

'This is inconvenient,' Ben says.

Hades' green blast comes at us. I jump, pulling Ben with me. It barely misses, the webbing spreading over the ground and crumbling sections of the island into the lava below.

'Over there,' Ben says, pointing to the other side of the golden door. 'He won't be able to reach us.'

I wrap his arms around my shoulders and we limp over to the protection of Olympus' doorway. Heda's guards still surround the cable bridge and Heda ushers more into her lift. Then she, Marissa and Le-Li pile in.

'We can still bring down the seal,' she yells over, waving her black bangle. 'Stop shooting up the place. We'll be there in a minute.'

Nani closes the lift door, separating her from Heda. 'Oversee the injections,' Heda tells her. And Nani nods. I hate seeing her under Heda's control like this.

Le-Li punches something into his tablet and a robotic arm extends from the glass room, over the army of Hedonesses. Rows of tubing drop down like something from a cattle feed lot. Heda stands at the lift rails, holding the golden arrowhead in her good hand. 'Form lines and receive your final infusions. The hour is upon us. You will have your power again.'

No one cheers, no one claps. They herd into lines, one by one, making no hassle.

Le-Li punches another command into his tablet and the lift rises, the cable pulling in and changing direction, pointing at us. Ben is still too weak to fight. I don't know what we'll do when Heda's lift full of guards reaches the island.

Then out of the crowd of blue-clad Hedonesses, three silhouettes break formation and weave through the lines. I gasp when I see who it is – Ma, Dad and Kyle.

Nani steps in front of Ma and Ma stops instantly, still under her Hedoness control. Dad and Kyle rush past, jumping off the river's edge and grabbing the side of the lift.

Kyle pulls himself over the rails and wrestles with Marissa and two guards. Dad clings to the side near Heda, not able to make it over before she pushes him and his foot slips off the rails, his body falling. My heart falls too. Somehow Dad manages to grab her robe. He dangles under the lift from the sleeve of her robe.

'This,' she shouts as the cable pulls her higher above the fiery river, 'is why men especially need regular indifference injections. They have no connection or draw to the Hedoness power and love is such a pesky little thing.' Heda begins to strip her robe and Dad drops down further. Kyle is pinned to the corner by a handful of bolt rods.

The lift gets closer to the island. Dad dangles about a metre away. Just a few feet more and I'm sure I could catch him.

Before I can tell him to jump, Kyle springs forward, grabs a bolt rod and swings it like a bat. He takes shock after shock as they slam theirs into him, the brawl making the lift rock. Someone bumps into Le-Li and the tablet slips from his fingers. Heda lunges for it and trips, hanging over the rails, legs flailing wildly above her. It would be funny if it were any other situation.

Dad reaches up and seizes her arm – his fingers encircling the black armlet.

'Daniel,' Heda says with a growl. 'You are once again trying my last nerve.'

In the far corner of the lift, Marissa secures Kyle.

He struggles in her arms. 'I knew you were a liar!' he spits.

She shocks him again but he refuses to scream out in pain. Every time she hits him with the bolt rod, she smiles at me. My attention yo-yos between Kyle and my dad, worry filling me to bursting.

Guards grab Heda and try to pull her back but Dad's added weight makes it difficult.

'A little faster,' Heda says, her hair and robe hanging dangerously close to the licking flames, my father even closer.

A mass of golden curls catches my eye and I turn to see Eros swinging an axe in wide circles, making the guards by the bridge back up. He gets to the mouth of the cables and my heart relaxes. With his help, the three of us could grab my dad and pull him to the safety of the outcrop.

'Eros!' I call. 'Hurry!'

Heda clings to the rails with her splinted hand and turns to see him. 'Daddy!' she growls.

Eros steps on the bridge, sliding sideways like a pro. In no time he's on the island, passing the door to the Underworld. 'Hades,' he says, with a nod.

'You,' Hades hisses.

'Lift me,' I tell him. 'Then I can grab my father.'

'I can make that jump,' Eros says.

Ben shakes his head. 'It's not worth the risk.'

But Eros ignores him and backs up for a running start. He takes off, sprinting for the edge, pushing off his feet, arms raised. He makes it, slamming into the side of the lift with a smack. The compartment rocks. Everyone holds on as Eros climbs in.

He grabs Heda and pulls her far enough over the side that she won't fall then turns back to grab my dad. Through it all, Dad manages to get his foot on the rails, though he loses his grip on Heda's armlet.

'Drop him,' Heda commands.

'What?' Eros says, lifting my dad a little higher.

I gasp. 'Eros, no!'

'Actually wait.' Heda's voice booms into the cavern and a silence falls over us. She straightens her hair and robe, resting the golden arrowhead proudly on her chest – the once broken bow-cord retied in big sloppy knots – and stands at the edge of the railing, looking down at Dad then back at me, a smile twisting over her face like a cat pawing its prey. 'Will you be sad that he dies?' she asks me. 'Or that your chance of being mortal again is gone?'

'What do you think?' I snap back.

'What does she mean?' Ben asks.

'If it helps any, Daddy lied to you,' Heda continues. 'You don't have to eat your father's heart. That's ridiculous. There's another way to undo immortality.'

'H-how did you know?' I ask, thinking back to that conversation with Eros.

'Oh please, the ichor room had an intercom system. I heard everything you two shared. Besides, Eros told me himself. Daddy wouldn't leave me, even if given the chance.'

Heda nods to Le-Li and he shuffles over, slips a key out from under his shirt, reaches behind Eros's neck and unhooks the collar.

'Pull my dad up now!' I scream.

Eros's grip on my father falters as he takes a hand off to rub his neck. My legs give out but Ben holds me up.

'What are you waiting for?' I yell, refusing to believe what I'm seeing. Even without the collar, Eros doesn't disappear into the air like I know he can. 'Get my father up and away from them. Use your powers. You're free!'

Heda leans casually on the rails beside him. 'He won't leave me, Rachel.'

'Why?' I manage to say.

Marissa laughs. ''Cause we're fun,' she answers for him.

'That's not why and you know it,' Eros says, in the same manner that Nani scolds me when I'm being bratty. He turns back. 'There are many reasons my plans had to change, but the most important is because she's my daughter and she needs my blood. Without me she'll die.' His eyes fill with sadness as he watches Le-Li lay the

332

collar in the same box that held Heda's armlet. My father swings wildly in his grasp, struggling to pull himself up, managing to get his foot on the bottom rail. Eros does nothing more to help than offer one hand.

'But it burnt you. Your skin – she hurt you,' I mumble, trying to make sense of it all.

Eros drops his eyes to the river.

Dad's words fill my mind, when he said he'd give me his heart: *'No hesitation, no matter the cost.'*

Eros is doing that for Heda. But it's wrong – his daughter doesn't deserve that kind of love. Not after what she's done to him and everyone.

I've had enough of this conversation. My dad's dangling over the fire. Nani has Ma kneeling at the far riverbank under Heda's control, while the Hedonesses receive power-restoring injections. Electricity pours through me, mixing with my anger. I'm a sparked fuse, ready to blow.

'Well, what is it?' I ask.

'What is what?' Heda asks.

'You said there's another way to reverse immortality. Now tell me what it is.'

'My, you're a demanding little thing.' She holds out her arm, wags the bangle around for show. 'The arrow of indifference, created by Heph to undo the magic of the arrow of infatuation. And would you know it doesn't only do that. It just so happens to undo all magic.'

I hate myself for losing the shard.

Ben's eyes lock on me, so full of hope. Then it hits me. Even without the broken-off piece of the tail feathers, my dad could still live, and I could be mortal again. All I need to do is get the armlet from her.

Heda nods to Eros. 'Bring him up. I need to talk to him.'

Eros lifts Dad until he's face to face with Heda, only separated by the rails.

'You failed me time after time, Daniel. Now you must pay.' Dad reaches for the railing but Heda shoves him away, the momentum making Eros let go.

'No!' I scream, collapsing to my knees.

But Dad doesn't go down without a fight. He grabs Heda's arm, the armlet slipping off. His other hand pulls the cord and golden arrowhead from her neck. She screeches and claws for it back, managing to get the golden arrowhead, but the cord to Eros's bow stays strong in my father's grasp.

And together,

the black arrow,

the cord,

and my father,

. . . plummet into the flames.

I hang over the cliff's edge, tears evaporating before they fall past my cheek. My father forces back the pain and smiles up as the lava swallows the last of him, the armlet and cord sinking beneath the fiery deep at his side.

All that's left is a rising plume of steam.

Both my father and my chance at mortality are gone.

'No!' Hades shouts, green blazes rocketing out of the doorframe.

'Stop your tantrum,' Heda calls back, holding up the black and gold box. 'We have the collar. We can still open the seal.'

Sadness digs its claws back into me. My father died for no reason, and my ma never got to know how he felt for her. I want Heda to pay for what she did to him.

And the rubble from the door to Elysium is giving me an idea.

I pick up my sword and head for Hades, swinging madly at the wooden base – this doorway is coming down.

Hades shoots green energy blasts at my dome. But I chop harder, tears driving me further. Paisley is still on the ground behind him. The Blakes huddle together, their eyes never leaving Ben.

My next swing cuts one side right through, the frame twisting from the missing chunk.

'Stop!' Hades orders. He pulls the bident back for a recharge and sends his crow through the gap. It circles and dive-bombs Ben. He swings and fights it off. Hades brings the charged bident to the opening, aiming at me. He fires. The dome flickers off. His crow flies at me, claws slicing my face.

I turn to the other side and swing the sword down, hacking again and again. It's hard to see through the tears and blue blood and the claws of the crow that continues to attack. Ben hobbles over, swatting at the bird, trying to help. My arms burn from exertion. Each swing does less damage than the one before.

Hades aims his next bolt at Ben. I try to block it with the blade but miss. The green webbing covers Ben whole, making him shake so hard that blood trickles out of his mouth. He falls to the ground but I don't stop hacking to help him. 'I'm sorry, Ben,' I cry. Finishing this is more important now.

I swing fast and wide, trying to derail the crow's attacks, but it aims for my hands as Hades recharges the bident.

I'm only halfway through the frame when Heda orders her guards to form a human ladder to reach the outcrop. If I get hit by the webbing I won't be able to take down the doorway before she gets here.

I focus on Paisley, letting all the pain and loss I've endured under Heda fill me. My power flickers inside once again. I try to ignite the dome but it doesn't come. Hades' bident is glowing, ready to blast any second. I glance over to Nani, standing above Ma, and the lines of Hedonesses filing through the injection post. There's another power stirring in me now.

I reach in through the seal's opening, into the icy dark of the Underworld, and I grab Hades' arm.

My dormant Hedoness powers unleash into him.

He convulses. I scream. Heda screams. Then he falls to the ground.

Ben starts to move, the webbing now free from his body.

'My love,' Hades says to me.

'No!' Heda yells.

'Shoot her,' I say. 'And have your crow twist the injection lines.'

Hades sticks his bident out of the opening and aims for them.

Never have I loved the Hedoness power more.

'Get us out of here!' Marissa yells.

A guard grabs the crank and begins turning, backing the lift towards the glass room. Hades' blast misses, the angle too hard. The tail end of the webbing catches one of the guards forming the human ladder and spreads up her arms. She falls into the river, taking the others with her.

The crow flies past Heda.

'Stop it!' Heda yells, gripping the golden arrowhead in her fist.

Marissa throws her bolt rod at it, but the crow twists

out of harm's way. It gives Kyle an opening and he takes it. He rushes for the rails, climbs up and jumps. His feet fall short of the island but he manages to grip on to the edge with one hand.

'A little help here!' he struggles to say.

'Ben! Quickly!' I rush to Kyle and grab his hand, pulling with all my might. Ben stumbles over, and even though he's weak from the second webbing attack, he helps get Kyle up, mostly by anchoring me. I hurry to hug my cousin, and watch as the crow grabs the tubes, looping them into knots with its claws.

Hades' next blast heads straight for Heda. Eros grabs the collar from the box, using it to deflect the webbing. Hades fires again, quick steady pulses, and each time Eros dives to redirect it.

As the gods spar, Heda turns her attention to her army of Hedonesses on the other side. 'Someone stop the crow,' she yells.

A flurry of movement breaks out on the far riverbank as the Hedonesses try to catch the crow. They throw rocks at the bird and I cringe at every attack, hoping the tubes come down before any more of them manage to restore their Hedoness powers. There's nothing I can do to help the crow, but I can keep Hades' army from getting to those tubes.

I return to my job at the doorframe, swinging with all my might. With Kyle and Ben's help, we soon hack it off its base. It falls to the ground with a slap. Hades isn't angry, not even a little. He cries while we drag it over to the edge and prop it up ready to push.

We pause when we see Paisley and the Blakes huddled inside.

'Do it,' Ben's ma says.

'You were the best criminal BFF a girl could ask for,' Paisley says.

'I love you, son,' Mr Blake says.

Ben and I suck back tears and nod, our mouths no longer able to form the words for goodbye. The three of us put our weight into the final push. If we don't do it now, we never will.

'Stop, my love. Don't leave me,' Hades begs.

'Be good to everyone down there,' I tell him, and we shove the door into the flames. The weight of its absence fills me with a new kind of sadness, one mixed with hopelessness and loss. I'll never see them again. All of them are gone, for ever.

Heda and the lift are almost at the glass room. I can't let them get away with the collar. Who knows what she'll do with it.

'Stop them,' I yell. But the Hedonesses on the far side of the riverbank are as helpless as I am on this island. Even if they weren't under the spell of the golden arrowhead, there are no stairs leading to the glass room from their side, only the lift.

Heda grins and holds up the black and gold box.

Eros places the collar back inside, relief flooding his face the moment he lets go. Before she closes it, Heda places the golden arrowhead in too. 'I suppose you want this,' Heda calls to me. 'Seems you haven't won it all.'

Out of nowhere, a black feathery streak slams into Heda's bad hand. She screams, swatting at the crow, the box slipping from her grasp and arcing through the air. Hades' crow expertly manoeuvres around her attack and plucks the box out of the air, rerouting its flight direction towards me.

'That's your last chance of mortality,' Heda warns me.

I glance at the crow, knowing what the contents of the box mean, then I glance at Ben.

He nods, once, stiff, his eyes dropping to the ground – he doesn't want it, but he knows it's right.

I know it's right too.

'Drop it in the lava,' I yell, and the bird obeys. His claws unhook from the box, the lid hanging open and the contents spilling as it drops.

The sheet of blood-red velvet,

Eros's black collar,

the golden arrowhead,

and the box,

. . . all fall like kindling to the flames.

The far side of the riverbank breaks into chaos as Heda's control over the anklets disappears with the arrowhead. Those injected and sired by Heda use their new power to fight the others off.

Heda clutches the rails of her lift as it comes to a stop at the glass room, her chest heaving, her hair wild about her. 'I'll kill you,' she yells. I lock eyes with Marissa as she pushes her mother inside. So much passes between us – anger, disappointment, betrayal, sadness, loss – then she disappears after Heda and closes the door.

A new kind of rage fills me. I toss the sword and the hilt hits one of the stumps of wood where the door to the Underworld once was, and flops into the pile of stone rubble from Elysium. I'll never be able to see Paisley or my dad again. I'll never be mortal. I want Heda to feel the same fury. The same loss. All she wants is to overthrow Olympus, to make the gods bow. But I know how to take that from her and make sure she doesn't find any other ways to break down the seal. I grab the sword, step in front of the gold door and swing my blade.

Forty-Six

The three of us leave the rock island across the cable bridge and head over to the stairs leading up to the glass room. The door's unlocked and we push inside, the lights flicking on. Small splatterings of red and blue blood adorn the gurney where Nani once lay. I hope we can find a way to reverse the damage Heda caused.

'There's the door for the lift,' Kyle says, pointing across the laboratory to a balcony that looks out over the other side of the river, the side where the Hedonesses are gathering in groups, awaiting what comes next.

Something crashes behind us and a flash of purple bounces for the door.

'Oh hell, no,' Ben says. He sprints for the door, slides across the operating table, and dives to the floor.

There's a scuffle and next thing I know, Ben's yanking Le-Li to his feet and shoving him into the window. 'Look who was sneaking around for supplies.'

'Let's throw him in the river,' Kyle says.

'I can help you!' Le-Li says, his fingers twitching. 'I never wanted to work for her.'

'Probably a lie,' Kyle says.

'I had no choice.' Le-Li jerks his head around, staring desperately at each of us. 'She controlled my father's forge,' he adds in a panic.

Kyle crosses his arms. 'Sounds like a poor excuse to me. Let's see if he sinks or swims.'

'It's true,' he begs. 'Whoever controls the forge, controls me.'

I remember Heda telling us automatons did whatever they were told. 'Let's hold off for a bit, shall we,' I say, causing the boys to turn my way. 'We might be able to use him. He knows her plans.'

'Yes,' Le-Li says. 'Don't hurt me. You have control of the forge now. I'll tell you everything I know.'

'The forge?' Ben asks.

'Nah,' Kyle says, ignoring Ben's question, his face inches from Le-Li's. 'We don't need any more traitors in our midst.' He grabs him by the shoulders and knocks his chest in the process. The baseball game comes on. '. . . *Base, the first hit for the Colorado Rockies* . . .'

Le-Li quickly shuts it off.

Kyle stops mid-motion and cocks his ear. 'Was that their 1995 Shea Stadium game against the New York Mets?'

'You like baseball?' Le-Li hesitantly asks.

'Like it? I was going pro, even had scouts coming to my game, before I got sucked up in this drama and missed the playoffs.'

Le-Li starts to shake. 'Do-do you bleed purple?' he asks, like a kid who's found a new friend who understands his secret code.

Kyle's eyes trail up to Le-Li's hair. 'The purple's for team colours?'

'Is there any other reason?' Le-Li asks.

'OK,' says Kyle pushing away from Le-Li and turning to us. 'Anyone who likes my favourite team is worth a second chance.'

'I don't just like them, they're literally a part of me.' He lifts his shirt to reveal his patchwork metal torso and the tape deck he has for a heart – the skin around it puckered and stitched together in thick red string like a baseball's. I cringe at the sight. 'This is a recording of that game,' Le-li continues, 'and it's been stuck in there since I was made.'

'That's messed up,' says Kyle. 'But also kinda awesome.'

'All right,' Ben says, slow and exasperated like a mother who is trying to focus her hyper children. 'Show us how to get to the other side.'

Le-Li nods and hurries to the lift. A huge smile fills his face as he punches a command into a tablet. We load in and soon we're landing on the far riverbank surrounded by our family and friends. Ma rushes over and throws her arms around me before I'm even fully on solid ground. Kyle and Joyce embrace too. I can't help feeling bad for Ben, his hand protectively on Le-Li's shoulder, watching it all.

I lost my dad, but I have my ma and nani. He's all alone and had to grieve his family all over again.

Behind Ma, clusters of Hedonesses sit back to back on the ground, struggling to be free from the tubing they're tied up in.

'What's this?'

'This,' Ma says, 'is our way of stopping the ones who wanted to run off with Heda. We didn't get them all though.' I notice one of the sisters from St Valentine's and look away.

Ben's sad eyes fill my vision.

'I think we should have a moment of silence for the people who were lost,' I say, taking Ma's hand and leading her to the edge. We file along the bank, looking down into the flames. I'm surprised to see the wooden door still there, bobbing in the lava.

Something flickers in the opening. I grip on to Ma and lean over the cliff to get a better look.

My heart sinks when I realize it's Paisley.

'Rachel? Hey,' she says.

Forms move behind her as Ben's ma and family crowd around, watching their chance of leaving the Underworld sink into lava.

I choke back the urge to cry. 'Hey, you guys.'

'Mom?' Ben says. 'Dad?'

Soon more Hedonesses gather beside us on the cliff, watching the fire lick up over the edge. Mrs Turner joins us at the front, gripping Ma's arm for support. I don't know where Nani is.

'Hey, Mum,' Paisley says, jerking back as a large flame swipes at her. 'I'm OK down here, really. It's not so bad.'

Mrs Turner's reply is stifled by tears.

Something about Paisley's reaction to the river is puzzling. 'You can feel the fire?'

'Yeah,' she says, 'but it's OK. It's worth having one last goodbye.'

One last goodbye. I run the words in my head. One last goodbye. No matter how many times I replay them, they don't feel right. If she can feel the flame, then the doorway isn't properly sealed. If flames can get in . . .

She can get out.

My heart starts to race and I glance around the cavern for something, anything, to help. The cable I sliced from the bridge dangles into the fire across the way. It's long enough, but probably too hot and hard to use, plus I'd have to go all the way back there. We need a rope. My eyes land on the tied Hedonesses, then on the tangled injection tubes behind them. That's as close as we're gonna get.

'Grab those tubes.' I point to them and notice the crow perched on the metal arm above. 'Bring them to me,' I say. The bird flaps down from his seat on the arm and pecks at the tubing. One by one they drop.

'That's convenient,' Kyle says.

'Tell me about it.' As long as Hades serves me, I guess his crow does too. The Hedonesses get busy gathering the tubes and I look back to the river and Paisley. 'Just hang in there.'

Ma brings the pile to the river's edge. She frowns and glances between it and me and the door, which is now half submerged.

I start looping the tubes around my waist, tying the other sides together to make it long enough to reach her. When I tug on them they feel strong enough to pull someone up.

'Rachel, wait,' Ben warns, his hand firm on my back.

'Trust me,' I say, tying another two together and handing him the end. 'And hold on.'

His hands cement on my hips, my stomach flutters. I pick up the tube coil.

'Paisley, catch.'

'What?'

I toss the coil and it lands beside the doorway, fire searing the ends. 'No,' I growl, pulling it back and stomping on the flames to put them out.

'Here,' says Kyle, arm outstretched. 'Hand it over.'

The shoe-throwing incident was enough to prove he has better aim than me. I give the tubes to him right away.

'It's not long enough,' he says.

'Hurry,' a voice from the fire repeats. I glance over the edge. Dad's there now too, standing next to the Blake family. My hands scramble to unhook the tube from my waist. 'Everybody help!' I scream. Ben and I grab the end and Kyle swings the coil, aims between the licking flames at the three-foot opening, then tosses it. I hold my breath, worried it will miss and fall into the fire and more will burn. But it lands right in Paisley's hand.

'Good throw,' says Le-Li, standing obediently next to Ben.

'Climb up!' I squeal. I glance over my shoulder at Kyle. 'We're lucky to have you,' I say.

'I know.' He grins.

The slack in the tubing pulls taut and soon heavy tugs threaten to yank me over the edge. My feet slip on the rocky floor. Kyle grabs the tube too, helping Ben and I reel it in. We walk backward, feeling the weight on the other end, not caring that the tubes rub open our palms or that our arms ache – because our friends and family are on the other end. More of the tubing comes over the edge. Paisley struggles to lift herself up.

'Hold on – we'll haul you in.'

Other Hedonesses grab on, even Le-Li helps us pull. I turn to the boys and they secure their grip on the line and nod for me to go. I rush to the ledge, watching as she comes closer.

In the river below, the door's opening is almost completely engulfed in flames. I can barely make out the forms on the other side.

'Hurry!' I say, grabbing hold again. 'Or the others won't get through.'

We grunt with exertion, everyone breathing heavily, but soon Paisley's hand slaps on to the cliff's edge. I grab one arm, Sister Hannah Marie takes her other and together we lift Paisley to safe ground. 'Kyle! The tubes!'

Kyle immediately starts coiling them and I hug my friend. 'I never thought I'd see you again.'

'That makes two of us,' she says.

Mrs Turner grabs Paisley from me and the two of them cry into each other's shoulders.

The rest of the group crowds around the edge, excited whispers passing between them. My heart sinks when I look down to see how much of the door is submerged in flames. Ben's family and my dad crouch in the opening, watching up through the fire.

'Dad!' I shout. 'Hang in there!'

Ben's beside me, his body stiff. 'We won't be able to get them all.'

'Don't say that,' I say.

Ma puts her hand on my shoulder. 'He's right,' she says. 'We can't rescue them all. The door will sink any moment. We'll be lucky to get one more.'

'No, we—'

Ma taps my shoulder and leans over the edge. 'There's only enough time to save one of you,' she shouts down to them. 'We're sorry.'

Kyle tosses the coil, it misses and he pulls it right back up, stomping out the flames and recoiling it. I refuse to take my eyes off the door. The next toss, Kyle hits the target, and Ben's brother starts climbing from the flames.

'It's Luca,' I say, and Ben looks instantly happier. He pulls on the tubing with a new determination. I watch Luca struggle to hold on while putting out the fire that burns at his clothes.

'Pull! Everybody pull!'

I grab the tubes in front and, with the team behind me, Luca makes it up fast. Ben rushes to the edge and pulls him the rest of the way. Kyle recoils the pile and I rush to the edge.

Dad's face fills all that's left of the opening. He smiles up at me and then Ma. 'I love you both. I hope you know that.'

'Dad, please, just wait, we'll throw you the coil again.' But as I shout that down to him, the flames lick over the last corner of the door.

There's only fire.

They're gone.

All of them, for ever.

I collapse to the floor, next to Ben, who's kneeling and clinging to his brother like he's afraid he'll float away – or worse, sink.

Dad's voice pushes into my head, so faint I almost

miss it. *You're the best thing that ever happened to me, Rachel.*

'I love you, too,' I shout to the fire.

I cling to the edge, wishing for another whisper from my father, but it never comes. It's a strange feeling, having my friend and Ben's brother back but watching my father die all over again and knowing now that there are no more chances. I'm a mix of happiness and grief and my face doesn't know whether to smile or cry. But I look at Ben hugging his little brother and at Paisley and her ma, and I know we've been blessed.

My ma rests her hands on my shoulder. 'I never got to tell him how I feel,' she says.

'He knew,' I say.

'So,' Kyle says, pushing Le-Li over. 'What do we do with this one?'

'Please,' Le-Li begs before we say anything. 'I can help you. It's my nature to give you what you want.'

'What we want?' Ma says.

Le-Li shifts his glance from Ma to me and stutters something.

'What was that?' I ask.

He points to the rock outcrop. 'You destroyed the laser, but the shard of the black arrow is there somewhere.'

'The shard of the black arrow?' Ma repeats. 'Why would we want that?'

I glance down at my hand, rubbed raw from the tubes being dragged across it. Bright blue ichor pools in my palm.

'My mortality,' I say. 'The black arrow can give me back my mortality. But when I destroyed the laser, the shard fell into the flames.'

'What?' Ben says, coming over. 'Please tell me this isn't a joke. All we need is a piece of that arrow?'

'Yes,' Le-Li says.

'You're not hearing me,' I huff, more frustrated at my situation than the boys. 'The arrow, the collar and the laser's shard fell into the flames. It's all gone, OK? My chance of becoming mortal is over.'

A drop of blood from my wounded palm falls on to the toe of my shoe, staining the white with blue. It will be this colour for ever now.

Ben reaches into his grey guard jacket and pulls out a little jar, similar to the one he gave me with shavings from the shield of Achilles, for the skin under Eros's collar. He unscrews the lid, gold dust flying everywhere as he shakes the contents into his hand, brushing the dust away to reveal a small black object. 'You mean, like this?' he says, holding it up, his smile stretching bigger and wider than I've ever seen.

My eyes lock on his hand. 'Is that—'

'Yep,' he says proudly. 'I knew you took it and I retraced your steps until I found this piece wedged under Mrs Patel's shipping container. I almost missed it. Thought it was a rock at first.'

So that's what happened to the arrow shard I stole.

I'm so happy I could hug him. But I'm confused too. 'Why didn't you give it to me?'

'I wasn't sure what it did, and I didn't want you to hurt yourself with it.'

I half glare, half roll my eyes.

'You have a history of making self-harming decisions when it comes to magical items,' he says.

I can't argue with him on that.

'What the hell?' Kyle says.

We turn around to see him bend over to pick up something off the ground. He holds out what looks remarkably like a bloody Halloween prop.

'Ew!' Kyle says. He flings it in disgust. 'Who lost a finger?'

Everyone checks their hands, but before we get an answer an ear falls off Luca and slaps to the ground. Luca's hand shoots to cover the hole in his head, his eyes glued to the appendage at his feet.

I scan the group to see Paisley staring down at a four-fingered hand.

'No,' I gasp.

'They can't live outside of the Underworld?' Ma asks.

'No, it can't be that,' I say, refusing to believe it. We didn't come this far for them to fall apart on us now.

I watch Luca pick up his ear and the blue splatter on my toe catches my eye. My blood is healing, immortal.

Maybe . . . I glance to Ben's outstretched hand, where the last sliver of the black arrow lies, then to the ear in Luca's hand. 'Give me that,' I say.

He frowns, and not until Ben nods does he hand it over. I squeeze my palm over the ear, letting my blue blood coat the surface.

'What are you doing?' Luca says, trying to grab it back, but Ben holds him away.

'Here,' I say, handing Ben the ear. He crinkles his nose but takes it. 'Hold it in place.'

He puts it on Luca's head and holds it.

'How long will this take?' Kyle asks, sceptical.

'I heard that!' Luca says. 'In my ear. I can hear.' He pulls away from Ben and the ear remains on him. Paisley picks up her pinky and I repeat the process – bleed, stick, wait. Soon she's wiggling all five fingers.

'If I may,' Le-Li says. 'They'll likely require a regular dose of ichor, since they're technically dead and crossing out of the Underworld hasn't changed that.' He pauses until we all realize what he's saying, worried glances flying around the group. 'So, would you still like me to show you how to use the arrow shard?'

I look at Paisley and her ma, and Luca and Ben, and I know I cannot put myself above them.

'No. They're going to need my blood.' Mrs Turner, Paisley and Luca seem to relax at this. Ben's shoulders droop. He pats his brother's back, but one hand remains down at his side, fist clenched around the black arrow shard.

I wipe my forehead and watch the tired and weary group. 'Let's get out of here.'

Everyone nods in agreement.

'What do we do about this place?' Ben asks.

I stop and turn to him. 'My vote is, we burn it down.'

*'i am
a lioness
who is no longer
afraid to let the world
hear her
roar*

— an ode to me'

— Amanda Lovelace, The Princess Saves Herself In This One

Epilogue

The door to the end of the hall is open and warm sunlight streams through, breaking up the shadows with golden streaks. I take my first sulphur-free breath of air. It's salty like the ocean and reminds me of my time on the boat in the Atlantic with Ben. The feelings I had for him then were all-consuming. I wasn't sure how to live without him. Now I know I can live without him, but I'm still not sure I want to. Even after finding out he never was on Heda's side I feel a lot of things, and one of them is hurt.

The crow flies ahead of me, and Kyle grabs my arm and pulls me down the hall towards the light. When we exit on to a rocky hill overlooking the ocean, all the anxiety and fear stays behind in the facility. The grass is long and coarse and patchy, but I don't care. I pass a mowed section that looks like a helicopter landing pad and lie down, waiting for my eyes to adjust to the sunlight and staring up at the crisp blue sky and the fluffy white clouds. After everything we've been through, I want to treasure this moment of bliss.

Exhaustion weighs on me, and I close my eyes, letting the ocean breeze push my cares further away. Someone calls my name. At first I'm not sure if I'm dreaming, then my ears tune in over the sound of waves crashing into the rocky bluff and wind rustling the dry grass. It's no dream, not the good kind anyway. Ben's here, and by the sounds of it, Kyle's not happy.

'I don't know what your deal is, Kyle. You were fine with me inside.'

'Yeah, well, I remembered how douchey you were to Rachel.'

'You don't understand,' Ben says. 'I never wanted to hurt her. I was doing what I thought was best.'

'Don't understand?' Kyle says. 'You broke my cousin's heart. I'm not letting you anywhere near her.'

'No offence, man. But I've been concerned about her heart for much longer than you have.'

It skips a beat in my chest, the damn traitor that it is.

Kyle scoffs. 'Sure.'

'I made mistakes, I know, but I was always trying to help Rachel,' Ben says.

'Ha!' Kyle practically snorts. 'The same way you helped when you held Rachel down so they could stick a needle in her arm?'

'I can explain—'

'Then explain,' he says.

'It's . . . I . . . I really need to talk to Rachel. She should be the first to hear it.'

'Remember that time I thought you were badass when you fought off all those men at the church?' Kyle says.

'Yes?' Ben says, confused.

'I don't think that any more. Now I think you're a lame, pathetic excuse for a friend.'

'I deserve that.' He's quiet for a moment before letting out a big sigh. 'If you'd just let me talk to Rachel, she may—'

'What?' Kyle cuts him off. 'Agree with me?'

'Maybe,' Ben says, his voice so low I'm not sure I'm hearing right.

I peek over to see Kyle wave Ben my way, and glance back up at the sky. The crow dives and circles playfully above, and Ben's steps crunch on the dry grass.

'Hey, Rach,' he says, his voice a shaky whisper. 'We never got to finish our talk from earlier, and I'm wondering—'

I hold out my arms. 'Help me up?'

He flashes me one of his charming smiles and yanks me to my feet. The touch is electric and not in the bad way. He keeps hold of one of my hands and leads me away from Kyle, down a narrow path in the tall grass. I fight the urge to entwine my fingers with his. My body wants me to, but there's so much between us now. We're not the hopeful kids we were on that boat trip. We've been hurt and hurt each other. And yet, I can't seem to make myself take my hand away either. The path we're on is steep and his grip on me helps me balance – that's enough of a reason to keep holding his hand.

We continue down until the rock face is at our left and the ocean on our right. The wind blows my hair about and I savour the cool breeze as Ben's hand in mine has my entire body aflame.

We round the next bend, and I slip. He spins, catching me and hauling me up. My back is pressed into the rock. Our faces are inches apart.

My chest rises and falls like a tide.

His eyes stumble to my lips.

Electricity stirs my blood, but I don't fear that the Hedoness power in me will break him. I fear that the power he has over me will break me. He leans closer. We're a whisper away.

My lips tremble with need.

Pebbles fall down the side of the rock face, clinking as they go. My heart falls down after them. Ben's grip on my waist tightens. His warmth caresses my skin. When I don't move, he takes that as my yes, and closes the breath between us.

Our lips touch like coming home after a long trip. Like a weary head finding a pillow to rest. Or a blanket being wrapped around cold shoulders. His hand loosens from my waist and rises up the side of my body, over my shoulder and down my arm. His lips stay pressed tightly to mine. My heart feels like it's floating.

He wraps his hands around my wrist but instead of fingers I feel the leather straps he once fastened there. My mind spirals into a panic. 'Stop.' I push him away, trying to catch my breath.

The look in his eyes is utter fear. I'm tempted to open my mind and read his.

'I'm sorry,' I say. 'It's just—'

'You can't forget what I did to you.'

Flashes of him holding me to the bed, him threatening to harm my family – it's all there, swirling in my mind. 'I know you did what you thought you had to.'

'Rach.' He says my name with an exhale and brushes a stray curl behind my ear. I stiffen at his touch, not because I don't like it, but because I don't like that I can't control my body's desire to push deeper into it.

He drops his hand and turns, his back to the rock bluff next to me, looking out to the sea. 'When I learned about Heda teaming up with Hades I didn't know what to do, Rachel. But I—'

'You should have told me.'

'Yes,' he says, glancing over.

'Why didn't you?' I ask.

'So many reasons.' His eyes go distant like he's searching his mind for an answer. Finally he smirks. 'Because you're a terrible liar and there was so much at stake.'

I slap his arm. 'I am not.'

He stops smiling. 'I knew that you attacked Le-Li with the sleeping meds and snuck out of the room. I knew before I found the needle sticking out of my shirt, and I knew you already knew about Paisley's death.' He looks back up. 'Am I wrong?'

'No,' I say under my breath. I feel my walls slip down before I'm ready for that. 'You threatened to have my ma and nani beaten if I didn't comply.'

He jerks back, caught off guard at my sudden topic jump. 'It was a safe gamble. I knew you'd never let anything happen to them, and it made the guards stop beating you.'

My heart quickens. 'But then they took my blood.'

'They'd have taken it either way.'

He's right, they would have. But I'm not yet ready to let him off the hook. 'Well, what else did I lie about?' I ask.

His eyes shoot to me and I squirm under his analytical gaze. 'I saw you that night in front of the door with Marissa's key card in your hand.'

I slap him again, but hard this time. 'I knew you did and you made me believe I was imagining it.'

He laughs. 'I deserve that.' Then his face goes serious again. 'I wasn't sure I could trust her.'

'Her?' I ask, but then I realize who he means. *Marissa.* He never trusted Marissa. Something you'd think I'd have learned myself by now.

'Then why did you stop me from killing Heda? I could have ended everything. We might have been able to save your family and my dad.'

His eyes lower to his hands, twisted in knots over his stomach. 'She ordered the guards to shoot you if something happened to her, and I couldn't stand there and watch you gunned down in front of me again.' His blue eyes fill with tears.

'Oh,' I say, glancing away because the feeling in my chest when I look into those eyes comes with the need to pull him close and comfort him.

The side of his body presses into me, firm and intentional, but his eyes remain fixed on the ocean.

'I don't care that you're immortal. Yeah, it's not my favourite thing to happen to us,' he chuckles, airy and forced, 'but we can work it out. We can find a way to be together, if that's something you still want.'

He turns to me, his eyes searching my face as he waits for my response – and it's there, on the tip of my tongue, refusing to come out.

After a long awkward silence, he casts his eyes to our feet. 'If not now, I'll wait, Rach.' His entire body tenses. 'I'll wait as long as you need, because one lifetime with you is already more than I deserve.'

My reply still doesn't come, but I manage a scoff, and he looks up, those blue eyes holding mine. 'I mean it, you're incredible. I was trying to find a way to rescue you for weeks, and in days you managed to save us all, all on your own. You're the strongest person I know.'

'I had help,' I stammer, my cheeks heating in response to his praise.

'Sorry I wasn't able to do more, Rach. I thought I was doing the best—'

'Don't do that. You did what you thought was right. I can't fault you for that even if I don't understand why you took it so far and why you didn't just find a way to tell me.'

'I know,' he says. 'But in my defence, I tried to leave hints. Like the Punisher quote.'

I fight the urge to laugh. 'You should know I don't know anything about the Punisher!'

He takes my hand in his and traces around the rope burn on my palm. 'No more lies, no more distance.' His fingertips absently rub a dried trail of ichor. Suddenly his eyes flash with a mix of sadness and hope – it's such a strange look. One I've never seen on him before.

'Your blood . . .'

I immediately know what he's suggesting and I pull my hand back, more out of shock than disagreement. Being together for ever with him could be that simple. Whenever needed, he could drink my blood, *my ichor*, then death couldn't keep us apart.

He tucks his hands in his pockets. 'I'm sorry if that was pressuring you,' he says. He thinks I pulled away because I'm not ready to commit to us. It's the opposite really. I pulled away because I want to commit so badly my entire body hurts. But how can I ask him to do it, to drink my blood and become the very thing he's told me time and time again he despises – the very thing I despise too.

'I won't hold your hand, or do anything like that again,' he continues. 'Not until you're sure it's what you want.'

My heart flutters at the thought. For the first time in my life, my future is open. I actually get to choose what it is I want.

♥

There's a scuffle at the top of the rock bluff. 'Rachel?' Paisley calls.

'Down here,' I shout and turn to Ben. 'We should probably head back.'

He nods, though he doesn't want to leave before I give him a reply. It's obvious by the way he drags his feet and hangs back. But I don't know what to say yet. We have so much to work out still, so many unresolved feelings. Is the love I have for him enough to ask him to give me an eternity? It's too big a question to answer on an impulse.

I hurry up the hill to find Paisley, dressed in regular clothes – a T-shirt and jeans, a wild flower from the hill tucked behind her ear and her alien spaceship necklace.

I can't help the smile that comes to my face. It feels right seeing it on her again.

'Your mum asked me to come get you,' she says.

The crow flies down and pecks at the grass near us. 'You can stay here,' I tell it. 'I'll return for you soon.'

We follow Paisley into the facility, feeling the absence of sunlight like a punch. Ben and I walk close, our arms brushing, but our hands never reconnect. She leads us back through the demigod cavern to the fiery river, which she tells us used to be the heart of a volcano. There's another stairwell carved into the side of the cliff, the entrance hidden underneath the one to the glass room. We descend the steps, careful to hug the stone wall as there is no rail separating us from the riverbed. The heat from the flames makes it hard to breathe, and the fact I keep expecting to see the door, or my father, bobbing in the lava doesn't help either.

'Right this way,' Paisley says, waving to a room carved into the rock.

We enter an old-fashioned forge with an oven decorated in golden metal to resemble Zeus screaming and other garish metalwork hanging from the roof and worked into benches around the wall. Le-Li leans into Zeus's mouth, pouring molten metal into a mould. Ma, Sister Hannah Marie and Mrs Turner fill what's left of the small space.

'Where are Joyce, Luca and Nani?' I ask.

'Ah, Rachel,' Ma says, spinning to face me, Eros's unstrung bow slung over her shoulder. 'You're here. Welcome to Hephaestus's forge.'

Sister Hannah Marie smiles. 'Joyce and Luca went looking for Kyle.'

'And Nani?' I ask.

Ma's face hardens. 'We think she was taken by Heda along with some of the Hedonesses who received injections.'

And Marissa's one of them. At least now she's finally with her ma.

'How will we get them back?' I ask.

Ben glances at me, offering a look of comfort.

Ma adjusts the bow. 'Now that we have regained access to the Committee's technology and we manage the forge, giving us Le-Li's cooperation, it shouldn't take us long to hunt them down and overpower them. The trick will be detaining Eros before he has a chance to fight back.'

'The darts,' I say, remembering the fear that filled me as I watched Eros and then Ben get taken down by them at my fake funeral. Something like that wouldn't make me afraid any more, not after everything I've been through – it would make me mad.

'Yes,' Ma says. 'The Committee has access to many tools that can help contain gods and demigods.' When she says demigods, her eyes linger a little too long on me and it finally sinks in.

I'm a demigod now.

I'm what the Committee spent all those years hunting. At another time my skull would've been dipped in gold and mounted on the wall. But this time it offers abilities that can help get Nani and the Hedonesses back from Heda.

'What can I do to help?'

Ma gives me a look that says she wants to talk about it later, in private. Still, she says, 'For now your biggest help is to continue to donate your ichor. We're coming up with a way to save Nani.'

Ma seems to have everything under control, which makes my worry for Nani dissipate a little. I lift my chin and point to Le-Li. 'So, what's all this?'

He smiles up at me from under big welding goggles that only make his bug eyes more pronounced.

'Since Eros, Heda and her crew are still at large, we can't allow these weapons to sit idly and be easily stolen. We discussed it and have decided to divide the responsibility of care. Le-Li forged the anklets into these.' Ma waves to a table where six gold arrow armlets rest. I step closer, looking down at them and the danger they stand for.

'No,' I say, confused why they'd do this. 'Throw them all into the river. The last thing we need is her finding a way to control them.'

Ma's eyes widen. 'We didn't think of that,' she says.

Le-Li puts his latest work into a bucket of water. Steam fills the small space, and when it settles he pulls out his tongs. Pinched in their end is a black and gold armlet. 'I made this one specially for Rachel.'

The black folds through the gold, making it look like wood grain. It's strange to think my mortality is twisted up in there.

Ma must see the fear in my eyes. She puts her hand on my shoulder. 'You don't have to wear this.'

'I know,' I say.

Le-Li lowers the armlet. 'Whenever you're ready to revert, I will separate the metals and we can insert the black arrow shard into your heart.'

'Thank you,' I say, though it seems a strange thing to thank someone for. 'I want to use my ichor to help others.' Paisley grabs my hand and leans against my shoulder.

'You won't have to worry about the arrow of indifference taking away that ability. The magic from the gold arrow feeds it, so as long as these two are kept together like this they're no more powerful than any old chunk of metal.'

My body floods with relief. The last thing I want is the golden arrow encouraging my Hedoness abilities. If I have to have that power in me, I want it buried deep down. At least that way I have more control of when and where it is summoned.

The warmth of Ben brushes my arm. With him and Paisley and Ma, I have everything I need and more. 'I'll wear it,' I say.

The truth is, I do want to keep my mortality close.

Le-Li tests the armlet's heat with his fingers before picking it up. 'Roll up your sleeve.'

I do. As he twists the armlet tight to my arm, I reach out and grab Ben's hand, folding our fingers together, letting a small part of me have the closeness the rest of me craves. Ben smiles, knowing it's my answer.

Then the arrow's power once again knocks at my skin – but this time from both sides.

Acknowledgements

To David, thank you for showing me daily that good guys aren't exclusive to fairy tales. Your love and support make me feel like anything is possible. I love you.

To all my friends and family who know firsthand the deep well of my passion, and weirdness, and yet love me just the same, thank you. We've been through a lot together, some happy times and some sad, but I've never doubted that I'd have someone to hold my hand through the darkness or skip beside me in the light. I'm so blessed to do life alongside you.

Sarah Hornsley, aka, the best agent a girl could ask for. Thank you for always having my interests at heart and fighting to see my dreams realized. I'm so lucky to have you in my corner.

The team at Hodder Children's books; Lena McCauley, Naomi Greenwood, Sarah Lambert, thank you for taking a chance with me and patiently guiding me through this journey, and mostly thank you for seeing my heart in my words and helping bring that to the forefront. And to Sarah Jeffcoate, Natasha Whearity, Alice Duggan, your drive and vision to connect readers with stories never ceases to amaze, thank you, without you I'd just have a nicely bound coverless manuscript sitting on a dusty shelf wishing for readers. And to Mari Roberts, Ruth Girmatsion and the rest of the Hodder team that's worked on Heartstruck, thank you. I swear everyone at Hodder is secretly a magician – it's always a pleasure watching you do this bookish magic.

Alka, Natasha, Durriya, you've taught me so much, and opened your hearts and lives to me once again. I've said this before, and I will never stop thanking you for helping me make Rachel's story the most authentic I could.

To my Wattpad readers who've waited years to find out what happened with Rachel and Ben, thank you for your *many* messages, and emails, begging for me to update and continue their story – you can call off the dogs, it's finally here! … Jokes aside, your dedication and encouragement for me and Rachel, inspires me every day. Thank you. (I hope the wait was worth it)!

And to you, dear reader, dream giver, you've supported this wild dream of mine, and yet with every word readily at my fingertips, I can't seem to express how much you mean to me. Just know it's a lot.

Follow your arrows.
xo
Rebecca Sky

Rebecca Sky is a YA author who lives on an island
off the West Coast of Canada. When not writing,
she's reading and snuggling her Boston Terrier,
travelling to all sorts of off-the-map places,
or cheering side stage for her Rock Star hubby.

**Find out more about Rebecca
at www.rebeccasky.com**

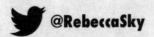 **@RebeccaSky**   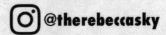 **@therebeccasky**

The Love Curse Series

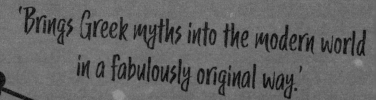

'Brings Greek myths into the modern world in a fabulously original way.'

BELLA H, ENGLAND

'Such an emotional rollercoaster read. Where can I get my own Ben?'

WINNIE B, USA

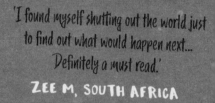

'I found myself shutting out the world just to find out what would happen next... Definitely a must read.'

ZEE M, SOUTH AFRICA

'Arrowheart is one of the most intriguing books I've ever read. Ever.'

TOPHIE J.S, NIGERIA